INDEX

I0671668

PROLOGUE

In the face of a zombie apocalypse, the ancient strategies of Sun Tzu's "The Art of War" can be adapted to guide survivors. This rulebook combines timeless wisdom with modern survival tactics to create a comprehensive guide for enduring a world overrun by the undead.

1. Know Your Enemy and Yourself:
• Understand the behavior of zombies: their strengths lie in numbers and relentless pursuit; their weaknesses are their lack of intelligence and slow movements.
• Assess your strengths and weaknesses. Knowledge, physical fitness, mental resilience, and emotional stability are key to survival.

2. The Supreme Art of War is to Subdue the Enemy Without Fighting:
• Avoid direct confrontations with zombies whenever possible.
• Use stealth and diversion tactics to navigate zombie-infested areas.
• Create safe zones and secure shelters without attracting zombie attention.

3. All Warfare is Based on Deception:
• Use decoys and noise to mislead and redirect zombie hordes.
• Be unpredictable in your movements and strategies to avoid detection.

4. The Opportunity of Victory is Provided by the Enemy Himself:
• Utilize the environment to your advantage (high ground).
• Exploit the predictability and limitations of zombies (traps).

5. He Will Win Who Knows When to Fight and When Not to Fight:
• Choose your battles wisely. Engage only when necessary and when the odds are in your favor.
• Conserve resources, including weapons, ammunition, and energy, for critical situations.

6. The Quality of Decision is Like the Well-Timed Swift of a Falcon:
• Make quick, informed decisions. Hesitation can be fatal.

THE ART OF WAR VS. ZOMBIES

THE COMPLETE TALES OF BRAINS AND MAYHEM

A series of bloody adventures
by Nero Badonis

- Continuously assess and adapt to the evolving situation.

7. In Chaos, There is Opportunity:
- Use the chaos of the outbreak to gather resources.
- Build a strong survival group.
- Be prepared to change plans and adapt to new threats and challenges.

8. The Greatest Victory is That Which Requires No Battle:
- Focus on long-term survival rather than short-term victories.
- Building a sustainable living situation (e.g., farming, fortifying) is more valuable than momentary triumphs over zombies.

9. Move Swiftly to Overcome the Drifting Clouds:
- Be mobile and flexible. Permanent settlements can become targets.
- Have contingency plans and escape routes for every situation.

10. If You Know Neither the Enemy Nor Yourself, You Will Succumb:
- Continuously learn and improve your survival skills.
- Stay informed about the behavior of zombies and the state of the world.

The principles of Sun Tzu, applied to the zombie apocalypse, emphasize strategy, intelligence, and adaptability. The key to survival lies not just in combat, but in understanding the nature of the enemy and oneself, using the environment to one's advantage, and maintaining the will to endure against all odds. Remember, in this new world, the greatest weapon is your mind.

Chapter 1

SO IT BEGINS

"In the midst of chaos, there is also opportunity."

The city's twilight had never seemed so foreboding to Damian, a young history student whose life was usually buried in the dusty pages of ancient tomes. On this particular evening, as he walked through the eerily quiet streets, his mind was absorbed not with the imminent threat of his upcoming exams, but with the peculiar silence that hung over the city like a shroud.

Damian's fascination with history, particularly military strategy, had always been his escape. Sun Tzu's "The Art of War" was his bible, its pages worn and dog-eared from countless readings. Little did he know, those very teachings were about to become his lifeline in a world that was unraveling faster than the frayed edges of his favorite book.

As he turned a corner, his phone buzzed with a flurry of notifications. Damian pulled it out, his brow furrowing as he scrolled through the messages. "Stay indoors - Emergency," read one. "Zombie outbreak in downtown!" exclaimed another. He chuckled at the absurdity, assuming it was some viral marketing stunt for a new movie. But as he lifted his eyes from the screen, the reality of the situation struck him with chilling clarity.

A woman, her clothes tattered and stained, staggered toward him. Her skin was an unnatural pallor, and her eyes... her eyes were vacant, devoid of humanity. She let out a guttural moan, sending a shiver down Damian's spine.

"Hey, are you okay?" Damian called out tentatively, taking a cautious step back.

The woman's response was a sudden lunge towards him, her arms outstretched, her fingers clawing at the air. Damian's heart raced as he stumbled backwards, his mind struggling to process the scene before him. This wasn't a stunt. This was real.

Dodging the woman with a swift sidestep, Damian's thoughts raced back to "The Art of War." "In chaos, there is opportunity," he muttered to himself, turning on his heels and sprinting towards his apartment.

Barricading himself inside, Damian watched from his window as the once-familiar streets turned into a tableau of horror. People ran screaming, chased by others like the woman he had encountered. The reality of the situation was undeniable now - the city was in the grip of a zombie apocalypse.

The initial shock gave way to a reluctant acceptance. Damian knew he couldn't stay hidden forever. He needed a plan, a strategy to survive. But as the night wore on, his confidence waned. The thought of venturing out into that chaos was overwhelming. He was a student of history, not a warrior. Doubt crept into his mind, whispering that he was not cut out for this.

As the first light of dawn crept through the cracks in his makeshift barricade, Damian's resolve hardened. Survival wasn't just about fighting; it was about outthinking the enemy. He needed to apply what he knew from his studies to this new, terrifying situation.

With a deep breath, Damian opened "The Art of War" once more, its pages offering a semblance of comfort in the madness. "All warfare is based on deception," Sun Tzu had written. Damian needed a plan, a way to use his knowledge to outsmart these creatures.

He started to map out his immediate surroundings, marking potential safe havens and sources of food and water. But as he plotted his course, a sudden crashing noise from the apartment below jolted him back to the harsh reality. They were inside the building.

The groans and shuffling footsteps grew louder, more insistent. Damian's heart pounded in his chest as he frantically searched for an escape route. He couldn't stay here - it was only a matter of time before they found him.

Gathering a small backpack with essentials and clutching his precious book, Damian steeled himself. He needed to move, to put his plan into action. It was time to step out of the pages of history and write his own story of survival.

With one last glance at his sanctuary, now breached by the relentless undead, Damian opened his door and stepped into the new world. A world where the lessons of the past were his only hope for the future.

Damian's first steps into the desolate morning were tentative, every sense heightened to the surreal nightmare that his world had become. The streets were littered with abandoned cars, their doors ajar, and windows smashed. Overturned trash cans and scattered belongings painted a picture of panicked flight. The moans of the undead echoed in the distance, a constant reminder of the peril lurking around every corner.

With Sun Tzu's teachings echoing in his mind, Damian moved stealthily, using the chaos to his advantage, blending into the environment. He recalled a line from the ancient text, "The supreme art of war is to subdue the enemy without fighting." Avoiding confrontation was his best strategy, given his lack of combat skills.

His first goal was to secure supplies. He remembered a small family-owned grocery store a few blocks away. As he approached, he noticed the door was slightly ajar. Heart pounding, he pushed it open, the bell tinkling eerily as he entered.

The store was in disarray, but thankfully deserted. Damian quickly gathered non-perishable food, water, and a first aid kit. As he was about to leave, a voice startled him.

"Thought I was the only one left," said a middle-aged man emerging from the back of the store. He was rugged, with weary eyes that spoke of things he'd seen.

Damian tensed, assessing the man. "I'm just looking for supplies," he said cautiously.

"Name's Rick," the man extended his hand, "I've been holed up here since this whole thing started."

They exchanged stories, and Damian learned that Rick had been a city maintenance worker. His knowledge of the city's infrastructure could be invaluable.

"Listen," Rick said, "I know a place, an old shelter. It's secure. We could hold up there, wait this thing out."

Damian weighed his options. Going with Rick meant deviating from his plan, but the offer was tempting. Strength in numbers, another of Sun Tzu's principles.

"Okay, let's do it. But we move carefully, avoid drawing attention," Damian replied.

Together, they navigated the city's labyrinth, avoiding zombies with a combination of stealth and quick thinking. Damian realized that despite his initial failures, he was learning, adapting.

The shelter Rick spoke of was an old bomb shelter beneath a derelict building. It was secure, with thick walls and a heavy door. Inside, they found canned food, water, and even a generator.

Emboldened by this small victory, Damian began to think bigger. He proposed fortifying the shelter, making it a base where they could gather more survivors. Rick agreed, impressed by Damian's strategic thinking.

Over the next few weeks, their duo grew into a small community. Damian, using his strategic mind, organized scavenging missions, fortification efforts, and even training sessions, teaching others basic self-defense and survival tactics.

But complacency became their greatest enemy. During a scavenging mission, they encountered a horde larger than any they'd seen. In the chaos, they lost two of their group, and barely made it back to the shelter. It was a harsh reminder of the reality they faced.

Undeterred, Damian devised a grander plan. He proposed finding a larger, more defensible location, gathering more survivors, and building a community that could withstand the zombie threat.

The plan was ambitious, and despite some reservations, the group rallied behind Damian's vision. They found an old school, its high walls and spacious grounds ideal for their needs. They worked tirelessly, reinforcing walls, setting up lookout posts, and gathering resources.

But their success was short-lived. They had underestimated their enemy. A massive horde, unlike any they had faced, descended upon them. The school was overrun in a matter of hours. The survivors scattered, many lost to the relentless tide of undead.

Damian, Rick, and a few others barely escaped, their spirits crushed, their grand plan in ruins. As they regrouped in the ruins of a nearby building, the weight of their loss and Damian's failed leadership was palpable.

"Why didn't we see this coming?" one of the survivors lamented.

Damian sat in silence, his confidence shattered. He had been so sure of their plan, so convinced in their ability to outsmart this enemy. But he had been wrong. They had underestimated the zombies, treating them like a predictable enemy. But this was a new kind of war, one that required not just strategic thinking, but an understanding of an unpredictable, relentless adversary.

As they sat in the dim light, licking their wounds and contemplating their next move, Damian realized that if they were to survive, he needed to change his approach. He needed to adapt, to evolve. The Art of War had taught him much, but this new world required more than ancient wisdom. It demanded innovation, creativity, and most importantly, an unyielding will to survive.

The remnants of their group huddled in the shadowed remains of an abandoned warehouse, a far cry from the hopeful sanctuary they had tried to build. The air was heavy with defeat and despair. Damian sat apart, his eyes fixed on the tattered pages of "The Art of War," but the words that once inspired him now seemed hollow echoes of a world long gone.

Rick approached him, his voice cutting through the silence. "We can't give up, Damian. We've lost too much to just roll over and die."

Damian looked up, his eyes weary. "I thought I had the answers, Rick. I thought I could outsmart them. But we're not just fighting mindless creatures. We're fighting an evolving enemy."

"It's not over yet," Rick insisted, his determination unyielding. "We regroup, we plan, we survive. That's what we do."

Damian nodded slowly, the spark of resolve reigniting in his eyes. They gathered the survivors, their faces etched with fear and fatigue, but still flickering with the embers of hope.

"We've been reacting, playing defense. It's time we take the fight to them," Damian said, his voice steady. "We've learned their patterns, their behaviors. They're not just mindless - there's a rudimentary intelligence, a pack mentality. We use that against them."

Plans were made, strategies formed. They would lure the horde into a trap, using themselves as bait. It was risky, but they had little to lose.

As night fell, they enacted their plan. The survivors moved through the city, a symphony of stealth and precision, each playing their part in the deadly dance. They reached an old industrial area, a maze of narrow streets and alleys, the perfect battleground for their final stand.

The horde came, drawn by their movements, a relentless wave of death. Damian and the others led them into the heart of the industrial maze, where they had prepared their trap. Explosives were set, choke points identified, escape routes planned.

The battle was ferocious. The zombies, driven by insatiable hunger, swarmed into the trap. Explosions rocked the night, fire lighting up the darkness, casting monstrous shadows against the crumbling buildings. The survivors fought with desperate bravery, but the tide seemed unending.

Just as victory seemed within their grasp, the worst fear materialized. From the depths of the horde emerged a figure - the Alpha, the leader of the undead, a towering, grotesque creature of nightmare. It moved with purpose, with intelligence, its eyes fixed on Damian.

Damian faced the Alpha, his heart pounding, his mind racing. This was the embodiment of their true enemy - not just the zombies, but the relentless, evolving nature of the apocalypse itself.

The Alpha lunged, and Damian dodged, leading it through the maze, using his knowledge of Sun Tzu's strategies to outmaneuver the creature. It was a dance of death, each move calculated, each step a gamble. In a final, desperate move, Damian led the Alpha to a rigged building. With a swift motion, he activated the explosives, and the building came crashing down, burying the Alpha under tons of rubble.

The horde, as if connected to the Alpha, faltered, their movements becoming erratic, aimless. The survivors seized the opportunity, dispatching the remaining zombies with a renewed fervor.

As dawn broke, the survivors emerged, battered but alive. They had won, but the cost was high. The city lay in ruins, a testament to their struggle. Damian stood amidst the wreckage, his eyes reflecting the dawning light. They had survived, but the world they knew was gone. They would have to rebuild, to create a new life in the ashes of the old.

Rick clapped a hand on Damian's shoulder. "We made it, kid. Thanks to you."

Damian looked at the survivors, their faces marked with loss but also with determination. "We made it," he agreed. "But this is just the beginning. We've won the battle, but the war... the war goes on."

As they walked away from the ruins, a new day rising before them, they knew the road ahead would be long and fraught with challenges. But they also knew they had each other, and in a world ruled by death, that was a victory in itself.

CHAPTER 2

MACBETH VS. ZOMBIES

"In the darkest of times, even the bravest hearts can be seduced by the allure of power, forgetting that the shadow of greatness often holds the deepest of terrors."

Under the shadowed canopy of the Scottish highlands, where the mists whispered ancient secrets, stood Macbeth, a warrior whose valor was as renowned as the legends that cloaked these lands. The air was thick with the metallic scent of blood and victory, remnants of a battle fiercely fought and won under his command. His sword, still slick with the lifeblood of his enemies, hung heavily by his side, a testament to his unwavering bravery.

Beside him, Banquo, his loyal comrade-in-arms, gazed into the dense woods, an unease knitting his brow. "This land," he murmured, "it harbors more than just the spirits of fallen men."

Macbeth, whose mind was as sharp as his blade, nodded silently, his gaze lost in the rolling mists that seemed to dance with ghostly forms. It was in this eerie silence that they heard the unsettling chorus of whispers, like leaves rustling against the call of the wind.

Drawn by a morbid curiosity, Macbeth led the way into the heart of the woods. The trees stood like silent sentinels, their gnarled branches clawing at the sky. It was here, amidst the unnatural chill, that they stumbled upon a sight that would haunt Macbeth's dreams henceforth.

Three figures, grotesque and ghastly, emerged from the fog. Their eyes, void of life, bore into Macbeth's soul. These were not mere women, but witches, their flesh decaying, their lips curling into sinister smiles. "All hail, Macbeth," they croaked in unison, "thane of Glamis, thane of Cawdor, and future King of Scotland."

Banquo's voice, tinged with fear, broke the heavy air. "What foul sorcery is this? Speak, if you dare!"

The witches cackled, their laughter echoing through the woods. "Your future, great thane, is drenched in blood," one hissed, her voice as cold as the grave. "The throne shall be yours, but it comes with a price."

Shaken, Macbeth stepped back, his mind a whirlwind of doubt and ambition. "And what of me?" Banquo demanded, his hand gripping the hilt of his sword.

"You shall father kings, but never be one," the second witch replied, her voice a deathly whisper.

As quickly as they had appeared, the witches vanished, leaving behind a silence that weighed heavily upon the warriors' hearts. Banquo turned to Macbeth, his eyes searching for reason in the madness. "What do you make of this devilry, Macbeth?"

Macbeth, his face a mask of contemplation, finally spoke, "These are but shadows of what may be. We must not let them cloud our judgment."

Yet, as they made their way back to their encampment, the seed of destiny the witches had sown began to sprout in Macbeth's heart, watered by a desire that he dared not admit.

In the days that followed, news arrived that King Duncan had named Macbeth Thane of Cawdor, just as the witches had foretold. This uncanny truth gnawed at Macbeth's resolve, the prophecy echoing in his mind like a siren's call.

At his castle in Inverness, Lady Macbeth awaited his return, her ambition burning as fiercely as the hearth's flames. "My dearest husband," she greeted him, her voice laced with a hunger for power that matched his own.

Macbeth looked into her eyes, seeing the same dark desire that now plagued his thoughts. "The witches spoke of a future drenched in blood," he confessed, the words heavy on his tongue.

Lady Macbeth's eyes gleamed with a predatory light. "And shall we let mere prophecies dictate our fate? We are the masters of our destiny, my love. If the throne is within your grasp, would you not seize it?"

Her words ignited a fire within Macbeth, the flames of ambition fanned by her relentless will. Yet, a part of him recoiled at the thought of regicide, the sacred bond of loyalty to his king battling the rising tide of his desire for power.

As night fell upon Inverness, Macbeth found himself wandering the castle's halls, his thoughts a tempest. The ghostly words of the witches haunted him, their prophecy a melody that played incessantly in his mind.

It was then that Lady Macbeth found him, her determination as unyielding as iron. "This is our moment, Macbeth. We must strike swiftly and without mercy. Duncan's death will be our ascent to greatness."

Macbeth, torn between honor and ambition, felt the last of his resistance crumbling under the weight of his wife's words. "If we should fail?" he whispered, the gravity of the deed weighing upon him.

"We shall not fail," Lady Macbeth declared, her conviction unwavering. "Fortune favors the bold, my husband. Let us embrace our destiny and forge our path to the throne."

And so, under the cloak of night, a plan was hatched, one that would stain the hands of Macbeth and his lady with the blood of a king. The castle of Inverness, once a symbol of loyalty and nobility, stood on the precipice of a dark and treacherous path, a path that would lead Macbeth into the very heart of darkness and awaken a curse that would bring the realm to its knees.

As the stars blinked coldly in the night sky, a sense of foreboding settled over the land, the winds whispering of a storm that would shake the foundations of Scotland and awaken horrors beyond mortal comprehension.

The air in Inverness Castle was heavy with the scent of treachery as Macbeth and Lady Macbeth plotted in the shadows. The walls, which had stood witness to many secrets, now echoed with the sinister whispers of regicide. In the dead of night, Macbeth, his soul torn between honor and ambition, made his way to King Duncan's chamber. The deed that followed was as swift as it was brutal, leaving the king lifeless, his blood a crimson stain upon the royal linens.

As dawn broke, the castle was rife with chaos and confusion. Macbeth, his face a mask of feigned shock and grief, declared, "Our noble king has been slain in his sleep!" The court erupted in horror, and amidst the turmoil, Macbeth ascended to the throne, his crown heavy with the weight of his guilt.

Yet, the fulfillment of the witches' prophecy brought no peace to Macbeth. His mind, once a fortress of resolve, now crumbled under the onslaught of paranoia and fear. He saw threats in every shadow, heard whispers in every corner. In a desperate attempt to secure his reign, he ordered the murder of his once friend, Banquo, and the family of his perceived rival, Macduff.

But with each life taken, a strange phenomenon began to manifest across the kingdom. The dead, restless in their graves, rose as if called by some unseen force. The land of Scotland, once vibrant and alive, now echoed with the groans of the undead.

In Dunsinane, Macbeth fortified his castle, turning it into a bastion against both the living and the dead. "We must protect our reign against all threats," he declared to his lords, his eyes betraying the madness that gnawed at his soul.

Lady Macbeth, watching her husband's descent into madness, felt the first stirrings of fear. "What have we unleashed, my love?" she whispered one night as they stood upon the battlements, gazing out at the dark, zombie-infested landscape.

"We did what was necessary," Macbeth replied, his voice hollow. "The throne is ours, and we shall defend it against all, living or dead."

Yet, as the undead horde grew, so too did the dissent within the kingdom. Reports of Macbeth's tyranny and madness spread, and whispers of rebellion began to stir. Macduff, seeking vengeance for his family's murder, rallied forces against the mad king.

The siege of Dunsinane was unlike any seen before. The undead, drawn by the scent of the living and the darkness within Macbeth's heart, converged upon the castle. The night sky was alight with the flames of battle, the air filled with the clash of steel and the cries of the dying.

Inside the castle, Macbeth fought with the ferocity of a man possessed, his sword cutting through both rebel and undead alike. "This throne is mine!" he roared, his eyes alight with the fire of insanity.

As the battle raged, Lady Macbeth wandered the halls of the castle, her mind a maelstrom of guilt and terror. In a moment of lucidity, she realized the horror of what they had done. "We are damned," she cried out, her voice echoing through the stone corridors. "Our hands are stained with blood that will never wash clean!"

In the heat of battle, as Macbeth fought his way through the chaos, he encountered the witches once more. Their decaying forms were a grotesque mirror to the decay of his soul. "The throne was never yours to keep," they hissed, their voices a chorus of doom. "Your reign ends tonight, and with it, the curse you have wrought upon this land."

Macbeth, his heart pounding with fear and rage, screamed his defiance. "I will not be undone by shadows and superstition!" He swung his sword with a warrior's skill, but the witches vanished into the night, leaving behind a chilling laughter that echoed in the depths of his soul.

As dawn approached, the battle reached its climax. The undead, relentless in their assault, breached the castle's defenses. Macbeth, cornered and desperate, fought with the strength of a man who had nothing left to lose.

But in that moment of chaos, when death seemed certain, a figure emerged from the shadows. It was Lady Macbeth, her eyes wide with madness, her hands clawing at her own flesh. "I cannot be cleansed," she wailed, her voice a testament to their shared damnation. "The blood is everywhere!"

Macbeth, seeing the depth of her despair, felt the last of his resolve crumble. "What have we become?" he whispered, his voice lost in the cacophony of battle.

The castle, once a symbol of power and ambition, now stood as a tomb, a testament to the folly of man's greed and the terrifying power of prophecy. As the sun rose over the blood-soaked fields of

Dunsinane, it cast its light upon a kingdom forever changed, its king and queen lost to the madness of their own making, and the land cursed by the horrors they had unleashed.

In the end, Macbeth stood alone amidst the ruins of his kingdom, a broken man haunted by the ghosts of his actions, his crown a hollow symbol of a reign marked by blood and terror. And as he gazed upon the destruction he had wrought, he realized the true cost of power and the devastating price of ambition.

As dawn crested the horizon, painting the sky with streaks of crimson and gold, Macbeth stood amidst the ruins of Dunsinane, a kingdom shattered by his own doing. The air was thick with the stench of death, the cries of the undead echoing in the hollow silence. Lady Macbeth, once a beacon of strength and ambition, now lay broken, her mind lost to the madness of guilt and despair.

Macbeth, his eyes hollow, gazed upon the destruction around him. The undead, once his unwitting allies in terror, now surged towards him, their hunger insatiable. The castle that had been his fortress now stood as his prison, its walls breached, its defenses overrun.

With sword in hand, Macbeth fought. Each swing was a desperate bid for redemption, a futile attempt to undo the horrors he had unleashed. "I have walked too far in blood to turn back now," he roared, cutting down the grotesque forms that lunged at him.

As the battle raged, the witches appeared once more, their decaying forms a ghastly reminder of the curse Macbeth had brought upon himself. "Behold the fruits of your ambition," they cackled, their voices a symphony of doom.

Macbeth, his heart pounding with fear and rage, faced them. "I am not yet defeated," he declared, his voice a defiant challenge. "I will fight until my last breath to undo this curse."

The witches laughed, their laughter a chilling sound that pierced the chaos of battle. "The curse can only be broken by your end," they taunted. "Only with your death will this nightmare cease."

In that moment, Macbeth understood the cruel irony of his fate. To save his kingdom, he must sacrifice himself. With a newfound resolve, he fought his way through the undead, his every move a dance of death.

As he battled, a figure emerged from the chaos. It was Macduff, his face a mask of vengeance. "This ends now, Macbeth," he shouted, his sword raised for the final blow.

Macbeth, his energy waning, faced his nemesis. "Then let it end," he said, his voice resigned. "I have already lost everything."

Their swords clashed, the sound echoing through the crumbling halls of Dunsinane. Blow after blow, they fought, their duel a testament to their shared hatred and sorrow.

In the midst of their battle, Lady Macbeth, her mind a whirlwind of madness, stumbled into the fray. "I cannot escape the blood," she cried, her eyes wild with terror. "It haunts me, it consumes me!"

Macbeth, seeing his wife's torment, felt a pang of remorse. "Forgive me," he whispered, his heart breaking at the sight of her despair.

But it was too late. In a moment of distraction, Macduff seized his chance, driving his sword through Macbeth's heart. "For Scotland," he whispered as Macbeth fell, his reign of terror ended at last.

As Macbeth lay dying, the witches' laughter faded, and the undead horde collapsed, the curse lifted with his final breath. The sun rose higher, casting its light upon a kingdom freed from the shadow of tyranny.

Lady Macbeth, her mind finally released from the grip of madness, fell to her knees beside her fallen husband. "What have we done?" she wept, her tears a silent testament to their tragic folly.

And so, the reign of Macbeth, the Thane of the Undead, came to an end. His ambition, fueled by prophecy and unchecked desire, had brought his kingdom to the brink of ruin. In his death, he found redemption, his sacrifice breaking the curse that had plagued the land.

The story of Macbeth, a tale of ambition, power, and the consequences of man's reach for greatness, would be whispered throughout the ages. A warning to all who would follow in his footsteps, a reminder that the shadows of greatness often hide the deepest of terrors.

As the new day dawned, Scotland began the long journey of healing, its people forever changed by the horrors they had witnessed. And in the heart of the highlands, where the mists still whispered ancient secrets, the memory of Macbeth lingered, a ghostly echo of a king who had dared to defy fate and paid the ultimate price.

CHAPTER 3

BEOWULF VS. THE UNDEAD

"In the shadow of legends, even heroes must tread with caution, for the tales of old hold truths far grimmer than the darkest night."

In the heart of Scandinavia, where the cold winds whispered secrets of the old gods and the land itself bore the scars of countless battles, there existed a realm where myth and reality were indistinguishably intertwined. It was a world of rugged beauty, where the roar of the ocean was a lullaby and the howl of the wolf a nightly serenade.

Beowulf, a man whose name was sung in the mead halls and whispered in awe across the lands, stood tall and broad-shouldered, his eyes reflecting the calm resolve of a seasoned warrior. Renowned not just for his strength but for his sharp mind, akin to a master chess player amidst the chaos of battle, Beowulf had faced and conquered challenges that would have broken lesser men. Yet, he was about to confront a terror that defied the boundaries of his understanding.

In the warmth of a bustling mead hall, where the fire crackled and spat sparks into the night, Beowulf listened intently as a weary traveler spoke of a new horror. "Grendel," they called it - a monster of nightmarish proportions, terrorizing King Hrothgar's kingdom. But what piqued Beowulf's interest was not the familiar thrill of battle against a formidable foe; it was the hushed, fearful whispers of something far more sinister - the dead walking among the living.

"I tell you, Beowulf," the traveler's voice quivered as he leaned closer, the firelight casting ghostly shadows on his face, "the creature is but a harbinger. The dead, they rise at night, their eyes hollow, their hearts cold as the winter frost. It's unnatural, a curse upon our land."

Beowulf's gaze lingered thoughtfully on the flickering flames, considering the implications. The undead were tales for old wives and frightened children, not the concern of a warrior. Yet the fear in the traveler's eyes spoke of a truth that could not be ignored.

Days later, as Beowulf and his most trusted warriors approached King Hrothgar's kingdom, a chilling sight awaited them. The land was shrouded in a palpable dread, the once vibrant fields now wilted under an unseen, malevolent force. The kingdom, a stronghold of men and valor, stood besieged not just by Grendel's wrath, but by an unceasing wave of the undead.

Within the walls of Hrothgar's great hall, where despair hung heavy like a shroud, King Hrothgar himself, a bear of a man brought to his knees by grief, welcomed Beowulf. "Beowulf, my friend," he said, his voice heavy with sorrow, "I fear we are cursed. Grendel is a terror I cannot fathom, but these... these walking dead... they are an abomination against the very essence of life."

Beowulf, clasping Hrothgar's hand in a firm grip, met his gaze squarely. "My king, I came for Grendel, a foe worthy of song and battle. But this," he gestured toward the darkened windows, beyond which an unnatural moaning could be heard, "this is a plight I cannot turn my back on. We face not just a monster, but a shadow that threatens to engulf us all."

That night, as Beowulf and his men prepared for the dual threats that loomed over them, a sense of foreboding settled in their hearts. The undead, a plague upon the land, defied the very laws of nature and the gods. Beowulf knew that to combat this new enemy, he would need more than his legendary strength and courage.

Under the cloak of darkness, Beowulf ventured forth, his trusted sword gleaming dimly in the moonlight. The undead, grotesque parodies of their former selves, roamed the land aimlessly, their presence an affront to life itself. Beowulf's first encounter with them was a brutal reminder that these were not foes that could be felled by steel alone.

As the first light of dawn broke over the horizon, painting the sky in hues of gold and crimson, Beowulf stood amidst a field of fallen undead, his heart heavy with the realization of the enormity of the task before him. This was a battle that would require not just physical prowess, but a wisdom and understanding that transcended the realm of mortals.

In the days that followed, Beowulf's resolve only grew stronger. He knew that to defeat this scourge, he would need to delve into the ancient lore of his people, to seek out knowledge long forgotten and alliances thought impossible. For in the shadow of legends, even a hero must learn to tread new paths, paths that would lead him into the very heart of darkness itself, challenging the very nature of what it meant to be a monster, and what it meant to be a man.

The days in Hrothgar's kingdom wore on under a cloud of unease, as the twin threats of Grendel and the undead loomed over the land. Beowulf, with his band of warriors, set out each night, their swords slick with the remnants of battles against the undead. Yet, for every creature they felled, it seemed two more took its place.

One night, as the moon cast a pallid light over the silent fields, Beowulf stood before the mist-laden forest, the lair of Grendel. His heart pounded with a warrior's anticipation and a strategist's caution. "Tonight," he addressed his men, "we face Grendel. Remember, this is no ordinary foe. He is as cunning as he is brutal."

The clash with Grendel was as fierce as it was revealing. Beowulf, grappling with the monster, saw in Grendel's eyes not just ferocity but a flicker of something else - an intelligence that bespoke of a deeper, more complex nature. The battle ended with Grendel retreating into the shadows, wounded but alive. Beowulf, panting and covered in the beast's foul blood, knew this was but the opening gambit in a much larger game.

In the following days, Beowulf's strategy shifted. He poured over ancient texts and consulted seers, seeking any knowledge that could turn the tide against the undead. It was during one such consultation, with an old blind seer, that Beowulf's path took an unexpected turn.

"The undead are bound to this land by a curse," the seer hissed, her blind eyes seeming to see through Beowulf. "A curse tied to Grendel's bloodline, entwined with the fate of the Norse gods."

Beowulf's mind raced with this revelation. A curse? Could it be that Grendel and the undead were linked in a way he had not yet understood?

Armed with this new knowledge, Beowulf formulated a bold plan. He would lure a large contingent of the undead into a trap - a valley known for its mystical properties, where his men would ambush them. But as the plan unfolded, the unexpected happened. The undead, seemingly drawn to the valley's mystical energy, grew stronger, their numbers swelling as if fed by the very land that was supposed to be their undoing.

The battle was a massacre. Beowulf's men fought valiantly, but they were overwhelmed by the sheer force of the undead horde. As the survivors retreated, battered and demoralized, Beowulf's mind was a whirlwind of frustration and anger. They had underestimated their enemy, and the cost was written in the blood of his fallen warriors.

In the aftermath of the defeat, Beowulf's resolve hardened. He knew now that brute force was not enough. He needed a new ally, one who understood the nature of their enemy better than anyone - Grendel himself.

Under the cover of darkness, Beowulf ventured alone into Grendel's forest. The air was thick with the scent of decay and unspoken secrets. "Grendel," he called into the darkness, "I seek a parley. We face a common enemy, one that threatens us both."

The response came not in words but in a low growl that reverberated through the trees. Grendel emerged from the shadows, his massive form a silhouette against the moonlit sky. The two stood face to face, the legendary hero and the monstrous fiend, bound by a shared fate.

"Grendel," Beowulf began, his voice steady, "the undead plague this land because of a curse tied to your bloodline. We must join forces to break this curse, or all will be lost."

Grendel's eyes, glowing faintly in the dark, narrowed. In a guttural voice, tinged with pain and a grudging respect, he spoke. "Beowulf, slayer of my kin. Why should I trust you, a man who seeks my head?"

"Because," Beowulf replied, meeting Grendel's gaze, "in this war, we are not each other's true enemy. The undead threaten to consume all in their path - man and monster alike. Together, we can end this curse and restore balance."

A tense silence hung in the air, broken only by the distant howls of the undead. Finally, Grendel nodded, a grudging agreement forged between two unlikely allies.

As they planned their combined assault, Beowulf and Grendel shared insights into their foes' nature. Beowulf learned of the curse's origin - a spiteful act by a forgotten Norse god, and Grendel revealed the key to the undead's power, a dark energy that fed on violence and despair.

The following night, Beowulf's men, alongside Grendel, launched a coordinated attack on the largest gathering of the undead. The battle was fierce, the air filled with the clash of steel and the guttural roars of combat. But just as victory seemed within grasp, disaster struck. Grendel, in the midst of battle, was gravely wounded, a dark arrow piercing his side.

Beowulf fought his way to Grendel's side, dispatching undead with brutal efficiency. "Hold on, Grendel," he urged, supporting the faltering monster. "We need you to break the curse."

Grendel's breath was ragged, his voice a mere whisper. "Beowulf... the curse... it's not just in the blood... it's in the land... the gods..."

As Grendel's words trailed off, Beowulf's heart sank. The tide of battle turned against them, the undead closing in. With Grendel incapacitated and their forces dwindling, Beowulf issued a retreat, his mind racing with Grendel's cryptic final words.

In the cold light of dawn, as the surviving warriors tended to their wounds and mourned their fallen, Beowulf stood apart, his gaze lost in the distance. The weight of their situation was crushing - the undead were stronger than ever, and now, even Grendel lay at death's door.

But in the depths of despair, a spark of determination ignited within Beowulf. He would not be defeated, not by Grendel, not by the undead, and certainly not by a forgotten god's curse. He would find a way to turn the tide, to break the curse and end the undead plague once and for all. For in the heart of every legend lies the truth of a hero's resolve, a resolve that can weather the darkest of storms.

Beowulf's eyes surveyed the haunted landscape, the once fertile lands now a morass under the relentless march of the undead. The air was thick with despair, the stench of decay mingling with the sharp tang of fear. But beneath it all, there lay something else - a flicker of hope, a flame that refused to be extinguished.

With Grendel grievously wounded, his monstrous form lying motionless in the secluded cave they had taken refuge in, Beowulf knew the time for their final stand was upon them. He knelt beside the fallen creature, the lines between friend and foe forever blurred.

"Grendel," Beowulf whispered, his voice a mixture of urgency and respect. "You must guide me. The curse - how do we break it?"

Grendel's eyes fluttered open, a dim light flickering within. "The gods... their power... in the land," he rasped. "The curse... it feeds on the conflict... on the bloodshed. You must reverse it... turn their power against them."

Beowulf's mind raced. Reverse the curse? But how? Then, like a thunderclap, it struck him. The valley - the site of their disastrous battle - it was not just a place of death; it was a nexus of ancient power, a conduit for the gods' will.

Rising to his feet, Beowulf called his remaining warriors to him. "We have one last battle," he declared, his voice resonating with a determination that belied the grim odds they faced. "We will lure the undead to the valley. There, we will use the gods' own power to end this curse."

The warriors, battered and bruised but unbroken in spirit, nodded in agreement. They would follow Beowulf to the ends of the earth, into the very jaws of death if need be.

As night descended, a grim procession made its way to the valley. Beowulf, his armor dented and his shield scarred, led the way. Grendel, weakened but resolute, limped beside him. Together, they would face the darkness.

The valley, bathed in the ghostly light of the moon, seemed to pulse with an unseen energy. Beowulf could feel it beneath his feet, a thrumming power that beckoned to the deepest part of his soul.

The undead, drawn by the promise of blood and carnage, swarmed into the valley, their moans a cacophony of the damned. Beowulf and his warriors stood ready, their faces set in grim determination.

"Tonight, we fight not just for our lives," Beowulf roared over the din, "but for the very soul of our land!"

The battle was a maelstrom of violence, a dance of death that tested the limits of Beowulf's skill and courage. But amidst the chaos, he kept his focus on the true objective - the reversal of the curse.

Channeling the energy of the valley, directing it with the force of his will and the power of his belief, Beowulf felt the tide begin to turn. The undead, once seemingly invincible, began to falter, their forms dissolving into mist as the curse's hold weakened.

But victory was not yet assured. From the depths of the horde emerged the leader of the undead, a creature of pure malevolence, its form a twisted echo of the Norse gods' wrath. Beowulf, his energy nearly spent, faced this final adversary, knowing that the fate of his land hung in the balance.

The duel was epic, a clash of titanic forces that shook the very foundations of the earth. Beowulf, pushed to his limits, fought with a ferocity that was both terrifying and awe-inspiring.

Just as the undead leader raised its hand for the killing blow, Grendel, using the last of his strength, lunged forward. With a roar that echoed through the valley, he struck the creature, his sacrifice turning the tide of battle.

The undead leader fell, its form dissolving into nothingness, and with it, the curse lifted. The remaining undead collapsed, their forms melting away as the land itself seemed to sigh in relief.

As dawn broke, casting its light on the weary but victorious warriors, Beowulf stood in the midst of the valley, his heart heavy with the cost of their triumph. Grendel, his body broken but his spirit unbound, lay beside him, a silent testament to the power of redemption.

The land was free, the curse broken. Beowulf had not only defeated his enemies but had rewritten the very nature of legend. Where once there stood a hero and a monster, there now lay two champions, united in their final victory.

And as Beowulf returned to Hrothgar's kingdom, the tales of his bravery and Grendel's sacrifice spread far and wide, a story of darkness, redemption, and the unyielding strength of

the human spirit. For in the annals of legend, it is not just the battles that are remembered, but the hearts of those who fought them.

CHAPTER 4

SHERAZADE: NIGHTS OF THE LIVING DEAD

"In the heart of darkness, the faintest light can hold the power of salvation."

Under the shadow of a crescent moon, the once-majestic kingdom of Zarapheth lay in ruin, its splendor buried beneath a relentless tide of the undead. Through the desolate streets, where eerie silence battled with the groans of the damned, there moved a figure not of death, but of desperate life.

Sherazade, her raven hair a stark contrast against her pallid complexion, treaded lightly but swiftly, a ghost amongst ghosts. Her eyes, dark pools reflecting a relentless will to survive, scanned the ruined facades of shops and homes she once knew, now hollowed out like the souls that roamed aimlessly through them.

The palace loomed ahead, a grotesque mockery of its former glory, illuminated by the ghastly light of the moon. The gargoyles perched atop its gates seemed to sneer at her approach, as if in on the cruel joke that was her fate. This was to be her prison, the lair of the creature they now called the zombie king.

Once, he had been a just ruler, loved and revered. But as the curse swept through the kingdom, it spared no one, not even the throne. Now, he was but a shadow of his former self, ruling over a kingdom of decay.

As Sherazade was ushered through the gates by guards whose flesh hung loose on their bones, a chill ran down her spine. She was not led to a cell, but to the grand hall, where the king awaited her arrival.

He sat upon his throne, a grotesque figure draped in royal garb that hung loosely over his decaying form. His eyes, once warm and kind, now glowed with a feral, unnatural hunger. Yet, somewhere within those depths, Sherazade glimpsed a flicker of something painfully human.

"You are the storyteller," his voice rasped, a sound like dry leaves scraping across stone. "Your tales have reached even my... ears."

Sherazade bowed, masking her fear with the grace that had always been her shield. "Yes, Your Majesty. I am Sherazade, keeper of tales and spinner of yarns. I bring with me stories from lands near and far, hoping they might please you."

The king leaned forward, the motion unsettling in its eerie slowness. "Stories..." he murmured, the word seeming to stir something within him. "Yes... the stories will keep the darkness at bay. For a while."

The air was heavy with unspoken threats. Sherazade knew the rules of this macabre game. She must weave a story each night, a story captivating enough to distract the king from his baser instincts. If she failed, she would join the ranks of the undead that roamed his kingdom.

As she began her first tale, her voice steady and clear, the king's eyes never left her. The story was one of adventure and bravery, of a hero who faced insurmountable odds to save his beloved from the clutches of a malevolent sorcerer. With each word, Sherazade painted a vivid picture, her narrative a tapestry of hope amidst despair.

The king listened, his expression an enigma. Was he moved by the tale, or merely amused by the efforts of his latest plaything? Sherazade dared not guess. As the story reached its climax, with the hero triumphing over darkness, a tense silence fell upon the hall.

Then, the king clapped, a slow, deliberate sound that echoed through the cavernous room. "Your tale has... pleased me," he said, his voice less harsh than before. "You will tell me another tomorrow night. And the next. Until I grow weary of your words."

Sherazade bowed again, her heart pounding. "Thank you, Your Majesty. I shall strive to keep your interest."

As she was led to her quarters - a small, dimly lit room with a narrow bed - Sherazade knew that her battle had just begun. She must not only survive the king's fickle moods but also find a way to escape this nightmare. For in her heart, she carried a secret, a glimmer of knowledge about the curse that had befallen the kingdom.

And so, under the watchful eyes of the moon and the stars, Sherazade prepared for the nights ahead, each story a step on the path to freedom, or to her doom.

Each night in the decrepit grandeur of the palace hall, Sherazade spun tales more intricate and captivating than the last. Her voice, a beacon in the dark, wove stories of distant lands, brave heroes, cunning villains, and impossible love. The zombie king listened, his undead heart stirred by the echoes of a life he could no longer remember.

Yet, with each passing night, the weight of her task grew heavier. Sherazade's initial attempts to weave subtle hints about the curse into her stories bore no fruit. The undead outside grew in number and ferocity, as if enraged by her attempts to bring light to this darkened realm. The kingdom's once formidable defenses were now little more than crumbling relics, barely holding back the tide of decay.

But Sherazade was not one to yield to despair. Drawing inspiration from a tale of an ancient general, she devised a daring plan. She began to tell a story of a great war, of a kingdom besieged and a cunning strategy that turned the tide against an overwhelming force. Her eyes flicked to the king, gauging his reaction.

The king, his interest piqued, leaned forward. "This general... what was his strategy?" he rasped, the glint of a tactical mind briefly surfacing in his undead eyes.

Encouraged, Sherazade wove her plan into the fabric of her tale. "The general knew he could not defeat the enemy by force alone. So, he lured them into the catacombs beneath the castle, using himself as bait. There, in the narrow corridors, the enemy's numbers meant nothing. They were picked off, one by one."

A spark of understanding flickered in the king's eyes. "Clever," he muttered. "Very clever."

Over the following nights, Sherazade subtly reinforced this strategy, her stories molding the king's thoughts. Under her guidance, the king ordered his undead army to prepare the catacombs, turning them into a trap for the encroaching undead hordes. Sherazade's heart raced as the plan neared fruition. If successful, this could be the turning point, weakening the undead enough for her to escape.

But on the night the trap was sprung, disaster struck. The undead, far more cunning than anyone had anticipated, avoided the catacombs, instead launching a direct assault on the palace. The trap, so carefully laid, was left useless, and the palace's defenses crumbled under the onslaught.

In the chaos, Sherazade was dragged before the king. His eyes burned with betrayal and rage. "You tricked me," he snarled, his voice a guttural growl. "You sought to use me!"

Sherazade's heart pounded in her chest. "Your Majesty, I sought only to protect your kingdom," she pleaded, her mind racing for a way out. "The strategy failed, but it was not my intention to deceive you."

The king's gaze held her, his inner turmoil a tempest of the man he once was and the monster he had become. Finally, he relented. "You will continue your stories," he decreed. "But no more tricks. Or your next tale will be your last."

Bound more tightly to her role than ever, Sherazade knew she needed a new approach. Delving deep into the lore of the kingdom, she began to craft tales that mirrored the king's past, stories of a noble ruler, loved and respected. Night after night, she watched as the tales seemed to reach something within him, a flicker of the man trapped inside the monster.

As the days turned to weeks, the tension in the palace grew palpable. The undead, now leaderless in their frenzy, clashed in brutal skirmishes throughout the kingdom. And in the midst of this chaos, Sherazade saw her chance.

One night, as she told a story of a great festival in honor of the king's past victories, the palace was attacked by a rival faction of the undead. In the ensuing battle, the king, driven by an instinct to protect what he once held dear, took Sherazade and fled into the labyrinthine catacombs beneath the palace.

There, in the suffocating darkness, surrounded by the echoes of the undead, Sherazade's situation grew more perilous. The king, though seemingly more lucid, was erratic, torn between moments of clarity and fits of rage.

But Sherazade did not falter. Each night, her stories became her lifeline, her voice a soothing balm to the king's tortured soul. She spoke of love and loss, of redemption and hope, each tale a subtle plea to the humanity that lingered within him.

And as the nights wore on, in the heart of the catacombs, beneath a kingdom lost to darkness, Sherazade's tales spun a fragile thread of connection between her and the zombie king, a thread that might yet lead them both to salvation or doom.

In the shadowed catacombs beneath the crumbling palace, where the chill of death lingered in the air like an unspoken curse, Sherazade continued her nightly

vigil. The stories she whispered in the darkness were more than mere tales; they were a lifeline, a fragile bridge spanning the chasm between life and the undead.

The zombie king, his form looming like a specter in the dim light of the flickering torches, listened with an intensity that belied his monstrous appearance. In his eyes, where once only a ravenous hunger had glowed, now flickered moments of lucidity, fleeting glimpses of the man he once was.

As the nights passed, the battles raging above seemed to grow more distant, the world of the living and the dead becoming blurred in the catacombs' sepulchral embrace. It was in this eerie quietude that Sherazade realized the moment of her final gamble had arrived.

One night, as she wove her tale, she reached into the depths of the king's past, into the heart of his humanity. "There was once a king, fair and just," she began, her voice a soft echo in the gloom. "He loved his people, and in return, they adored him. But tragedy struck, and he lost his queen, his heart, to forces beyond his control."

The king shifted, a tremor of recognition passing through his ravaged form. "The queen," he murmured, the words a ghost of a memory.

"Yes, your queen," Sherazade pressed gently, her heart pounding. "In his grief, the king made a pact, seeking to bring her back. But the price was heavy, for it brought a curse upon the land."

The king's eyes widened, the fog of his undead existence momentarily clearing. "The curse... my queen..." His voice trailed off, a mixture of sorrow and dawning horror.

Sherazade took a deep breath, her next words a key to unlock the shackles of his damned existence. "But the king, strong of heart and true of purpose, found a way to undo the curse. He needed only to remember who he was, to reclaim his soul from the darkness."

The king's gaze locked onto hers, a silent plea for salvation in his haunted eyes. "How?" he rasped, the word a desperate whisper.

"The king's blood," Sherazade answered, her voice steady. "It was the key, for the curse was bound to his lineage. Only a sacrifice, a final act of love and courage, could break the chains that bound the kingdom."

For a long moment, the king was still, his mind warring with the remnants of his humanity and the curse's relentless grip. Then, with a clarity that shone like a beacon in the dark, he spoke. "I... I remember. My queen, my kingdom... I must save them."

With trembling hands, the king drew a dagger from his belt, its blade gleaming dully in the torchlight. He looked at Sherazade, a silent farewell in his gaze, before plunging the blade into his heart.

As the king's form crumbled to dust, a great shudder passed through the catacombs, a wave of energy that surged upward, breaking the curse's hold over the kingdom. The undead, released from their torment, lay still, their time of damnation at an end.

Sherazade, tears streaming down her face, emerged from the catacombs into the light of dawn. The kingdom, though forever scarred, was free. The people, gathering in the pale morning light, looked upon her with awe and gratitude.

In the days that followed, Sherazade took up the mantle of leadership, her wisdom and compassion guiding the kingdom through its time of healing. She ruled not from a throne of gold, but from a place of understanding and strength, her tales a reminder of the resilience of the human spirit.

And so, in a land where darkness had once reigned, a new era dawned, born from the ashes of tragedy and the power of redemption. Sherazade, the savior of the kingdom, became a legend, her stories echoing through time, a testament to the enduring light that lives within every tale, every heart.

CHAPTER 5

CAPTAIN NEMO VS. THE UNDEAD OF ATLANTIS

"In the heart of the ocean, where the depths hide more secrets than the stars above, lies the truth about our world."

The Nautilus, a marvel of engineering and a testament to human ingenuity, cut through the waters of the Atlantic like a sleek predator. Inside its hull, Captain Nemo, a man whose eyes held the glint of unquenchable curiosity and a hint of unspoken sorrow, stood before a large, brass-rimmed window, gazing into the abyss. His crew, a collection of the world's most daring and skilled individuals, moved with well-practiced efficiency through the narrow corridors of their underwater home.

"We've picked up something unusual, Captain," Lieutenant Aronnax, Nemo's trusted second-in-command, called out, breaking the submarine's rhythmic hum. His voice was a mix of excitement and caution, a tone well-earned from years of navigating the uncertainties of the deep sea.

Nemo turned, his cloak swirling around him, a ghostly silhouette against the backdrop of machinery and dimly lit gauges. "On screen, Lieutenant," he ordered, his voice carrying the weight of a man who had known both the triumphs and tragedies of the sea.

The crew gathered around a flickering screen, where a series of cryptic symbols and an incomplete map of an uncharted region beneath the Atlantic Ocean materialized. The symbols, ancient and unfamiliar, spoke of a civilization lost to the depths, a city shrouded in mystery and legend. Atlantis.

"A fool's errand," grumbled Master Harpoonist Ned Land, his arms crossed skeptically over his broad chest. "Chasing after fairy tales and ghost stories."

"Perhaps," Nemo replied, his eyes not leaving the screen. "But imagine if the tale is true, Ned. The discovery of Atlantis would redefine our understanding of history."

The crew exchanged uncertain glances, the allure of discovery wrestling with the fear of the unknown. Rumors of cursed waters and the unexplained disappearance of explorers in this region of the Atlantic had long been the subject of whispered conversations among seafarers.

As the Nautilus approached the coordinates, the ocean seemed to come alive with strange phenomena. Lights flickered in the depths, and the sonar picked up inexplicable readings. Nemo, feeling a pull he could not resist, ordered the submarine to dive deeper, towards the heart of the mystery.

It was then they found the artifact. A piece of craftsmanship so ancient, yet so advanced, it could only belong to the lost city of Atlantis. It was a small, intricately carved trident, glowing with a faint, otherworldly light. The crew huddled around it in awe, the artifact silencing any remaining doubts.

"We are on the brink of rewriting history," Nemo whispered, his voice barely audible over the sound of their excitement.

But as they neared the source of the transmission, the Nautilus was suddenly caught in a powerful underwater current. It was as if the ocean itself had come alive, determined to pull them into its deepest, darkest secrets.

"Engines at full reverse!" Nemo shouted, but it was no use. The current was relentless, dragging the submarine into an abyss that seemed to have no end.

The crew braced themselves as the Nautilus spiraled uncontrollably. Instruments flickered and alarms sounded, a cacophony of warning that went unheeded. They were no longer explorers but prisoners of the deep, drawn into an adventure that none of them had signed up for.

When the Nautilus finally stabilized, they found themselves in a vast underwater cavern, its walls glistening with bioluminescent algae. And there, in the distance, shrouded in shadows and mystery, lay Atlantis.

"We've done it," Aronnax breathed, a mix of disbelief and awe in his voice.

"Indeed, we have," Nemo replied, his face a mask of determination. "But remember, we tread upon a world lost to time. Caution will be our closest ally."

The crew nodded, understanding the gravity of their discovery. They were no longer just explorers. They were pioneers on the brink of the greatest discovery mankind had ever known. But unbeknownst to them, the shadows of Atlantis hid more than just forgotten history. They concealed a curse, a terror so ancient and so deadly, that it would test the very limits of their courage, their sanity, and their will to survive.

As the Nautilus ventured further into the lost city, the true adventure, fraught with danger and wonder, was about to begin.

The Nautilus, with its crew brimming with a mix of dread and excitement, glided through the ghostly streets of Atlantis. The city, submerged and silent, was a hauntingly beautiful maze of coral-covered buildings and statues, their once-majestic splendor now yielding to the relentless embrace of the sea.

As they ventured deeper, Captain Nemo's eyes remained fixed on the sonar and navigation screens, the green blips and lines painting a picture only he seemed to fully understand. "The heart of the city should be just ahead," he murmured, more to himself than anyone else. His crew stood by their stations, each man's breath caught in his throat as they approached the unknown.

It was then that they first saw them - the guardians of the deep. Figures, once human, now twisted and grotesque, their movements jerky and unnatural. Aquatic zombies, cursed inhabitants of this sunken world. They swarmed around the Nautilus, their eyes void of life, yet burning with an insatiable hunger.

"We need to back off, Captain," urged Aronnax, his voice tense. "We're not prepared for this."

Nemo's jaw tightened. "No, we press on. There must be a way to get past them."

But the initial skirmishes were disastrous. The undead creatures, relentless and seemingly impervious to harm, clung to the Nautilus, their grotesque fingers scraping against the hull. Each attack left the crew more shaken, their weapons and tactics proving futile against this underwater nightmare.

In the aftermath of the skirmishes, a heavy gloom settled over the crew. The excitement of discovery had been replaced by the cold, creeping fingers of fear. In the dim light of the control room, Nemo stood in silent contemplation, the weight of their situation etching deeper lines into his weathered face.

"We need a new plan," he finally said, his voice a low rumble in the tense air. "These creatures... they're not just mindless beasts. There's a pattern to their movements, a strategy we're not seeing."

Inspired by the ancient tactics of 'The Art of War', Nemo devised a daring plan. "We'll use the Nautilus as a lure," he explained. "Lead them into the Great

Canyon off the eastern ridge. If we can trap them there, we may have a chance to explore the city and find answers."

The crew set to work, their resolve hardened by their captain's unwavering determination. But as they executed the plan, an unforeseen horror emerged from the depths. The undead king of Atlantis, a colossal creature whose very presence seemed to warp the water around him, appeared. His attack was brutal and swift, shattering the Nautilus's defenses and throwing the crew into disarray.

The plan had failed. The Nautilus, damaged and vulnerable, retreated to a hidden alcove to lick its wounds. The crew, battered and demoralized, struggled to comprehend the power of their adversary.

"It's like fighting a force of nature," Aronnax said, his voice hollow. "We underestimated them."

In the midst of their despair, Nemo sought solitude in the Nautilus's library, pouring over ancient texts and forgotten lore. It was there that he found a glimmer of hope - a communication from a being unlike any other.

The captured zombie sage, once a wise Atlantean scholar, reached out to Nemo through telepathic whispers, its voice echoing in the depths of his mind. "The curse... it was our doing," the sage revealed. "Atlantis was a paradise, but our quest for knowledge led us down a dark path. We unleashed this horror upon ourselves."

Nemo listened, the sage's words painting a tragic picture of a civilization destroyed by its own hubris. The realization that brute force would never be enough to overcome this threat dawned on him. He needed a new approach, one that combined strength with wisdom.

As he shared this revelation with his crew, a new sense of purpose took hold. They began to study the movements and behaviors of the undead, searching for weaknesses, for patterns that could be exploited. The Nautilus, once a vessel of war, became a laboratory, a place of learning and strategy.

But just as hope began to flicker anew, disaster struck. The undead king, having tracked them to their hiding place, launched a ferocious assault. The crew fought valiantly, but they were outmatched. The king's power seemed to grow with every attack, his command over the undead legions unyielding.

In the chaos, Nemo was captured, dragged from the Nautilus and brought before the king in the heart of the drowned city. There, surrounded by the

decaying grandeur of Atlantis, the king revealed his ghastly plan. With Nemo and the Nautilus, he would break free from his watery prison, spreading the curse to the world above. Nemo, bound and helpless, could only watch in horror as his crew fought desperately to save him, and themselves, from a fate worse than death. The battle raged, the waters around Atlantis churning with violence and despair.

The Nautilus lay crippled, its crew shattered, and their captain in the clutches of an enemy whose power seemed as vast and unfathomable as the ocean itself. The dream of discovery had turned into a nightmare, and the depths of the undead held them in their merciless grip. The Nautilus, battered and bruised, sat quietly in the murky depths, a wounded beast in the lair of its enemy. Inside, the air was thick with despair. The crew, once buoyed by the thrill of adventure, now faced a reality they could scarcely comprehend. Their captain, their leader, was in the clutches of a creature as ancient and merciless as the sea itself.

In the heart of Atlantis, Captain Nemo stood before the undead king, his spirit unbroken despite the dire circumstances. The king, a towering figure of decay and malevolence, gazed down at Nemo with eyes that burned like the deepest ocean vents.

"You are a formidable adversary, Captain Nemo," the king's voice echoed through the waterlogged halls. "But your resistance is futile. With you and your ship, I will finally be free to claim the world above."

Nemo, his hands bound, met the king's gaze. "You may break my body, but my will remains my own. Your curse will not reach the surface. I swear it."

Back on the Nautilus, Lieutenant Aronnax rallied the remaining crew. "We cannot abandon the Captain," he declared, his voice cutting through the gloom. "We must fight, not just for him, but for all humanity."

The crew, inspired by Aronnax's words, prepared for their final stand. Using the ancient knowledge they had gleaned from the Atlantean sage, they set about reactivating the city's long-dormant defense mechanisms.

As the battle began, the Nautilus moved with a purpose, its torpedoes and electrical charges finding their marks against the undead hordes. The crew, fighting with a newfound understanding of their foe, pushed back against the seemingly endless waves of attackers.

In the throne room, Nemo struggled against his bonds. The undead king, sensing the turn of the tide, grew furious. "You cannot win, Captain," he roared, his voice a tempest. "My power is eternal."

But Nemo had one last trick up his sleeve. With a swift, calculated movement, he freed himself, lunging towards the mystical orb that hung suspended above the king's throne. His fingers closed around it, and with all his might, he shattered it. A shockwave rippled through Atlantis. The king, his power source destroyed, let out a wail of agony as he began to crumble into the abyss. The undead, suddenly leaderless, faltered in their assault. The crew of the Nautilus, seizing the moment, fought with renewed vigor. They pushed forward, inch by inch, towards their captain. The waters around Atlantis boiled with chaos and conflict, the fate of the world hanging in the balance.

As Nemo rejoined his crew, the city began to collapse around them. They raced back to the Nautilus, their hearts pounding in their chests. But as they made their escape, Nemo noticed something that filled him with dread. His crew, his brave and loyal men, showed signs of infection. The curse of Atlantis had claimed them, too. With a heavy heart, Nemo realized what he must do.

"Set course for the deepest trench," he ordered, his voice barely a whisper. "We cannot risk bringing this curse to the surface."

The crew, understanding the gravity of their captain's words, complied. As the Nautilus dove deeper, Nemo sent out a final transmission, a warning to the world about the horrors that lay beneath the waves.

As the trench loomed before them, a mutiny broke out. Some of the crew, their minds twisted by the curse, sought to return to the surface. A fierce battle erupted, the Nautilus a battleground between the will of its captain and the dark desires of the infected. In the chaos, Nemo initiated the self-destruct sequence. The crew, those still loyal and those lost to madness, stopped, realizing the end was near. As the countdown began, Nemo took one last look at his beloved Nautilus, his home and sanctuary in the deep.

The explosion, when it came, was a brilliant burst of light in the dark abyss. The Nautilus, along with the secrets of Atlantis and its cursed inhabitants, was swallowed by the sea, a sacrifice to ensure the safety of the world above.

In the silence that followed, the depths reclaimed their secrets, the legends of Captain Nemo and the lost city of Atlantis fading into the whispers of the ocean currents. But the final transmission of the Nautilus lingered, a haunting reminder of the mysteries and dangers that lie in the unexplored corners of our world.

CHAPTER 6

GULLIVER VS. TINY ZOMBIES

"In the heart of the vast ocean, where man's dominion has yet to reach, nature unfolds her mysteries."

The Hopeful, a vessel as sturdy as her name, sliced through the indigo waves of the uncharted sea, her sails billowing like the lungs of the deep. Lemuel Gulliver, the ship's navigator, stood at the helm, his eyes reflecting the endless expanse of water and sky. The journey had been long, and Gulliver's thoughts often wandered to his home, to the faces of those he left behind. Yet, there was a spark in his gaze, a hunger for the unknown that kept him steadfast on this perilous voyage.

As night descended, a tempest brewed in the distance, a monstrous swirl of clouds and wind, like the maw of some colossal beast. The crew, seasoned men of the sea, scrambled across the deck, securing ropes and battening hatches. Gulliver barked orders, his voice barely rising above the howling wind. "Steady, lads! We've weathered worse than this!" he shouted, gripping the wheel with a determination that belied his growing unease.

The storm hit them with the fury of an enraged titan. Waves, mountainous and merciless, crashed against The Hopeful, tossing her about as if she were a mere toy. The ship groaned and creaked, her timbers strained against nature's onslaught. Amidst the chaos, Gulliver fought to maintain control, his every muscle tensed against the tempest's wrath.

"Navigator! The mast!" cried out Mr. Bates, the first mate, his voice laced with terror. Gulliver's eyes widened as he saw the mainmast, a proud column of wood and canvas, splintering and crashing down. The impact threw him off his feet, and the world turned into a maelstrom of shouts, crashing waves, and darkness.

When consciousness returned to Gulliver, it was a slow, groggy awakening. His body ached as if every bone had been remade. His eyes fluttered open, revealing a sky of the clearest blue. He was lying on a beach, the sand beneath him warm and comforting. With great effort, he pushed himself up, his mind clouded with confusion. "Where am I?" he murmured, scanning the unfamiliar terrain.

The island was lush, verdant greenery stretching as far as the eye could see. In the distance, he could make out structures, tiny and intricate, like the creations of a meticulous artisan. As he stumbled towards them, driven by a mix of curiosity and desperation, he began to notice the scale of everything around him. The trees were like tall grass, the leaves like small shrubs. A surreal realization dawned upon him - he was a giant in this land.

Suddenly, he heard voices, high-pitched and frantic. Hiding behind a cluster of what seemed like tiny trees, he peered out to see a group of minute human figures, no taller than his fingers, armed with what looked like miniature spears and swords. They were in a state of disarray, some tending to the wounded, others forming battalions.

One of them, a figure who seemed to command authority, was rallying his troops. "The undead have breached the Eastern Wall!" he exclaimed. "We must fortify our defenses!"

Gulliver's mind raced. Undead? He had heard tales of such creatures in sailors' yarns, but to witness such a phenomenon was unthinkable. Compelled by a mix of empathy and adventure, he decided to reveal himself.

Standing up, he addressed the tiny crowd. "I mean you no harm," he boomed, modulating his voice to not startle them further. The Lilliputians recoiled in shock, their faces a mix of fear and awe.

The leader, braver than the rest, stepped forward. "Giant, from whence do you come? Are you a friend or foe to Lilliput?" His voice, though faint, carried a tone of defiance.

Gulliver knelt, bringing himself closer to their level. "I am Lemuel Gulliver, a navigator of the sea. I come in peace, and wish only to understand where I find myself, and perhaps, offer my aid in your plight."

The Lilliputian leader eyed him warily, then nodded. "I am General Redressal. Our land is in peril. The undead, once our own people, now threaten to overrun our kingdom. We are at a loss, giant Gulliver, for their numbers grow and our strength wanes."

Gulliver looked at the tiny faces around him, seeing determination and fear intermingled. He thought of his own crew, lost to the sea, and a sense of kinship stirred in him. "Then let us fight together," he said, a resolve kindling in his heart.
"

With your knowledge of this enemy and my... advantage in size, perhaps we can find a way to turn the tide."

General Redressal exchanged looks with his men, a silent conversation passing between them. Finally, he turned back to Gulliver. "Very well. We shall welcome your aid, Lemuel Gulliver. Together, we shall face this scourge."

As the tiny soldiers cheered, Gulliver felt a weight lift off his chest. He was no longer just a castaway on a strange land; he was an ally in a battle for survival. And in the depths of his mind, a thought lingered, perhaps this journey was not just about finding his way home, but about discovering a purpose far greater than he had ever imagined.

The alliance between Gulliver and the Lilliputians, once formed, grew into a bond of camaraderie and respect. Gulliver, with his vast size and strength, brought a new ray of hope to the beleaguered inhabitants of Lilliput. Yet, with every passing day, the undead horde seemed to swell, their numbers growing like a dark tide threatening to engulf the land.

General Redressal and his council met with Gulliver under the shade of a mammoth leaf, which to them was akin to a grand pavilion. Maps, miniature to Gulliver but detailed and intricate, were spread out before them. The General pointed to various locations, explaining their strategies and the challenges they faced.

"The undead are relentless," General Redressal said, his voice tinged with weariness. "They feel no pain, no fear. And they are cunning, far more than mere mindless creatures. We need a strategy that combines strength with ingenuity."

Gulliver listened intently, his mind working. "In my world, there is an ancient text, 'The Art of War.' It speaks of using the enemy's strength against them, of fighting not just with force but with strategy. Perhaps we can adapt its teachings to our situation."

The Lilliputians looked at each other, intrigue sparked in their eyes. "Tell us more, Giant Gulliver," urged the General.

Gulliver leaned closer, his voice a gentle rumble. "For instance, if the undead are attracted to movement or noise, we can create diversions, lead them into traps. We have the advantage of intelligence, and we must use it."

The council murmured in agreement, and plans were quickly formed. Gulliver, with his immense strength, began constructing traps and barricades.

Guided by the Lilliputians' knowledge of their land and the behavior of the undead, they built pitfalls covered with leaves, giant snares from twisted vines, and walls made from sturdy tree trunks.

Days turned into nights, and nights into days, as they toiled together. Gulliver found himself growing fond of these resilient little beings, admiring their courage and ingenuity. He learned their language, laughed at their jokes, and shared stories of his own world.

Then came the day of the first major confrontation since Gulliver's arrival. A large horde of the undead, drawn by their activities, approached from the east. The Lilliputians, armed and ready, took their positions. Gulliver, armed with a giant club fashioned from a tree limb, stood ready.

As the undead came into view, a sea of decaying flesh and soulless eyes, a shiver ran down Gulliver's spine. He had faced many dangers at sea, but nothing like this. At General Redressal's command, the first trap was sprung. A section of the ground gave way, swallowing a large number of the undead. Cheers erupted from the Lilliputians, quickly silenced as more of the horde pressed forward.

Gulliver swung his club with precision, taking care not to harm the tiny allies fighting beside him. Each swing felled several of the undead, but they kept coming.

"Retreat to the second line of defense!" ordered General Redressal. The Lilliputians fell back, luring the undead into another series of traps.

Amidst the chaos, Gulliver noticed a group of undead moving differently, almost strategically. They were avoiding the traps, guiding others. An icy realization struck him - these undead were once Lilliputian soldiers, their skills in warfare still ingrained in their cursed forms.

"General, some of them remember their training!" Gulliver bellowed, pointing out the group.

General Redressal's eyes narrowed. "Then we must adapt. Focus on those ones!"

The battle raged on, Gulliver and the Lilliputians adapting to each twist and turn. As the sun began to set, painting the sky in hues of fire and blood, the horde finally began to thin. Exhausted but victorious, the Lilliputians let out a triumphant cry.

That night, as they tended to their wounded and honored their fallen, Gulliver sat with General Redressal, looking over the battlefield. "Today, we won a battle," said Gulliver, "but the war is far from over."

General Redressal nodded. "True, Giant Gulliver. But with you by our side, we have hope. And sometimes, hope is the mightiest weapon of all."

In the days that followed, Gulliver and the Lilliputians continued their campaign against the undead. With each victory, their bond grew stronger, and Gulliver's respect for the Lilliputians deepened. He learned from them, as much as they learned from him.

But as they fought side by side, a gnawing thought grew in the back of Gulliver's mind. The undead were unlike anything natural. There was a sinister intelligence behind them, a malevolent will. And the more he observed, the more he began to suspect that the source of this plague might be more complex, and more terrifying, than they had imagined.

The air was thick with tension as dawn broke over Lilliput. Gulliver and the Lilliputian army stood ready, facing the open field that had become the stage for their most crucial battle yet. The enemy they were to face was like none other - a colossal tiny zombie, a grotesque mutation that seemed to embody the very essence of the plague.

General Redressal stood beside Gulliver, his face set in a grim line. "This creature, it's unlike anything we've ever seen. It's as if our collective fears gave birth to it," he said, his voice barely above a whisper.

Gulliver nodded, his eyes fixed on the horizon. "We'll defeat it together. We must."

As the sun rose, casting a golden light over the land, the ground began to tremble. The colossal tiny zombie emerged, a towering figure even to Gulliver. Its eyes, void of any soul, locked onto the army before it.

The Lilliputians let loose their arrows, tiny yet deadly in their precision. Gulliver charged forward, a giant sword in hand, crafted specially for this battle. The zombie roared, a sound that chilled the bravest of hearts, and met Gulliver's charge.

The clash was titanic. Gulliver's sword struck against the zombie's flesh, tearing through decayed sinew. The Lilliputians maneuvered around it, attacking with coordinated strikes. But the creature was relentless, its strength seemingly inexhaustible.

In the midst of the battle, Gulliver found himself face to face with the zombie. He swung his sword with all his might, but the creature caught it, its grip unyielding. With a swift motion, it struck Gulliver, its teeth sinking into his flesh.

Pain seared through Gulliver, but it was not the agony of a deadly wound. His vision blurred, and the battlefield around him faded into a nightmarish vision. He saw his own world, his home, ravaged by a similar plague. The streets were filled with the undead, and the sky was a tapestry of despair.

Shaking his head, Gulliver broke free from the creature's hold, the vision clearing from his eyes. "It's showing me my world," he gasped, realization dawning on him. "The plague... it's there too."

General Redressal, fighting nearby, overheard him. "Gulliver, focus! We need you here, now!"

Gathering his wits, Gulliver rejoined the battle with renewed vigor. The Lilliputians, inspired by his resilience, rallied around him. Together, they pushed the zombie back, driving it towards a trap they had prepared - a deep pit, filled with spikes and fire.

With a final, concerted effort, Gulliver and the Lilliputian soldiers managed to topple the monstrous zombie into the trap. It fell with a deafening crash, its roars silenced as the flames consumed it.

The battlefield fell quiet, the threat vanquished. Gulliver, breathing heavily, looked at the faces of the Lilliputians around him. They were bruised and battered, but alive and victorious.

General Redressal approached Gulliver, his expression one of mixed relief and concern. "You were bitten. Are you...?"

Gulliver shook his head. "I'll be fine. But General, the visions I saw... the plague is not just here. It's in my world too. Somehow, it's connected."

The revelation hung heavily in the air, a new shadow cast over their hard-won victory. The battle was over, but a larger war loomed - a war that spanned worlds.

As the Lilliputians tended to their wounded and mourned their fallen, Gulliver stood apart, his thoughts turbulent. The connection between the

plagues, the visions he had seen - there were pieces of a puzzle he needed to solve. And he knew, deep in his heart, that the key to it all lay in his own world. The journey he had thought was an escape had become a mission, one that he could not turn away from.

In the fading light of the day, as the Lilliputians gathered around him, a sense of unity and purpose took root. Together, they had faced the unimaginable. And together, they would face whatever came next.

In the aftermath of the battle, a solemn air hung over Lilliput. Gulliver, now seen not just as a giant but a leader and a protector, joined forces with the kingdom's wisest scholars. Together, they delved into ancient texts and obscure lore, seeking the root of the undead scourge that had so ravaged their land.

In the grand library of Lilliput, a room filled with scrolls and tomes so small that Gulliver had to use a magnifying glass to read them, they pored over every piece of knowledge available. Days turned into nights, and nights into days, as they searched for answers.

One evening, as a storm raged outside, casting flickering shadows across the walls of the library, a breakthrough came. A scholar named Allectus, his eyes wide with a mixture of fear and excitement, called Gulliver over to a dusty corner of the library.

"Gulliver, look at this," Allectus said, pointing to an ancient scroll. "It speaks of a 'Dark Relic,' a cursed artifact from another world. The descriptions match those of an object from your realm."

Gulliver leaned in, studying the intricate drawings and cryptic texts. The Dark Relic was depicted as a small, unassuming object, but the aura around it was drawn with dark, menacing strokes.

"Yes, I've seen this before," Gulliver murmured, a chill running down his spine. "It's a compass, an old maritime one, from my world. But how did it end up here, and how is it linked to the undead?"

Allectus shuffled through more scrolls. "The legend says it was brought here through a 'tear' in the worlds, a breach caused by a great storm. It speaks of a curse that spreads like a plague, bringing the dead back to life."

A sense of dread settled over Gulliver. The storm that had shipwrecked him in Lilliput, the visions he had seen - it was all connected.

"We need to find this compass, this Dark Relic," Gulliver said, determination steeling his voice. "It's the key to everything."

The search began in earnest. Gulliver, accompanied by a team of Lilliput's bravest soldiers and scholars, scoured the island. They searched through ancient ruins, delved into forgotten caves, and even ventured into the territories still haunted by the undead.

Finally, in a hidden cave beneath the island's tallest mountain, they found it. The compass lay on a stone pedestal, its surface dull and unremarkable. But the air around it was thick with an invisible menace, a palpable sense of malice.

Gulliver reached out, his hand hesitating inches from the compass. "This is it," he said, his voice barely above a whisper. "The source of our nightmare."

As his fingers touched the cold metal, a surge of images flooded his mind - visions of his world, of a darkness spreading across the oceans, of the undead walking the streets of cities far and wide. And he understood. The curse was not bound to one world; it was a bridge between them, a dark thread weaving through the fabric of both realms.

"We must find a way to break the curse," Gulliver said, turning to the Lilliputians. "The cure... it's not here. It's in my world."

The revelation was a heavy burden, but it brought clarity. The Lilliputians, with their newfound knowledge, began to work on a plan. They would help Gulliver return to his world, armed with the cursed compass and the understanding of the plague that bound their fates together.

In the days that followed, as they prepared for Gulliver's departure, a bond of deep respect and friendship had formed between the giant and the tiny inhabitants of Lilliput. They had faced the darkness together, and now they were united in a quest to end it.

As Gulliver set sail on a raft built by the Lilliputians, a crowd gathered at the shore. General Redressal stepped forward, his expression solemn yet hopeful.

"You have become more than a friend, Gulliver. You are a brother to us," he said, his voice steady. "Go, and may the winds guide you to your home. Find the cure, for both our worlds."

Gulliver nodded, a lump in his throat. "I will return, I promise. And I will bring back the light to banish this darkness forever."

With those final words, he pushed off the shore, the raft carrying him towards the horizon. Behind him, Lilliput faded into the distance, but the memory of its brave people, their courage and their plight, remained etched in his heart.

The journey back was a race against time, with the fate of two worlds hanging in the balance. As the raft bobbed on the vast

ocean, Gulliver held the cursed compass in his hand, its needle spinning wildly. He knew that his adventure was far from over - it was just the beginning of a greater quest, a quest to save all that he held dear.

The sun dipped low on the horizon as Gulliver's makeshift raft, crafted with the ingenuity and aid of his Lilliputian comrades, bobbed gently on the tide. The Lilliputians, gathered on the shore, watched with a mixture of pride and sorrow. In their eyes, Gulliver was no longer a mere giant, but a hero, a friend, a part of their very soul.

As he prepared to depart, General Redressal stepped forward, a small yet dignified figure against the vast expanse of the sea. In his hands, he held the highest honor of Lilliput - a tiny medal of bravery, wrought in the finest gold.

"Gulliver, in recognition of your courage and the deep bond you have forged with our people, we bestow upon you the Order of the Lilliputian Star," General Redressal announced, his voice carrying across the water.

Gulliver knelt, allowing the General to place the medal around his neck. It was a poignant moment, the weight of the tiny medal feeling like the heaviest burden he had ever borne.

"Thank you," Gulliver said, his voice thick with emotion. "I carry with me not just this medal, but the spirit of Lilliput. You have my word, I will return."

With those final words, he pushed off, the raft drifting away from the island. As the shores of Lilliput receded into the mist, Gulliver felt a deep sense of purpose. The journey ahead was fraught with danger and uncertainty, but his resolve was unshaken. He would find a way to break the curse, to save both his world and the world he had come to cherish.

Days turned into nights, and nights into days, as Gulliver navigated the endless sea. The cursed compass, secured safely in his pocket, was his only guide, its needle spinning erratically, as if caught in an unseen struggle.

One foggy dawn, as a mist hung heavy over the waters, Gulliver's keen eyes spotted a shape looming in the distance. It was a ship, or rather, the ghost of a ship - derelict, its sails tattered, drifting aimlessly on the current.

A chill ran down Gulliver's spine as he recognized the vessel. It was The Hopeful, his ship, the very one that had carried him on this fateful journey. With a mix of dread and determination, he steered his raft towards the ghostly remains.

Climbing aboard, Gulliver's heart pounded in his chest. The deck was silent, save for the creaking of old wood and the moan of the wind. He moved cautiously, a sense of foreboding growing with each step.

Then, he saw them - his crew, or what was left of them. They roamed the deck, their movements sluggish, their eyes devoid of life. They were undead, like the creatures he had fought in Lilliput.

Horror and realization struck Gulliver in the same breath. The curse, the undead plague, it had originated from his world, not Lilliput. The storm, the tear between worlds - it was all connected.

As the undead crew shambled towards him, Gulliver backed away, his mind racing. He understood now the true nature of the curse - it was a bridge between worlds, a dark force that had ensnared both Lilliput and his home.

In a moment of desperate clarity, Gulliver grasped the cursed compass, the key to it all. He knew what he had to do. With a mighty cry, he hurled the compass into the sea, watching as it sank beneath the waves.

A blinding light erupted from the spot where the compass disappeared, a shockwave rippling across the water. The undead crew halted, their movements ceasing as the curse that bound them unraveled. One by one, they collapsed, finally at peace.

Gulliver stood on the deck of The Hopeful, the sun breaking through the fog, casting its light on a world forever changed. He had set out to find adventure, but what he found was a destiny entwined with the fate of two worlds.

As he set sail once more, this time towards his home, Gulliver knew that his journey was not just a tale of survival, but a testament to the unbreakable bonds of friendship and the enduring power of hope. And though the seas ahead were uncharted, he sailed on, a man forever changed by a land of tiny people and a battle against the shadows.

CHAPTER 7

ROMEO & JULIET VS. THE UNDEAD

"In love and war, the first casualty is always the truth."

The moon hung low over Verona, casting a ghostly pallor on the cobbled streets. A city once vibrant with the colors of noble banners now lay shrouded in the ominous shadow of a timeless feud, the houses of Montague and Capulet locked in a bitter struggle for supremacy. Yet, as the night deepened, a more sinister force than the pride of feuding nobles crept silently through the alleyways.

Romeo Montague, heir to a legacy of warriors and poets, wandered the deserted streets. His heart, a tempest of emotions, grappled with a sense of foreboding that clung to the air like a shroud. His cloak billowed behind him, the sword at his side a mere whisper of security against the unseen terrors of the night.

As he turned into an alley shrouded in darkness, Romeo's thoughts were not of the ancient grudge that marred his family's name but of a pair of eyes that sparkled like stars in the Veronese sky. Juliet Capulet, a name that should have tasted of venom on his tongue, yet it sang like a sweet melody in his heart. Their meetings were fleeting, stolen moments in the shadows, away from prying eyes, a secret symphony in a city of discordant screams.

Suddenly, a chilling howl pierced the night, snapping Romeo back to the grim reality. He drew his sword, the steel glinting under the moon's watchful gaze. From the shadows emerged a figure, or what once was a figure, now a grotesque parody of humanity. Its eyes, devoid of life, glared hungrily at Romeo.

"Stay back, creature of the night!" Romeo's voice echoed through the alley, strong yet tinged with an unspoken fear.

The creature hissed, its movements jerking unnaturally as it lunged towards him. With a swift, practiced motion, Romeo thrust his sword forward, piercing the creature's heart. It fell with a thud, lifeless once more.

Breathing heavily, Romeo wiped his blade on his cloak. This was the third undead he had encountered this week. The plague, as the townsfolk whispered in hushed, fearful tones, was no longer a distant rumor. It was here, in Verona, turning friend and foe alike into mindless cadavers driven by a hunger for the living.

He hastened his steps, eager to leave the scene of death behind. As he emerged onto the broader street, he saw the light of a torch approaching. Benvolio, his cousin, came into view, his expression grave.

"Romeo, thank the stars you're safe! The streets are no longer ours once the sun sets," Benvolio said, gripping Romeo's shoulder.

"I know, cousin. The undead... they are increasing in number," Romeo replied, sheathing his sword.

"The city is in chaos. Our families' quarrel seems petty in the face of this scourge. We need a plan, Romeo. You must speak to your father."

Romeo nodded, his mind racing. The art of war was in his blood, but this was a foe unlike any his ancestors had faced. He needed to be innovative, cunning.

As they walked back to the Montague residence, Romeo's thoughts drifted back to Juliet. In these dire times, their love was a beacon of hope, a reminder of what they were fighting to preserve. He knew that their secret meetings could not continue for much longer. The city needed him, and he could not afford the luxury of a love, however pure, that the world deemed forbidden.

Upon reaching his home, Romeo found Lord Montague in deep discussion with his advisors. The room fell silent as Romeo entered. All eyes turned to him, some with expectation, others with undisguised concern.

"Father, we need a new strategy. The old ways of war will not suffice against this plague. We must unite, Montague and Capulet alike, to fight this greater enemy," Romeo declared, his voice steady, betraying none of the turmoil in his heart.

Lord Montague regarded his son with a mixture of pride and worry. "You speak of unity in times of division, my son. Do you believe the Capulets will lay aside centuries of hatred for this cause?"

"They must, for the sake of Verona. I will meet with Lord Capulet, seek a truce. We have a common enemy now, one that threatens to devour us all if we do not stand together."

The room erupted in murmurs. The idea of a truce with the Capulets was radical, almost unthinkable. Yet, the fear of the undead was a powerful motivator, stronger than the bitterness of old grudges.

Romeo's proposal was a gamble, a flicker of hope in the encroaching darkness. The night was far from over, and the shadows held more than just secrets. They harbored a threat that could end not just a feud, but the very existence of Verona itself.

Romeo's journey through the night-laden streets of Verona was fraught with peril, his every step shadowed by the lurking dread of the undead. The moon, a silent witness to his turmoil, cast an eerie glow over the city, its light flickering like the last breath of hope in a world succumbing to despair.

He arrived at the Capulet estate just as dawn was breaking, the first rays of the sun piercing through the darkness. The grandeur of the house stood in stark contrast to the chaos that reigned outside its walls. Romeo's heart pounded in his chest, not just from the fear of the undead, but from the prospect of seeing Juliet.

Stealing inside, he found his way to the orchard, their secret meeting place. The air was filled with the sweet scent of blossoming flowers, a fleeting reminder of the beauty that once was Verona.

"Juliet," Romeo whispered, his voice barely audible.

From the shadows emerged a figure, her beauty undiminished by the surrounding gloom. Juliet Capulet, a vision of hope in a world teetering on the brink of despair.

"Romeo, you came. I feared the worst," Juliet said, her voice trembling with a mix of fear and relief.

"We must speak quickly. The city is overrun. My plan... I need to unite our families against this common foe. It's the only way," Romeo said urgently.

Juliet's eyes widened in disbelief. "Our families? United? Romeo, do you understand what you're asking?"

"I do, and I know it seems impossible. But love, look around us. This feud, our families' pride, what does it matter against the tide of death at our doors? We need to stand together, or Verona will fall."

Juliet's gaze met his, a storm of emotions swirling in her eyes. "I will speak to my father, Romeo. I cannot promise he will listen, but I will try."

Their hands met, fingers intertwining in a silent vow. The moment was brief, for the dawn was no longer safe, and they parted with heavy hearts, each to face their own daunting task.

The meeting with Lord Capulet was as tense as Romeo had anticipated. The grand hall of the Capulet estate felt like a battlefield, with words as weapons and pride as shields.

"Lord Capulet, I come to you not as a Montague, but as a citizen of Verona, pleading for unity against a threat that endangers us all," Romeo began, his voice resonating with a conviction that surprised even him.

Lord Capulet, a man of imposing stature and fierce demeanor, regarded Romeo with a mixture of curiosity and disdain. "You expect me to believe that a Montague comes to my house, not to scheme or gloat, but to parley for the good of Verona?"

"It is the truth, my lord. The undead plague respects neither Montague nor Capulet. It seeks to devour all. Our feud must be set aside, for the survival of our city," Romeo implored.

The conversation was arduous, with suspicion and age-old grudges clouding every word. Yet, the urgency of Romeo's plea, the sincerity in his eyes, began to chip away at the walls of enmity that had stood for generations.

Meanwhile, the streets of Verona grew ever more perilous. The undead, once solitary predators, now roamed in packs, their numbers swelling as the plague claimed more victims. Romeo's initial attempts to rally the citizens and defend the city were met with failure. The traditional tactics of warfare were futile against a foe that felt no fear, no pain, no hesitation.

In a desperate bid, Romeo gathered a small band of fighters, a mix of Montagues, Capulets, and brave souls who dared to stand against the tide of death. Inspired by the legendary battles of old, he devised a plan to lure the undead into the open fields beyond the city, where they could be fought en masse.

The plan was bold, perhaps too bold. As the undead swarmed the fields, the living warriors found themselves overwhelmed. The creatures were relentless, their numbers far greater than anticipated. The battle turned into a massacre, with Romeo and his fighters barely escaping with their lives.

This defeat was a bitter pill to swallow. Romeo realized that brute strength and conventional strategies were not enough. He needed something more, something unpredictable, something as unorthodox as the enemy they faced.

The revelation came from an unlikely source. In the depths of the city's library, Romeo found ancient texts on mystical warfare, treatises on psychological manipulation, and strategies that blurred the line between the physical and the supernatural. It was a new kind of art, a fusion of intellect and instinct, perfectly suited to combat the undead.

As he poured over the texts, Juliet's words echoed in his mind, a reminder of the stakes. "We fight not just for ourselves, Romeo, but for the promise of a future where our love can exist in the light of day."

Armed with this newfound knowledge, Romeo began to retrain his fighters, instilling in them the principles of this unconventional warfare. The city's defenses were bolstered, traps and deceits laid in the streets, and the people of Verona braced for the coming storm.

Yet, in the midst of their preparations, tragedy struck. A horde of undead, larger and more ferocious than any before, descended upon the city. The battle that ensued was apocalyptic. The streets ran red with blood, both living and undead.

Romeo fought with a ferocity that belied his despair, his sword a blur of steel and vengeance. But as the sun set, casting long shadows over the battlefield, a dreadful realization dawned on him. Juliet was missing. In the chaos, she had vanished, and a dreadful rumor spread like wildfire - Juliet Capulet had been turned.

As the night closed in, and the screams of the living and the undead melded into a symphony of horror, Romeo stood alone amidst the carnage, his heart breaking. The woman he loved, the beacon of his life, lost to the very darkness they had vowed to fight.

The battle for Verona had reached its lowest ebb, and Romeo Montague, warrior-poet, lover, and fighter, faced the abyss, not knowing if the dawn would ever come again.

The darkness of the night enveloped Verona like a shroud, a city once vibrant with life now teetering on the brink of annihilation. The air was thick with despair, the streets echoing with the cries of the undead and the living alike. Romeo Montague, his heart a barren wasteland of grief and fury, stood amidst the ruins, his eyes reflecting the inferno that raged within.

The rumor of Juliet's fate, a dagger twisting in his soul, propelled him forward with a reckless determination. He rallied the remnants of his forces, a motley crew of desperate souls clinging to the faintest glimmer of hope. They were not just fighting for survival now; they were fighting for the memory of a love that had dared to dream in a time of nightmares.

"Tonight, we make our final stand," Romeo declared, his voice cutting through the despair like a beacon. "For Verona, for our fallen, for Juliet."

The survivors, inspired by Romeo's unwavering resolve, took up arms. The city, their city, was a labyrinth of death, but in Romeo, they saw a leader who could guide them through the darkness.

As the sun dipped below the horizon, the undead began their relentless march, a tide of death surging towards the heart of Verona. Romeo and his fighters met them head-on, their battle cries rising above the din of clashing steel and snarling beasts.

The fight was brutal, a dance of death that left no room for mercy. Romeo, his sword an extension of his will, moved through the undead with a grace born of desperation. Each strike was a tribute to Juliet, a testament to a love that had burned too brightly to be extinguished by the darkness.

In the midst of the carnage, a figure emerged, cutting a path through the undead with a ferocity that matched Romeo's own. It was Juliet, her eyes blazing with an unworldly light, her movements lethal and precise.

"Juliet!" Romeo cried out, his voice laden with disbelief and relief.

Their eyes met across the battlefield, a moment of clarity in the midst of chaos. Juliet fought her way to Romeo's side, her blades singing a deadly duet with his.

"I thought I had lost you," Romeo said, his voice a whisper amidst the storm of battle.

"I was lost, Romeo, but I found my way back. For you, for us," Juliet replied, her gaze fierce and unwavering.

Together, they turned the tide, their love a weapon against the darkness. The undead, sensing the strength of their bond, faltered and fell back. The night, once an ally to the creatures, now seemed to stand with Romeo and Juliet.

As dawn approached, a glimmer of hope on the horizon, the final wave of the undead descended. It was a monstrous horde, led by a creature more terrifying than any they had faced. Its eyes glowed with a malevolent fire, its presence chilling the very air.

Romeo and Juliet stood side by side, their hearts beating as one. "Together, to the end," Romeo said, gripping her hand.

"Together," Juliet echoed, her voice a vow.

The battle that followed was a maelstrom of fury and fear. Romeo and Juliet fought with a desperate strength, their swords weaving a deadly dance around the creature. In the end, it was Juliet who delivered the killing blow, her blade piercing the creature's heart. As the creature fell, a deafening silence descended upon the city. The sun broke over the horizon, its rays banishing the darkness and revealing the extent of the devastation.

Verona was saved, but the cost had been grievous. The streets were littered with the fallen, the air heavy with the scent of loss. Yet, in the midst of the ruins, Romeo and Juliet stood, a testament to the enduring power of love. As they surveyed the aftermath, a revelation dawned on them. Their blood, mingled in battle, held the key to the cure. Juliet, who had been on the brink of turning, was the living proof.

Romeo, realizing what needed to be done, turned to Juliet. "Our love has been our strength. Now, it can be Verona's salvation."

With a heavy heart, Juliet nodded. Romeo, bitten in the battle and slowly succumbing to the plague, used his last moments of humanity to transmit the cure through his bite to Juliet.

As his humanity faded, Romeo looked into Juliet's eyes, seeing not just the woman he loved, but the future of Verona. "I love you, now and forever," he whispered, his voice fading into the light of the new dawn. Juliet, tears streaming down her face, held Romeo as he transformed, her heart breaking and yet filled with a fierce determination. She became the vessel of the cure, her blood the antidote to the plague that had ravaged their city.

In the days that followed, Juliet, with the help of the survivors, administered the cure to the afflicted. The plague receded, and the city, though forever scarred, began the slow process of healing.

The feud between the Montagues and Capulets, once the heart of Verona's discord, was forgotten in the face of their shared victory. Romeo and Juliet, in their sacrifice, had united the city in a way no peace treaty ever could.

Their story, a tale of love and valor, became a legend, whispered in the streets and sung in the taverns. Romeo and Juliet, the undying guardians of Verona, their love a beacon of hope in a world that had known too much darkness.

As Juliet stood on the balcony where she had first declared her love for Romeo, she looked out over the city, a solitary figure of resilience and strength. Their love had conquered death, and in doing so, had given life to a new Verona, a city reborn from the ashes of calamity by the power of undying affection.

CHAPTER 8

MONKS VS. THE UNDEAD

"In the heart of every winter lies an invincible spring," whispered the ancient walls of the Lotus Monastery, veiled in the mist that hung like a silken curtain over the craggy mountains.

Liang, a young monk whose spirit was as unyielding as the stone beneath his bare feet, moved with a grace that belied his formidable strength. In the monastery's shadowed halls, his figure was often seen gliding silently, an embodiment of peace and discipline. His days were a rhythmic dance of meditation, study, and the art of combat - a martial prowess that had become the stuff of whispered legend among his brothers.

One evening, as amber hues of sunset bled into the deep blue of twilight, a disturbance rippled through the tranquility of Lotus Monastery. A solitary figure, haggard and bloodied, emerged from the forest that cradled the sacred grounds. The stranger, a pilgrim bearing wounds that spoke of unspeakable horrors, collapsed at the monastery's gates.

The monks, led by Liang, rushed to aid the fallen traveler. As they carried him to the infirmary, Liang couldn't shake a gnawing sense of unease. The monastery, a haven for seekers of enlightenment, had never before been touched by such palpable shadows.

Under the flickering light of oil lamps, the monks tended to the pilgrim. His breaths were shallow, his eyes clouded with pain and fear. Liang, with hands as skilled in healing as they were in combat, worked tirelessly to soothe the pilgrim's suffering. Despite his efforts, the man's murmurs grew increasingly delirious, whispering of shadows that walked and hungered.

That night, Liang found no peace in meditation. His thoughts were haunted by the pilgrim's words, a foreboding sense of a looming threat that transcended their understanding. As dawn approached, the monastery was shaken by a blood-curdling scream. Liang was the first to reach the infirmary, only to witness a scene that chilled his soul.

The pilgrim, now a grotesque version of his former self, his eyes hollow and hungering, had turned. His hands, twisted into ghastly claws, were clasped around the throat of Brother Jun, one of the younger monks. Liang's heart raced as he confronted a nightmare made flesh.

Without a moment's hesitation, Liang leaped forward, pulling the transformed pilgrim away. The creature snarled, its teeth bared in a grotesque parody of a smile. Liang's training took over, his movements a blur of precision and force, yet he was mindful to spare the creature's life, constrained by his vow to do no harm.

"Brother Liang, what... what is this abomination?" gasped Brother Jun, terror and confusion etched on his youthful face.

"I do not know, Brother," Liang replied, his voice steady despite the tumult in his heart. "But we must protect the monastery. Alert the others. We must prepare."

As Brother Jun hurried away, Liang faced the creature, his mind racing. The transformation was beyond natural ailments or injuries. It was as if the very essence of the pilgrim had been corrupted, twisted into something unholy.

The monastery, once a bastion of serenity and wisdom, now echoed with the sounds of panic and preparation. Liang, standing before the ancient altar, couldn't help but feel a profound sense of responsibility. The peace they had known was shattered, and a dark, uncharted path lay ahead.

He gathered the monks, their faces a tapestry of fear and resolve. "Brothers," he began, his voice cutting through the murmurs, "we face an unknown evil. Our compassion bids us to aid the suffering, but our duty now is to protect these sacred grounds and each other. We must stand united, as guardians of light against this darkness."

The monks nodded, their faith in Liang unshaken. They had always seen in him a leader, though he had never sought the role. Now, as danger encroached upon their sanctuary, Liang found himself at the forefront of a battle he never imagined - a battle not just for their lives, but for their very souls.

As the sun rose, casting a golden glow over the monastery, Liang stood resolute, a lone sentinel facing the unknown. The Lotus Monastery, a haven of peace for centuries, was now the stage for a struggle between life and death, light and shadow. And Liang, the reluctant warrior-monk, was at its heart.

The monastery, once a bastion of serenity, now echoed with the sounds of chaos and fear. The monks, robed in their traditional saffron and maroon, moved

with a sense of urgency they had never known. Under Liang's direction, they fortified the ancient walls and secured the sacred halls against the abomination that had infiltrated their sanctuary.

Liang, while orchestrating the defenses, was plagued by a gnawing sense of inadequacy. His skills in martial arts, though unparalleled, seemed futile against this unnatural foe. He remembered the teachings of his elder, Master Chen, who often spoke of the need for wisdom in battle, not just strength.

As dusk fell, a spine-chilling howl echoed from the forest, a harbinger of the impending onslaught. The transformed pilgrim, now a grotesque harbinger of death, led a horde of undead towards the monastery. Their eyes glowed with a hunger that was both terrifying and unnatural.

The monks, standing shoulder to shoulder, braced themselves. Liang stood at the forefront, his staff in hand, his heart heavy with the weight of impending conflict. "Remember your training, brothers. Let your inner peace be your strength," he called out, trying to steady the trembling hands and wavering spirits around him. The first wave of the undead crashed against the monastery's gates like a tide of despair. Liang leaped into action, his staff whirling in a dance of precision and power. The monks followed, their chants a resonant backdrop to the chaos. But for every undead creature they felled, another took its place. It was a battle they were not prepared for, a battle against an enemy that knew no fear, no pain.

Retreating behind the gates, Liang's mind raced. The traditional methods of combat were failing them. They needed a strategy, a way to outsmart this relentless enemy. In a moment of inspiration, he recalled a passage from "The Art of War": *Know your enemy and know yourself, and you can fight a hundred battles without disaster.* Gathering the remaining monks, Liang outlined a plan. Using the monastery's labyrinthine architecture to their advantage, they would lure the undead into the inner courtyards, where they could be isolated and dealt with more effectively. The monks, their faith in Liang unwavering, set about preparing traps and barricades.

As night deepened, the plan was set into motion. The undead, drawn by the monks' chants, mindlessly entered the trap. For a moment, it seemed they would prevail. But the unforeseen intelligence of the undead, especially the transformed pilgrim, turned the tide. He seemed to anticipate their moves, directing the horde with a cunning that was chilling.

The monastery's walls, which had stood for centuries, trembled under the onslaught. Liang watched in horror as the undead breached their defenses, tearing through the traps as if they were mere cobwebs. The monks fought bravely, but they were being overwhelmed. The courtyard, once a place of meditation and peace, was now a battleground stained with both living and undead blood.

In the midst of the chaos, Liang's eyes met those of the transformed pilgrim. There was a moment of eerie recognition, a flicker of something almost human, before it was drowned in the abyss of its undead hunger. Liang realized then that they were not just fighting reanimated corpses; they were fighting something far more sinister, something that had taken control of the dead. The night wore on, a relentless wave of terror and despair. Liang fought with a desperation he had never known, his staff a blur of motion. But it was not enough. The undead kept coming, their numbers seemingly endless.

As dawn approached, bringing with it the promise of light, Liang and the surviving monks found themselves cornered. The undead had overrun the monastery, and their numbers were dwindling rapidly. Liang, bloodied and exhausted, looked at his brothers, their faces etched with fear and fatigue.

"This may be our last stand," Liang said, his voice steady despite the hopelessness of their situation. "But we will stand together, as brothers, as guardians of this sacred place. Let our courage be our legacy."

The monks, inspired by Liang's resolve, prepared for one final, desperate battle. They formed a circle, their backs to each other, as the undead closed in. Liang raised his staff, ready to meet his fate with dignity and valor. But fate, it seemed, had other plans. As the first rays of dawn pierced the darkness, a sudden, deafening explosion rocked the monastery. The ground shook, and a bright light engulfed the courtyard. The undead, caught in the blast, were incinerated, their ashes carried away by the wind.

Liang and the monks, shielded by the monastery's walls, looked on in stunned disbelief. The courtyard, once filled with the undead, was now empty, a scorched testament to the night's horrors. In the silence that followed, Liang realized that their battle was far from over. The source of the explosion was a mystery, one that hinted at forces beyond their comprehension. The monastery, their home and sanctuary, lay in ruins, a shadow of its former self.

As the monks gathered around Liang, their eyes filled with questions and fear, he knew that the path ahead was fraught with danger and uncertainty. But one thing was clear: they had survived the night, and in surviving, they had discovered a strength they never knew they had. The battle against the undead was over, but the war for their souls had just begun.

CHAPTER 9

BILLY THE KID VS. THE UNDEAD

"All Warfare is Based on Deception." Sun Tzu

The sun hung low over the Dustbowl, painting the sky with strokes of crimson and gold. It was a quiet evening in the small western town, a kind of quiet that made folks uneasy, like the calm before a storm. Nestled between the rugged mountains and the arid desert, the town was a haven for those who sought riches from the earth. But that evening, as the sun dipped behind the mountains, an ominous shadow fell over the town, a prelude to the darkness that was about to engulf it.

In the heart of this desolate landscape, behind the bars of the town's jail, sat Billy the Kid. The infamous outlaw, notorious for his cunning and his quick draw, was now a caged animal. His reputation had preceded him, a legend whispered in saloons and around campfires, but here, he was just another prisoner awaiting his fate.

Billy leaned against the cold stone wall, his eyes fixed on a small spider weaving its web in the corner of his cell. The methodical nature of the creature's work fascinated him. It was an artist at its craft, much like he was with a revolver. The irony wasn't lost on him.

The clanging of boots on the wooden floor outside his cell snapped Billy out of his reverberation. Sheriff Collins, a man as tough as the land he governed, stood before the cell, keys jangling in his hand.

"Billy," the sheriff said, his voice a gravelly drawl. "Never thought I'd see the day when Billy the Kid would be caught by the likes of me."

Billy smirked, his eyes never leaving the sheriff's. "Everyone gets lucky once, Sheriff. But it's staying lucky that's the hard part."

The sheriff grunted, unamused. "Luck's got nothing to do with it. You're here because you're a menace. A danger to every honest folk in this town."

"Honest folk? In this town?" Billy chuckled. "That's as rare as a rainy day in the desert, Sheriff."

Before the sheriff could retort, a sudden commotion outside caught their attention. Shouts and screams pierced the evening air, followed by a sound that chilled the blood - a guttural, inhuman moaning that seemed to rise from the very bowels of the earth.

Sheriff Collins hurried to the window, peering out into the growing darkness. What he saw made his seasoned heart skip a beat. People were running in a frenzied panic, chased by figures that seemed to shamble and stagger with a grotesque, unnatural gait. The undead, risen from their eternal slumber, were upon the town.

"God Almighty..." the sheriff muttered, his face turning ashen.

Billy stood up, his interest piqued. "Sounds like you got bigger problems than an outlaw, Sheriff."

The sheriff turned, his eyes meeting Billy's. In that moment, an unspoken agreement passed between them. The town was under siege, and every gun was needed, even one wielded by an outlaw.

With a heavy sigh, Sheriff Collins unlocked the cell. "I'm letting you out, Billy. Not because I trust you, but because we need every gun against... whatever those things are."

Billy stepped out of the cell, stretching his legs. "Well, Sheriff, looks like we're partners now."

Grabbing his hat and gun belt from the sheriff's desk, Billy felt a rush of adrenaline. This was more than an escape; it was a call to a different kind of adventure, one that he had never imagined.

As they stepped outside, the full horror of the situation unveiled itself. The townsfolk were in disarray, fighting off the advancing horde of zombies with anything they could lay their hands on. The creatures, their bodies decayed and their eyes void of life, moved relentlessly towards the living.

Sheriff Collins and Billy stood back to back, their guns at the ready. "Remember, aim for their heads," the sheriff instructed.

Billy nodded, a sly grin on his face. "Never thought I'd be taking orders from a sheriff."

With a deep breath, they plunged into the fray, their guns blazing. Each shot from Billy's revolver was precise, dropping a zombie with every pull of the trigger. Beside him, Sheriff Collins fought with equal ferocity, his shotgun roaring in the night.

As they fought, a bond formed between them, a bond forged in the heat of battle. They were no longer lawman and outlaw; they were two men standing against a tide of darkness, fighting for their very survival.

But as they soon would learn, this was just the beginning. The horrors that emerged from the ancient gold mine were more than just mindless undead. They were a force that would test Billy the Kid's cunning and survival instincts to their limits. And in this battle, it wasn't just the zombies he would have to outwit.

The night air was thick with the smell of gunpowder and death as Billy and Sheriff Collins fought back-to-back against the relentless tide of the undead. The once peaceful town had transformed into a macabre battleground, illuminated only by the sporadic flashes of gunfire.

In the midst of chaos, Billy's mind was surprisingly clear. His past life as an outlaw had prepared him for moments like this - moments where survival hinged on quick thinking and quicker reflexes. But this was different. These creatures, with their rotting flesh and soulless eyes, were unlike any adversary he had faced before.

As they fought their way towards the safety of the Sheriff's office, a plan began to form in Billy's mind. "Sheriff," he shouted over the din of the battle, "we need to regroup and come up with a real strategy. We can't keep shooting blindly into the night!"

Sheriff Collins, reloading his shotgun, nodded in agreement. "You're right, Kid. Follow me!" he yelled, leading Billy through a maze of alleyways, dodging the groping hands of the undead.

Once inside the office, they barricaded the doors and windows. The room was filled with a handful of survivors, each wearing a look of terror and disbelief. Among them was Emily, the town's schoolteacher, a woman of both wit and courage; Tom, the young blacksmith, strong and steadfast; and Doc Simmons, the elderly town doctor, his hands trembling not from age but from fear.

"We need a plan," Sheriff Collins stated, his voice heavy with the burden of leadership.

Billy stepped forward, the gears in his mind turning. "These things... they seem to be coming from the old gold mine," he began, drawing curious glances from the survivors. "What if we lure them back there and seal it off?"

The idea was met with a mix of skepticism and hope. Emily spoke up, her voice steady. "But how do we lure them all back there? And how do we seal the mine?"

Billy's eyes sparkled with a dangerous kind of intelligence. "Explosives. We use bait to draw them into the mine and then blow it sky-high."

Tom, the blacksmith, chimed in, "I can make the explosives, but we'll need gunpowder, lots of it."

Doc Simmons, looking more composed, added, "And I can create a concoction that should attract them. It'll be risky, but it might just work."

The plan was set. Over the next few hours, they worked tirelessly. Tom fashioned makeshift bombs from the gunpowder stored in the sheriff's office, while Doc Simmons mixed a foul-smelling concoction designed to mimic the scent of living flesh.

As dawn broke, painting the sky with hues of purple and orange, they were ready. Billy, Sheriff Collins, Tom, and a few other brave souls prepared to execute their plan. Emily and Doc Simmons stayed behind to tend to the wounded and protect the survivors.

The group made their way to the gold mine, the bait in hand. The plan was simple yet perilous - lay the bait, draw the zombies inside, set the explosives, and get out before everything came crashing down.

As they neared the mine, the ground trembled with the shuffling steps of the undead. The air was filled with their grotesque moans, a symphony of the damned. Billy felt a chill run down his spine, but he pushed the fear aside. This was their only chance.

They laid the bait at the entrance of the mine, the stench attracting the zombies like moths to a flame. As the creatures stumbled into the dark maw of the mine, Billy and the others retreated to a safe distance.

Tom lit the fuse, and they waited with bated breath. Seconds felt like hours until finally, the ground erupted in a massive explosion, sending a plume of fire and debris into the sky. The mine collapsed, sealing the zombies within.

Cheers erupted among the group, but Billy's celebration was cut short. A guttural roar echoed from the rubble, and out of the smoke emerged a figure - a zombie, larger and more grotesque than the others, with eyes that glowed with a malevolent intelligence. It was the zombie leader, and it was clear they had underestimated their foe.

The creature charged, and the group scattered. Billy and Sheriff Collins stood their ground, firing round after round, but the bullets seemed to have little effect. In the ensuing chaos, the zombie leader grabbed Billy, its grip like iron.

Sheriff Collins aimed his shotgun, but he was too late. The creature hurled Billy against a rock, knocking the wind out of him. As he lay there, dazed, the reality of their situation sank in. They had succeeded in trapping the horde, but in doing so, they had awakened something far more dangerous.

As the zombie leader advanced towards Billy, his mind raced. He needed a plan, and he needed it fast. His eyes caught a glint of metal - the explosives Tom had left behind. A risky idea formed in Billy's mind, one that would require all his cunning and a bit of luck.

With the last ounce of his strength, Billy rolled towards the explosives, pulling the pins as the creature loomed over him. The world slowed down, and in that moment, Billy made peace with his fate. He had lived as an outlaw, and he was ready to die as a hero.

But fate, it seemed, had other plans for Billy the Kid.

The ground beneath Billy the Kid trembled as he lay dazed, the zombie leader towering over him like a specter of death. In the fraction of a second that seemed to stretch into eternity, Billy's hand closed around the pins of the makeshift explosives. His fingers, so accustomed to the cold steel of a gun, now held the key to their salvation or their end.

Just as the creature lunged forward, Billy yanked the pins out, a defiant glare in his eyes. The explosion that followed was cataclysmic, a roar that seemed to shake the very foundations of the earth. Fire and debris erupted around them, a hellish inferno consuming all in its path.

Miraculously, Billy was thrown clear from the blast, his body battered but alive. As he struggled to his feet, his ears ringing and his vision blurred, he saw the aftermath of his desperate act. The mine was now a smoldering crater, and the zombie leader was nowhere to be seen.

Sheriff Collins, along with Tom and the others, rushed to Billy's side. Their expressions were a mix of shock and awe. "You did it, Billy! You took down that monster!" Tom exclaimed, his voice tinged with disbelief.

Billy managed a weak smile, his body aching in protest. "Seems like I did, kid. Seems like I did."

As they stood there, amidst the wreckage of their once peaceful town, the sound of approaching hooves broke their moment of triumph. A cavalry unit, led by a stern-faced captain, rode into town. The townspeople, weary and battered, looked on with a mix of hope and apprehension.

The captain dismounted and approached Billy and Sheriff Collins. His gaze was steely, his voice authoritative. "Sheriff Collins, we received word of an outbreak here. We've come to secure the town and eliminate any remaining... threats."

The sheriff nodded, relief evident in his eyes. "We appreciate the help, Captain. But thanks to Billy here, the threat has been taken care of."

The captain's eyes narrowed as they landed on Billy. "Billy the Kid, the infamous outlaw. You are under arrest. There's a bounty on your head, and the law has a long memory."

The reality of the situation dawned on Billy. The battle with the undead might be over, but his fight for survival was far from finished. He exchanged a knowing glance with Sheriff Collins, a silent acknowledgment of their shared predicament.

"Sheriff, are you going to let them take me after all we've been through?" Billy asked, his voice laced with a hint of betrayal.

Sheriff Collins looked torn, his sense of duty clashing with the debt he owed Billy. "Billy, you saved this town, but I can't go against the law. I'm sorry."

As the soldiers moved to apprehend Billy, the outlaw's mind raced. He had faced death head-on and emerged victorious. He wasn't about to let his fate be sealed by the very people he had just saved.

With a swift movement, Billy disarmed the nearest soldier, his instincts taking over. "Sorry, boys, but I ain't going down without a fight," he declared, his voice steady despite the odds stacked against him.

What followed was a blur of motion, a dance of desperation and survival. Billy moved with a grace and agility that belied his injuries, dodging bullets and taking down soldiers with an efficiency that was almost artistic.

Sheriff Collins, caught in the middle, hesitated. His loyalty to the law was unwavering, but he couldn't bring himself to raise his weapon against the man who had just saved his town, his people.

In the chaos, Billy made his way to a horse, his escape route clear. He paused for a moment, looking back at the town that had become an unlikely battleground. "You might not see it now, Sheriff, but you and I, we're not so different. We both fight for what we believe in."

With those final words, Billy spurred the horse into a gallop, disappearing into the horizon, leaving behind a legacy that would be remembered for generations.

The town slowly recovered from the nightmare it had endured. Sheriff Collins, forever changed by the events, would often find himself gazing into the distance, wondering about the outlaw who had become an unlikely hero.

In the end, Billy the Kid had not only fought the dead but had also outwitted the living. His legend, born in the fires of battle and the shadows of an outlaw life, would continue to echo through the annals of time, a testament to the thin line between hero and outlaw.

CHAPTER 10

SAMURAIS VS. ZOMBIES

"In a world darkened by despair, the faintest light of honor can illuminate the path of many."

The wind howled through the desolate landscape, carrying with it the stench of decay and the whispers of the undead. It was a world unrecognizable, torn asunder by a plague that left nothing but ruin in its wake. Amidst this chaos, a solitary figure moved with purpose, his silhouette etched against the setting sun. Kaito, once a proud samurai, now the last of his kind, wandered these ravaged lands, a ghost haunted by memories of a past life.

As Kaito approached a small, beleaguered village, the sight of the tattered banners flapping in the wind stirred something within him. The villagers, gaunt and weary, watched him with a mix of fear and hope. An old man, his face lined with the hardships of this new world, stepped forward. "Sir, are you... could you be... a samurai?" he asked, his voice trembling.

Kaito's eyes, which had seen too much death, softened. "I am," he replied, his voice a whisper of its former glory.

The villagers gathered, their eyes alight with a flicker of hope. A young woman, her face smeared with dirt, clutched a child to her chest. "Please, we need your help. The undead... they come every night. We're not fighters, we can't..."

Kaito's gaze drifted to the child, who stared back with wide, innocent eyes. They reminded him of his own daughter, lost to the same monsters that now plagued this village. A pang of pain shot through his heart. He had sworn never to wield his sword again, the weight of his failures too heavy to bear. Yet, in the child's eyes, he saw a reflection of the past he could not escape.

"I cannot help you," Kaito said finally, turning away. The desperation in the villagers' eyes grew, but he walked on, his steps heavy with guilt.

That night, as Kaito camped in the nearby woods, the distant screams of the villagers pierced the night. He tried to shut them out, but they echoed the screams of his own family, ripped away by the same fate. His resolve wavered.

The next morning, Kaito returned to the village, only to find it under siege by a horde of zombies. Among the chaos, a young girl, no older than his daughter would have been, stood defiantly against a zombie, armed with nothing but a broken piece of wood. Her bravery, in the face of certain death, rekindled a fire in Kaito's soul.

With a cry that seemed to tear the very air, Kaito drew his sword, an extension of his will, and charged. The blade sang as it cut through the undead, each strike a testament to his skill and sorrow. The villagers, inspired by his bravery, rallied and fought back with renewed vigor.

As the last of the undead fell, the villagers surrounded Kaito, their faces alight with gratitude. The old man approached him, tears in his eyes. "You have saved us," he said, his voice heavy with emotion.

Kaito sheathed his sword, the weight of it feeling different now. "I have only delayed the inevitable," he replied solemnly. "These creatures... they will return."

The young woman with the child stepped forward. "Then teach us to fight, to defend ourselves. You can't just leave us now."

Kaito looked at the faces around him, seeing in them not just fear, but a willingness to fight, to survive. He saw in them a reflection of himself, of the warrior he once was. "I will train you," he said, his voice resolute. "But know this, the path ahead is fraught with peril, and I cannot promise survival."

The villagers nodded, understanding the gravity of his words. Kaito set about training them, teaching them the basics of combat, of how to move and strike, and most importantly, how to stay alive. As the days passed, Kaito felt a change within him. The guilt that had shackled his soul began to lift, replaced by a sense of purpose he had long thought lost.

But as they prepared for the coming night, an unsettling truth gnawed at the back of Kaito's mind. These zombies, relentless and seemingly with a hint of cunning, were unlike any he had encountered before. A deeper, more sinister threat loomed over them, hidden in the shadows of this apocalypse. Kaito knew that the true battle was yet to come.

The days melded into each other as Kaito trained the villagers, his sword cutting through the air with a precision born of a lifetime of discipline. Each swing, each stance he demonstrated, was imprinted in the minds of his impromptu students. The villagers, though initially clumsy, began to show signs of improvement, their movements growing more confident, their strikes more assured.

As night fell, they readied themselves, a motley crew of farmers, blacksmiths, and mothers turned warriors by necessity. Kaito watched them, a silent guardian, his heart heavy with the knowledge of the horror that awaited them.

The first attack came under the cloak of darkness, a tide of groaning, shuffling undead. The villagers, guided by Kaito's tactics, held their ground. The air was filled with the sounds of clashing weapons, desperate cries, and the ungodly moans of the zombies. Despite their bravery, the villagers were pushed back, the sheer number of the undead overwhelming.

Kaito, amidst the chaos, fought like a demon possessed, his blade a whirlwind of death. But even he could not be everywhere, and slowly, inexorably, the undead gained ground. As dawn broke, the zombies retreated, leaving behind a village shaken but still standing. The cost, however, was clear in the faces of the villagers as they counted their dead.

In the aftermath, Kaito realized that traditional tactics would not suffice. He retreated into himself, poring over ancient texts and strategies, seeking a solution. It was in these moments of solitude that an idea began to form, inspired by the legendary 'Art of War.'

He gathered the villagers, his eyes alight with a fierce determination. "We cannot outfight them," he said, his voice cutting through their despair. "But we can outthink them. We will use the environment, set traps, create illusions. We will strike where they least expect it."

The villagers listened, their spirits lifted by Kaito's confidence. They worked tirelessly, setting up defenses, digging trenches, and preparing their homes to be fortresses. Kaito taught them the value of psychological warfare, how fear could be a weapon used against their mindless foes.

The night of their grand plan arrived. The villagers, hidden in shadow, waited as the undead approached. At Kaito's signal, the traps were sprung. Flames erupted, trenches collapsed, and chaos reigned among the undead ranks. For a moment, victory seemed within grasp.

But the tide turned swiftly. From the shadows emerged a new horror - zombies unlike any they had faced. These creatures moved with a terrifying purpose, dodging traps and tearing through defenses. The villagers' morale shattered, and their lines broke under this unexpected onslaught.

Kaito fought desperately, his sword a blur, but even he could not stem the tide. The village was overrun, its defenses breached. Amidst the screams and bloodshed, Kaito saw the truth - these were not mere mindless zombies, but something far more sinister.

In the aftermath, the village lay in ruins, the survivors few and huddled in fear. Kaito, wounded and exhausted, could only watch in despair. He had underestimated the enemy, and the price was paid in blood.

As he tended to the wounded, a shadow fell over him. Looking up, he saw a figure standing at the edge of the village, an enigmatic presence amidst the destruction. The figure approached, revealing himself to be a scientist, his clothes incongruous in this wasteland.

"You fight a war you do not understand, samurai," the scientist said, his voice cold and detached. "These creatures, they are but pawns in a greater game."

Kaito gripped his sword, suspicion and curiosity warring within him. "Explain," he demanded.

The scientist looked around at the devastation, his expression unreadable. "The zombies, they are the result of a failed experiment, a government project gone awry. But what you faced tonight, they are different. They are drawn here, controlled by something else."

"A signal," Kaito said, realization dawning. "You mean to say there is a device controlling them?"

"Precisely," the scientist replied. "Destroy the device, and you free the village."

The revelation hit Kaito like a physical blow. All this time, they had been fighting an enemy they did not understand, led to slaughter by an unseen hand. He looked at the faces of the survivors, their eyes filled with fear but also a flickering hope.

"I will destroy this device," Kaito declared, his voice resolute. "But I will need your help."

The scientist nodded, a hint of a smile playing on his lips. "Then we must act quickly. The horde will return, and in greater numbers."

Kaito set out the next day, accompanied by a handful of the bravest villagers. The scientist led them through the ravaged countryside

, towards an abandoned military facility. As they approached, the air grew heavy with an ominous feeling, the silence oppressive.

They found the device, a sinister contraption of wires and metal, pulsing with a malevolent energy. Kaito stepped forward to destroy it, but the world exploded into chaos. From every shadow, every corner, the undead surged, drawn by the device's signal.

The battle was brutal and unforgiving. Kaito fought with a ferocity born of desperation, but it was not enough. The undead were relentless, and one by one, the villagers fell. Kaito, surrounded and outnumbered, fought on, but it was a losing battle.

As the undead closed in, a monstrous figure emerged, towering over the others - a super-zombie, grotesque and seemingly invincible. Kaito faced it, knowing this was the end. The creature struck, and pain exploded through Kaito's body as he was thrown to the ground, his sword skittering away.

Lying there, defeated and broken, Kaito saw the faces of the villagers, of his lost family, and of the young girl who had inspired him to fight. In that moment, he understood the true cost of this battle, not just in lives lost, but in the hope extinguished.

As the super-zombie loomed over him, ready to deliver the final blow, Kaito closed his eyes, ready to join his ancestors. But the blow never came. Instead, a deafening silence fell, and Kaito knew no more.

Kaito's eyes fluttered open to a world blurred and spinning. The weight of his defeat pressed down on him like the heavy air of a storm. He lay there, broken, the shadow of the super-zombie towering over him. But in that moment of anticipated death, the creature halted, its grotesque head tilting as if listening to a distant call. With an unnatural growl, it turned and lumbered away, leaving Kaito in a pool of his own despair.

Struggling to his feet, pain lancing through his body, Kaito's gaze fell upon the remnants of his sword, shattered in the melee. He reached for it, his fingers wrapping around the cold steel. The broken blade was a reflection of his own shattered spirit, yet it reignited a spark within him.

The scientist, who had watched the scene from a safe distance, approached cautiously. "You're lucky to be alive," he remarked, a note of genuine surprise in his voice.

"Luck had no part in this," Kaito grunted, pushing himself upright. "That creature... why did it spare me?"

The scientist's eyes darted away, hiding something unspoken. "Perhaps it sensed you were no longer a threat. But this is our chance. The horde is dispersing. You need to destroy the device, now."

Kaito nodded, a sense of finality settling over him. With the scientist's guidance, he limped towards the device. Each step was a battle, but his resolve was unwavering. Reaching the contraption, he raised the broken blade and brought it down with all his remaining strength. The device sparked, sputtered, and then fell silent, its ominous pulsing light dying away.

For a moment, there was stillness, a calm that felt foreign in this ravaged world. Kaito collapsed, his mission complete, his body and spirit spent. As he lay there, the scientist's shadow fell over him once more.

"You've done it," the scientist said, his voice laced with an emotion Kaito couldn't place. "You've saved them."

But Kaito's eyes, clouded with pain, saw something more in the scientist's demeanor, a hidden truth lurking beneath the surface. "Who are you, really?" he asked, his voice barely a whisper. "Why guide me to this?"

The scientist hesitated, then sighed, as if a mask were being removed. "I was part of the project that created them," he confessed. "I believed we were advancing science, but we unleashed hell instead. I thought I could control it, use it, but I was wrong."

Kaito's heart sank. The realization hit him with the force of a thunderclap. This man, this scientist, was the true architect of their suffering. Anger flared within him, but his body was too weak to act.

"You... you led them here," Kaito managed to say, betrayal and horror mingling in his voice.

The scientist nodded, remorse etched on his face. "Yes, and I regret it every moment. But you've ended it. You've..."

His words were cut short as a guttural roar echoed through the air. The super-zombie, thought to be gone, re-emerged from the shadows, its eyes burning with a malevolent intelligence. The creature charged, fueled by a rage that was more human than zombie.

Kaito, summoning every ounce of his fading strength, stood to face this final adversary. The scientist scrambled away, his role as observer reclaimed.

The super-zombie was upon him in a heartbeat, but Kaito, driven by a mixture of fear and determination, met it with the ferocity of a cornered animal. The broken sword in his hand danced a deadly ballet, cutting into the creature's flesh. But for every wound he inflicted, the zombie seemed only to grow stronger. They fought, a blur of movement and violence, a dance of death under the apocalyptic sky. Kaito's every move was guided by instinct and training, the legacy of a samurai facing his final battle.

In the end, it was not skill but sheer will that turned the tide. Kaito, seeing an opening, thrust the jagged remnant of his sword into the creature's heart. With a final, ear-splitting howl, the super-zombie collapsed, its body disintegrating into dust. Kaito stood over the remains, breathing heavily, his body on the brink of collapse. He had won, but the victory was hollow. He turned to find the scientist, the man responsible for so much pain, watching him with a mix of fear and awe.

"You created monsters," Kaito said, his voice steady despite his exhaustion. "But in doing so, you forged a warrior."

The scientist nodded, accepting his judgment. "What will you do now?" he asked, a tremor in his voice.

Kaito looked out over the land, the sun rising over a world forever changed. "I will protect what remains," he declared. "I will be the guardian this world needs."

As he walked away, leaving the scientist to his guilt, Kaito knew his journey was far from over. There were more battles to be fought, more innocents to protect. But he also knew that in this broken world, there was still a place for honor, for bravery, for the way of the samurai.

And with that thought, Kaito, the last samurai, disappeared into the rising sun, his broken sword by his side, ready to face whatever new horrors this world had to offer.

CHAPTER 11

CAMELOT VS. THE UNDEAD

"In the heart of every legend lies a grain of truth, a seed that blossoms into a story that outlives time itself."

The sun was setting over Camelot, casting long shadows across the courtyards of the mighty castle. It was a kingdom of legends, where tales of chivalry and magic were not mere stories, but the very fabric of life. In the Great Hall, where banners fluttered gently in the evening breeze, knights and nobles gathered, their voices a symphony of laughter and lively debate.

At the Round Table, sat Sir Lancelot, the bravest among the knights, a man whose deeds were sung by minstrels across the land. His gaze, however, was distant, lost in thoughts that weighed heavily on his soul. The clatter of the hall seemed to fade as he dwelled on the vision that had haunted his dreams for nights on end. The Lady of the Lake, emerging from the depths of mist-shrouded waters, had spoken to him of a quest that would shape the destiny of Camelot.

King Arthur, noticing Lancelot's pensive mood, approached with a kingly grace. "Lancelot, my most trusted knight, what troubles you on this fine evening?" Arthur's voice was warm, yet carried the weight of a ruler well aware of the perils facing his kingdom.

Lancelot lifted his gaze, meeting the king's eyes. "My liege, I have been visited by a vision. The Lady of the Lake has revealed the location of the Holy Grail," he confessed, his voice tinged with awe and trepidation.

A hush fell over the hall. The Holy Grail, the most sacred of relics, had been a subject of many quests, but its discovery remained elusive, shrouded in mystery and danger.

Arthur's eyes lit up with a fire that spoke of both excitement and concern. "The Grail... its power could be the salvation our kingdom needs. But the path to such a relic is fraught with peril. Are you prepared to lead this quest, Lancelot?"

Lancelot hesitated, the weight of responsibility pressing down on him. "I fear the journey will be more perilous than any we have known. The Lady warned of great danger guarding the Grail. I worry for the lives of our brothers-in-arms."

Sir Gawain, overhearing the conversation, stepped forward, his youthful face alight with determination. "Where you lead, Sir Lancelot, we will follow. The bonds of brotherhood shall carry us through whatever trials await."

As the knights rallied around Lancelot, pledging their swords and lives to the quest, a sudden commotion at the castle gates interrupted their vows. A messenger, breathless and wide-eyed, burst into the hall. "My lords! The kingdom is under attack! Dark forces lay siege at our borders!"

The hall erupted into chaos. Knights rushed to their feet, drawing swords and donning armor. Arthur's expression hardened into that of a battle-hardened king. "To arms, my knights! Camelot shall not fall this day!"

Lancelot, his premonition of doom now a stark reality, knew there was no turning back. He donned his armor, a magnificent suit of silver and blue, and took up his sword, a blade that had tasted the blood of many foes.

As he rode out to meet the enemy, the weight of the vision bore down on him. This was no ordinary foe, but a harbinger of the darkness that lay ahead. The quest for the Holy Grail was no longer just a pursuit of glory; it was a race against time to save the kingdom he loved.

The battle raged through the night, a storm of steel and sorcery under the moonlit sky. Lancelot fought valiantly, his sword a blur as he cut down enemy after enemy. But even as they drove the invaders back, he knew this was but the first of many battles to come.

As dawn broke over the smoldering battlefield, Lancelot stood amid the fallen, his heart heavy with the cost of victory. Turning to King Arthur, who surveyed the aftermath with a mix of relief and sorrow, Lancelot spoke with a resolve born of necessity. "We must seek the Grail, my king. It is our only hope."

Arthur placed a firm hand on Lancelot's shoulder. "Then go, my bravest knight. Find the Grail and bring back the hope our kingdom so desperately needs. You have my blessing, and the prayers of all Camelot."

With that, Lancelot gathered a select group of knights, each a hero in their own right, and set off on the quest that would become legend. The journey to the Holy Grail had begun, a path fraught with unknown dangers and dark magic. But in their hearts, the knights carried the unyielding spirit of Camelot, a light that would guide them through the darkest of times.

As the morning sun crested the hills, Lancelot and his knights ventured into the heart of a land shrouded in ancient mystery. The path to the Holy Grail was uncharted, a journey across treacherous terrains and through forgotten realms. Each knight bore the burden of the quest, their hearts a blend of valor and apprehension.

The first trial they faced was the Forest of Whispers, a dense thicket where the trees themselves seemed to watch with unseen eyes. Sir Gawain, ever brave, led the way, his sword ready. "Stay sharp, brothers. The legends speak of spirits that guard these woods," he warned, his voice barely above a whisper.

As they delved deeper, ghostly voices filled the air, whispering secrets and temptations. Several knights strayed, lured by the promises of the voices, only to be saved by the swift intervention of their comrades. It was a harrowing ordeal, one that left them shaken but unbroken.

Emerging from the forest, they faced their next challenge at the Cliffs of Despair. A narrow path wound perilously along the cliff face, with a sheer drop to the roaring sea below. Sir Bedivere, the most level-headed among them, took the lead. "Keep your eyes forward, and trust in your footing," he advised, guiding them with a steady hand.

Their resolve was tested as the path crumbled beneath them, forcing them to leap perilous gaps and cling to the rocky face. With determination and brotherly aid, they overcame the cliffs, each trial forging their spirits like steel in fire.

But their greatest test lay ahead. As twilight descended, they reached an ancient crypt, nestled in a valley forgotten by time. The air was thick with the scent of age and decay. The Grail, according to the map they possessed, was hidden within.

Lancelot led them inside, the torches in their hands casting eerie shadows on the walls. The crypt was a labyrinth, its corridors lined with the statues of knights long dead.

In the heart of the crypt, they found it - an altar upon which the Holy Grail shimmered with a light that seemed to pierce the very darkness of the tomb. But as Lancelot reached for it, a chilling wind swept through the chamber, extinguishing their torches and plunging them into darkness.

From the shadows, an unholy moan echoed, growing into a cacophony of screams and wails. The knights drew their swords, standing back to back as the crypt came alive with the undead - a horde of ancient zombies, once knights themselves, cursed to guard the Grail for eternity.

The battle that ensued was like none they had ever faced. Blades passed through the spectral forms of the undead with little effect. Sir Bors, a giant of a man, was the first to fall, his body dragged into the darkness by clawing hands.

Lancelot, his heart heavy with the loss, rallied his knights. "We must think like warriors, brothers! Use the terrain to our advantage!" Inspired by the wisdom of Sun Tzu's "The Art of War," he led them in a strategic retreat, setting traps and using the narrow corridors to bottleneck their foes.

They fought through the night, their swords alight with magical flames conjured by Merlin's spells that had been imbued into their blades. But for every undead knight they felled, two more seemed to take its place.

As dawn broke, the knights found themselves surrounded, their strategies failing against the relentless tide. Lancelot, realizing the futility of their efforts, took a desperate gamble. He called upon Merlin through a magical talisman, a gift from the wizard himself for dire times.

Merlin's ethereal voice filled his mind. "The Grail, Lancelot! It is the key! Its holy light can banish these cursed souls to their final rest!"

With renewed purpose, Lancelot fought his way to the altar, his remaining knights covering him with fierce determination. Grasping the Grail, he raised it high, its light exploding in a blinding radiance that filled the crypt.

The zombies recoiled, their spectral forms dissolving in the holy light. But as the knights made their way out of the crypt, they realized the true extent of their plight. The Grail's light had awakened more of the undead, an army that had lain dormant in the earth, now clawing its way to the surface.

The knights, weary and wounded, stood on the brink of despair. The army of the undead stretched as far as the eye could see, a sea of death that threatened to engulf them. And then, in the midst of their darkest hour, the ground shook. From the direction of Camelot, a thunderous roar filled the air. Merlin, having sensed the peril his knights faced, had come to their aid.

Riding a chariot of fire, drawn by steeds of pure light, the wizard arrived, his power a beacon in the darkness. His staff raised high, he unleashed torrents of fire and lightning, decimating the undead ranks.

But even Merlin's might could not stem the tide completely. As he fought, a figure emerged from the undead army - the Grand Master of the cursed order, a knight of formidable power, driven by centuries of betrayal and rage.

Merlin, his strength waning, faced the Grand Master in a duel of magic and might. The ground cracked under the force of their battle, but it was a fight Merlin could not win alone.

Lancelot, realizing the grim truth, made a decision that would forever mark his destiny. "To me, knights!" he shouted, rallying his brothers. "For Camelot, for Merlin, we make our stand!"

Together, they charged into the fray, the Holy Grail's light their beacon, their courage the last hope against the unending darkness. The battle for the Grail, for Camelot, had reached its climax, a clash of light and shadow that would echo through the annals of time.

CHAPTER 12

THE UNDEAD OF SHERWOOD

"In the darkest of times, the faintest light can hold the power of the sun," whispered Robin Hood, his eyes surveying the moonlit expanse of Sherwood Forest, a shadowed haven in a world gone mad. He stood like a sentinel, his gaze piercing through the dense canopy of ancient oaks and elms, their branches swaying in the ghostly wind.

The forest, once a place of merry gatherings and joyful hunts, had transformed into a fortress, a sanctuary against the horrors that had befallen England. The undead, once mere figments of nightmarish tales, now roamed the land, their insatiable hunger turning the once-proud kingdom into a realm of despair. These creatures, the Undead Elite as they were bitterly dubbed, had not only robbed the people of their lives but had usurped their places of power, ruling from their grotesque courts in the shadows.

Among the living, there was one who dared to defy this new order. Robin Hood, once a lord of noble birth, now the leader of a band of outlaws known as the Merry Men. Under his command, these brave souls had become the unseen guardians of the oppressed, the last flicker of hope in a world smothered by darkness.

"It's not right, Robin," muttered Little John, his burly frame barely contained by the tree he leaned against. "The living suffer while those...things...feast and fatten in their castles."

Robin's eyes never left the forest, but his voice carried the weight of his resolve. "Aye, John. It's a world turned upside down. But we'll set it right, mark my words."

The plan had been simple at first: strike at the undead where it hurt, their hoarded treasures, and distribute it among the starving people. But as the nights grew longer, so too did the shadows that stretched across their souls.

A rustling in the underbrush announced the arrival of another of Robin's trusted men, Will Scarlet, his face etched with urgency. "Robin! The undead have taken more villagers. The people are scared, hungry. They look to us for help."

Robin turned, his face a mask of determination. "Then we shall not fail them. We've played the part of the fox for too long, stealing scraps from under the lion's nose. It's time we bared our teeth."

Little John's eyes gleamed at the prospect. "What do you propose?"

"We strike at the heart of their power. The Sheriff of Nottingham, that vile puppet of the undead, hoards the wealth in his tower, guarded by those creatures. We take it from him."

"But Robin," Will interjected, "that's a fortress. We've been lucky so far, but this... this is certain death."

Robin's gaze hardened, his voice a low growl. "Every night we delay, more innocents perish. We must act, not for glory, not for riches, but for the very soul of England."

The men exchanged uneasy glances, the weight of their task settling upon them like a shroud. They knew the risks, the almost certain doom that awaited them. Yet in their hearts, the fire that Robin Hood had ignited burned fierce and unyielding.

It was a young recruit, barely more than a boy, who broke the silence. His voice trembled, but his eyes shone with a fervor that belied his years. "I lost my family to the undead. You took me in, gave me a purpose. I'll follow you, Robin, to hell if need be."

Robin's gaze softened as he looked at the young lad, seeing in him the reflection of all they fought for. "Then we shall go into the belly of the beast, together. But make no mistake, this is no mere theft. It's a declaration of war."

As the first light of dawn crept through the trees, casting long shadows upon their huddled forms, Robin Hood and his Merry Men readied themselves for the greatest heist of their lives. Not for gold, not for fame, but for the glimmer of hope in a world devoured by darkness.

In the heart of the forest, where whispers of ancient magic still lingered, they plotted their course. The tower of the Sheriff of Nottingham loomed in their minds, a monolith of greed and corruption. But within its walls lay not just the wealth of a kingdom, but the key to its salvation.

For Robin Hood and his band of outlaws, the time for hiding in the shadows was over. The time for action, for bold and daring deeds, had dawned. And as the sun rose over Sherwood Forest, so too did the spirits of its protectors, ready to face whatever horrors awaited them, for the sake of a world that had forgotten how to hope.

The air in Sherwood Forest was thick with anticipation as Robin Hood and his Merry Men prepared for their perilous mission. The forest, usually a haven of tranquility, now buzzed with the energy of a war camp. Men sharpened blades, strung bows, and exchanged grim looks of determination. The stakes were higher than ever; this was not merely a raid for survival but a bold strike against the heart of darkness itself.

As night cloaked the forest, the band of outlaws moved like shadows, their steps muffled by the dense undergrowth. They were a motley crew, each man with a story, a reason to fight, united under Robin's unwavering leadership.

The Sheriff's tower, a monolithic structure of stone and iron, loomed ahead, its silhouette cutting through the night sky. It was a fortress in every sense, surrounded by high walls and patrolled by the undead, creatures whose mere presence sent shivers down the bravest of spines.

"Remember," Robin whispered, his voice barely audible, "stick to the shadows, move with silence. We strike swiftly and disappear into the night."

Their first task was to infiltrate the tower undetected. Will Scarlet led a small group to create a diversion at the east gate, drawing the undead guards away from the main entrance. The plan was simple but fraught with danger. One misstep, one noise out of place, and they would be swarmed by the undead.

The diversion worked. The guards, mindless in their pursuit, shuffled towards the noise, leaving the main gate momentarily unguarded. Robin, Little John, and a handful of others seized the moment, slipping through the shadows like phantoms.

Inside, the tower was a maze of corridors and chambers, each turn a potential trap. They navigated the labyrinth with caution, guided by a map stolen from a careless guard days earlier. Their target was the central vault, a room rumored to be filled with the wealth of the kingdom.

But as they neared the vault, disaster struck. An unseen alarm was tripped, and the corridors were suddenly flooded with the undead. The Merry Men fought fiercely, their arrows finding their marks with deadly precision. But for every undead that fell, two more took its place.

The situation grew desperate. Little John, wielding his staff with the ferocity of a wild bear, bellowed, "We can't hold them off forever, Robin!"

Robin's mind raced. The plan was unraveling, and they were running out of options. In a moment of clarity, he shouted, "Retreat! Back to the forest!"

The Merry Men fought their way out, their retreat a chaotic scramble of close calls and narrow escapes. As they emerged into the safety of the forest, the grim reality of their failure sank in. Several men were missing, likely captured or worse.

Around the flickering campfire, the mood was somber. Robin, his face etched with guilt, addressed his men. "We underestimated the enemy. I underestimated them. This was my mistake, and I vow to make it right."

Will Scarlet, his face shadowed by the firelight, spoke up. "We need a new plan, something they won't expect. We can't outfight them, but maybe we can outsmart them."

The men leaned in, their spirits reignited by Will's words. They began to plot anew, their minds weaving a tapestry of strategies and tactics. The Art of War, once a mere text, became their guide, its teachings fueling their resolve.

Their new plan was audacious, a complex web of deception and guile. They would use the forest to their advantage, turning its pathways into a labyrinth of traps and ambushes. They would strike not as a unified force but as elusive shadows, hitting the undead from all sides, sowing chaos and confusion.

The night of the second assault arrived, a moonless sky providing the perfect cloak for their operations. The Merry Men, now more than mere thieves, were warriors in a battle for the soul of their land.

The forest came alive with the sounds of battle, each trap springing, each ambush executed with precision. The undead, confounded by the guerrilla tactics, fell in droves.

But as they approached the tower once again, a chilling realization dawned upon them. The Sheriff, far from a mere puppet, was a cunning adversary. The tower was a trap, and they had walked right into it.

A horde of undead, greater than any they had faced before, descended upon them. The Merry Men fought valiantly, but they were outnumbered and outmatched. One by one, they fell, their cries echoing through the night.

Robin, surrounded and overwhelmed, fought with the desperation of a man with nothing left to lose. But as the undead closed in, his bow snapped, and he was thrown to the ground, the cold, clammy hands of the undead dragging him into darkness.

As consciousness slipped away, Robin's last thought was

of his men, of the people they had sworn to protect. He had led them into this nightmare, and now he had failed them, failed himself. The night sky above, once a canvas of infinite stars, now seemed to close in on him, the darkness claiming him as its own.

The darkness that engulfed Robin Hood was not just the physical absence of light but the overwhelming despair of defeat. He lay there, bound and bruised, in the damp, cold dungeon of the Sheriff's tower. The stench of decay filled the air, a constant reminder of the undead that roamed above.

His thoughts wandered to his Merry Men, to the people they had vowed to protect. In his heart, he knew he had led them to this catastrophic end. Guilt gnawed at him, more torturous than the physical pain that wracked his body.

As he lay in that abyss of despair, a faint sound reached his ears. At first, he thought it a trick of his mind, but then the sound grew clearer - the soft, melodic hum of a woman's voice. He strained against his bonds, turning his head towards the source. There, in a cell opposite his, shrouded in shadows, was a figure.

"Who's there?" Robin croaked, his voice a mere whisper.

"A friend, perhaps," the voice replied, gentle yet tinged with a strength that resonated in the gloomy cell. "Or maybe just another prisoner of the Sheriff's cruelty."

"Are you... are you real?" Robin asked, fearing his mind had finally succumbed to madness.

"As real as the chains that bind us," she replied, moving into the dim light. It was then Robin saw her clearly - a woman of regal bearing, despite her ragged appearance. Her eyes, bright and defiant, held a spark that belied her grim surroundings.

"Who are you?" Robin asked, a flicker of hope igniting in his chest.

"I am Marie-Anne," she said, "once a princess, now nothing more than a pawn in the Sheriff's wicked game."

The name struck a chord in Robin's memory. Rumors had whispered of a princess, spirited away by the Sheriff, her fate a mystery to all. And here she was, alive, a glimmer of light in the overwhelming darkness.

"Why are you here?" Robin asked, his mind racing with the implications of her presence.

"The Sheriff seeks to use me as a tool in his vile necromancy. He believes my royal blood will grant him powers untold," she explained, her voice laced with disgust.

Their conversation was cut short by the sound of approaching footsteps. The cell door creaked open, and the Sheriff himself stood there, a cruel smile playing on his lips.

"Ah, the great Robin Hood," he sneered. "How the mighty have fallen."

Robin glared at him, his spirit unbroken despite his predicament. "You won't get away with this. The people will rise against you."

The Sheriff's laugh was cold and humorless. "The people are nothing. With the power I will soon wield, I will be unstoppable."

As the Sheriff left, Robin's mind worked furiously. He needed to escape, to stop the Sheriff's plan, but how?

It was Marie-Anne who provided the answer. "The Sheriff is arrogant in his perceived victory. He has overlooked the old passages beneath the tower. If we can reach them, we can escape."

With renewed determination, Robin and Marie-Anne worked to free themselves. Using a loose stone from the cell wall, they managed to pick the locks of their chains.

Stealthily, they navigated the dark corridors of the tower, moving towards the hidden passages Marie-Anne spoke of. The tower was eerily silent, the only sound their soft footsteps echoing off the stone walls.

They found the passage, hidden behind an ancient tapestry, and descended into the bowels of the tower. The tunnel was narrow and dark, but it was their only chance.

As they emerged from the tunnel, the first light of dawn greeted them. But there was no time to savor their freedom. The Sheriff's plan had to be stopped.

Gathering the remnants of his Merry Men, Robin laid out his final stand. They would use the Sheriff's arrogance against him, strike during his ritual, and end his reign of terror.

The battle was fierce and brutal. The Merry Men, fueled by desperation and the righteous fury of their cause, fought with a ferocity that turned the tide. Robin, with Marie-Anne by his side, confronted the Sheriff in the midst of his dark ritual.

The Sheriff, caught off guard, was no match for Robin's skill and Marie-Anne's courage. As the ritual collapsed around him, the power he sought to wield turned against him, consuming him in a maelstrom of dark energy.

As the dust settled, the tower lay in ruins, the undead horde vanquished. The people, free from the Sheriff's tyranny, emerged from their hiding, their eyes filled with tears of gratitude and newfound hope.

Robin Hood and Marie-Anne stood amidst the ruins, their hearts heavy with the cost of their victory but lightened by the promise of a better future."

We did it, Robin," Marie-Anne said, her hand in his. "The people are free."

Robin nodded, a smile breaking through his weariness. "Aye, we did. But this is just the beginning. There are still many who suffer under the yoke of tyranny. Our fight is far from over."

As they turned to face the rising sun, a new day dawned over England. A day of freedom, of hope, a day where the legend of Robin Hood and his Merry Men would be told for generations to come. And in the heart of that legend, a spark of something more, a promise of adventures yet to unfold.

CHAPTER 13

ZOMBIES VS. TARZAN

"In the heart of the jungle, even silence has a voice."

Tarzan stood motionless, perched high on a sturdy branch of an ancient tree. The dense canopy of the rainforest stretched endlessly below, a vibrant tapestry of life. Yet, today, something was amiss. The usual symphony of the jungle - the chattering of monkeys, the rustling of leaves, the distant roar of a lion - was eerily subdued. It was as if the jungle itself held its breath, awaiting an unknown threat.

The Lord of the Jungle narrowed his eyes, scanning the verdant expanse. His keen senses, honed by years of survival in this untamed wilderness, alerted him to a subtle, yet distinct change. The air was different, tinged with a scent unfamiliar and unsettling. Tarzan's intuition, an unerring guide in the labyrinth of the jungle, whispered of danger, a peril unlike any he had faced before.

Suddenly, a piercing shriek shattered the quiet. It was a sound Tarzan knew well - the distress call of the jungle's inhabitants. Yet, this cry carried a tone of sheer terror that he had never heard. Without a moment's hesitation, he swung down from the tree, his powerful arms propelling him through the foliage with the grace of a panther.

As he neared the source of the commotion, a chilling sight unfolded before him. A group of monkeys, normally playful and mischievous, were fleeing in panic. Their eyes wide with fear, they scampered past Tarzan, paying him no heed. This alone was unusual, for the animals of the jungle were familiar with him, their guardian and ally. But what followed was beyond belief.

Emerging from the underbrush was a sight that made Tarzan's blood run cold. A tiger, its once majestic form now grotesque and decaying, lumbered forward. Its eyes, clouded and lifeless, were fixed in a deathly stare. The creature moved with an unnatural gait, its limbs jerking in a macabre dance of death.

Tarzan's instincts screamed at him to act, but for a moment, he stood frozen, disbelief grappling with the reality before him. This was no ordinary threat. This was a perversion of nature, a defilement of the sacred balance of the jungle.

With a fierce roar, Tarzan leaped into action. He knew he must drive this abomination away, protect the innocent lives under his care. Yet, as he engaged the creature, he quickly realized that his usual tactics were futile. The tiger, devoid of pain or fear, fought with relentless ferocity, impervious to his blows.

In the midst of the struggle, Tarzan heard a rustling in the nearby bushes. Expecting more undead monstrosities, he braced himself. Instead, out stepped a figure from his past, a trusted friend and ally - the wise shaman, Mbaya.

"Tarzan!" Mbaya's voice, usually calm and measured, was tinged with urgency. "You must not fight this battle alone. This is a curse that has befallen our land."

Tarzan, grappling with the undead tiger, responded through gritted teeth. "A curse? What madness speaks through you, old man?"

Mbaya stepped closer, his eyes filled with a grave seriousness that Tarzan had seldom seen. "This is no madness, son of the jungle. It is an evil that has seeped into our world, corrupting the living and the dead alike. I have seen it in the stars, a darkness that spreads like a plague."

Tarzan finally managed to subdue the creature, his strength overpowering the unholy force that animated it. Breathing heavily, he turned to Mbaya, his expression a mix of confusion and concern.

"What do we do?" Tarzan asked, the protector in him rising above the shock. "How do we fight this darkness?"

Mbaya looked at him, his eyes reflecting the wisdom of the ages. "We must seek the source of this curse, Tarzan. Only by confronting the root of this evil can we hope to restore balance."

Tarzan knew that the shaman's words rang true. Yet, a part of him resisted, a primal fear of this unknown enemy. The jungle had always been his home, his domain where he reigned supreme. Now, it had become a land of shadows and unknown terrors.

But as he gazed upon the desecrated form of the tiger, a resolve kindled within him. He was the guardian of this jungle, its protector. He could not, would not, let this darkness consume his world.

"Lead the way, Mbaya," Tarzan said, his voice steady with newfound determination. "We will face this curse together."

As they ventured deeper into the heart of the jungle, the shadows seemed to grow darker, the air heavier. Yet, Tarzan's step was unwavering, his resolve unbreakable. The Lord of theof the Jungle was not one to cower before the unknown.

As they delved deeper, the signs of the curse grew more prevalent. Animals, once vibrant and full of life, now roamed as hollow shells of their former selves, their eyes empty and their movements jerky and unnatural. The air was thick with a sense of wrongness, a perversion of the natural order that Tarzan held so dear.

"Mbaya," Tarzan said, his voice low, "this curse, it is like nothing I have faced before. The animals, they suffer, yet they are not alive. How can this be?"

Mbaya walked beside him, his eyes scanning the dark undergrowth. "It is an old magic, Tarzan, dark and twisted. It consumes the life force, leaving behind only a puppet, a shadow of the living."

Tarzan clenched his fists, anger and sorrow warring within him. "We must find the source. We must end this."

Their journey took them to the heart of the jungle, where the trees grew so tall and thick that little light penetrated the dense canopy. Here, the curse seemed even stronger, its presence almost tangible in the air.

Tarzan tried to use his usual tactics to fend off the undead creatures they encountered. He relied on his strength, his agility, his intimate knowledge of the jungle. But time and again, he found his efforts lacking. The undead were relentless, impervious to pain, and seemingly tireless.

In one particularly harrowing encounter, Tarzan and Mbaya were ambushed by a horde of zombified tribesmen. Tarzan fought valiantly, using his raw strength and speed, but the sheer number of the undead overwhelmed him. He watched in horror as Mbaya was knocked to the ground, the lifeless eyes of the undead tribesmen fixed on him.

With a burst of adrenaline, Tarzan leaped into the fray, pulling Mbaya to safety. But the realization hit him hard - his strength alone was not enough.

"We need a new plan," Tarzan said, panting as they retreated to safety. "My strength, my speed, they are not enough against these... these things."

Mbaya nodded, his face grave. "You are right, Tarzan. We must be cunning. We must use the jungle itself as our weapon."

Inspired by the wisdom of the Art of War, Tarzan began to devise a new strategy. He set traps, using the natural hazards of the jungle to his advantage. He employed guerrilla tactics, striking quickly and then disappearing into the foliage.

For a time, it seemed to work. They were able to thin the ranks of the undead, bring a momentary reprieve to the beleaguered jungle. But it was not to last.

As they neared what Mbaya believed to be the source of the curse, they encountered the leader of the undead - a colossal, decayed elephant, its eyes glowing with an unholy light. It was surrounded by a swarm of undead creatures, all moving in eerie unison.

Tarzan and Mbaya launched their attack, using all the cunning and skill at their disposal. But the undead elephant was unlike any foe Tarzan had ever faced. It seemed to anticipate their moves, counter their strategies with terrifying intelligence.

In the heat of the battle, Tarzan's grand plan backfired. The traps he had set were turned against them, the undead using them to their advantage. Tarzan watched in horror as his plan, his hope of ending the curse, crumbled before his eyes.

Defeated and demoralized, Tarzan and Mbaya barely escaped with their lives. They retreated to a secluded part of the jungle, where the curse seemed less pervasive.

Tarzan sat, his head in his hands, the weight of their failure crushing him. "I thought I knew the jungle," he said, his voice hollow. "I thought I could protect it. But this... this is beyond anything I have known."

Mbaya placed a hand on his shoulder, offering a silent comfort. "Tarzan, you are the heart of this jungle. But even the heart can falter in the face of such darkness. We need to find another way, a way to strike at the very heart of this curse."

Tarzan looked up, his eyes burning with a fierce determination. "Then that is what we will do. We will go to the source of this curse, face whatever darkness lies there. We will end this, once and for all."

With renewed resolve, Tarzan and Mbaya set out once again, delving deeper into the heart of the cursed jungle. The shadows seemed to press in on them, the air thick with the stench of decay. But Tarzan's step was firm, his resolve unshakable. He would not rest until the jungle was free of this curse, until the natural order was restored. The battle was far from over, and Tarzan was ready to face whatever horrors lay ahead.

The jungle's heart throbbed with an ominous rhythm as Tarzan and Mbaya advanced toward the source of the curse. The air was thick with a miasma of decay, the once vibrant foliage now wilted and blackened by the blight that had seized the land. Tarzan moved with a predator's grace, every sense alert to the dangers that lurked in the shadowy undergrowth. Beside him, Mbaya's presence was a steady beacon of wisdom and strength, the shaman's knowledge of ancient lore their only guide in this corrupted wilderness.

As they journeyed deeper, the very nature of the jungle seemed to warp and twist around them. Trees that once stood tall and proud were now gnarled and twisted, their branches reaching out like the fingers of the dead. The cries of the undead echoed through the forest, a haunting chorus that chilled Tarzan's soul.

Yet, in his heart, a fire burned brighter than ever. This was his home, his kingdom, and he would not see it defiled by this unholy plague. With each step, he steeled himself for the battle to come, a battle that would decide the fate of the jungle and all who dwelled within it.

Finally, they arrived at the heart of the darkness. Before them lay the ruins of an old shipwreck, its timbers rotted and covered in creeping vines. Around it swarmed the undead, their bodies a grotesque mockery of life. And there, towering above them all, was the colossal undead elephant, its eyes burning with malevolent intelligence.

Tarzan and Mbaya exchanged a determined glance, then charged into the fray. Tarzan leaped into the midst of the undead, his fists and feet a blur as he fought with the ferocity of the jungle itself. Mbaya, chanting ancient incantations, called upon the spirits of the forest to aid them in their fight.

The battle was fierce and brutal. Tarzan fought with a desperation born of love for his jungle, each blow driving back the tide of undead that threatened to overwhelm them. But for every creature he felled, two more took its place, an endless wave of death.

In the midst of the chaos, Tarzan locked eyes with the undead elephant. A silent challenge passed between them, a recognition of the struggle that was to come. With a roar that shook the very earth, Tarzan charged at the beast, determined to end its reign of terror.

The clash was titanic, a battle of primal forces that echoed through the cursed jungle. Tarzan, fueled by rage and sorrow, fought with a strength he had never known, his blows landing with the force of thunder. But the elephant was a monster of dark magic, its strength seemingly inexhaustible.

As the battle raged, Mbaya continued his incantations, his voice rising above the din of combat. The air shimmered with power, the ancient spirits of the jungle responding to his call.

Then, just when it seemed that Tarzan might finally prevail, the elephant struck with a devastating blow, sending him crashing to the ground. The beast loomed over him, its trunk raised for the killing strike.

In that moment, Tarzan's life flashed before his eyes. He saw the jungle in all its glory, the creatures he had sworn to protect, the friends he had made and lost. A surge of emotion welled up within him, a fierce love for this wild, beautiful land.

With a cry that was both a roar of defiance and a plea for strength, Tarzan summoned his last reserves of energy. He rolled out of the way just as the elephant's trunk slammed down, then sprang to his feet.

And then, the tide of the battle turned. Mbaya's incantations reached their crescendo, the spirits of the jungle manifesting in a blinding light that enveloped the battlefield. The undead creatures faltered, their movements becoming sluggish, their forms starting to dissipate.

Seizing the opportunity, Tarzan launched himself at the elephant, his fists glowing with the power of the jungle itself. With a final, thunderous blow, he struck the beast down, its form collapsing into dust and shadow.

As the light faded, Tarzan and Mbaya stood amidst the ruins of the shipwreck, the curse lifted, the jungle freed from its unholy grip. The natural sounds of the forest began to return, a symphony of life that filled Tarzan's heart with joy.

But as he surveyed the wreckage, something caught his eye. Among the rotted timbers and tattered sails, he found an ancient artifact, its surface etched with symbols of a long-forgotten language.

As Tarzan held the artifact in his hands, a chill ran down his spine. This was not the end, but the beginning of a greater mystery, a darker threat that loomed beyond the borders of his jungle. The artifact whispered of ancient evils and hidden dangers, a warning that the battle he had just fought was but a precursor to a greater war.

And so, with the jungle restored and a new quest burning in his heart, Tarzan turned his gaze to the horizon, ready to face whatever challenges lay ahead. For he was Tarzan, Lord of the Jungle, and he would stop at nothing to protect his home and unravel the mysteries of the ancient artifact. The end of one adventure was merely the beginning of another, and the jungle's heart beat strong and true within him.

CHAPTER 14

MARTIANS ZOMBIES

"In the war between worlds, our greatest weapon was the one we never saw coming." Dr. Elijah Reed

Under the cobalt skies of a bustling metropolis, in the year 2024, the world spun unknowingly on the brink of an unprecedented crisis. Dr. Elijah Reed, once a rising star in the field of astrobiology, now relegated to the fringes of scientific community, gazed through his telescope at the heavens. His eyes, reflecting the celestial dance, missed not a single streak that cut through the night.

That evening, as he recorded the coordinates of a peculiar meteor shower, a chill ran down his spine. These were no ordinary meteors. They descended with a purpose, a sinister precision that defied natural cosmic events. His heart raced as he pieced together the impossible puzzle. The Martians, subjects of fantastical tales and long-forgotten fears, were returning.

Morning light brought chaos. The city, a labyrinth of steel and ambition, awoke to a nightmare. News channels blared with reports of 'meteor' impacts across the globe. Elijah, with his unkempt hair and tired eyes, burst into the emergency meeting at the National Space Agency.

"They're not meteors!" he exclaimed, his voice echoing in the crowded room filled with skeptical glances. "They're spacecraft - Martian spacecraft!"

General Williams, a man whose demeanor spoke of wars fought and won, eyed Elijah with a mix of disdain and curiosity. "Dr. Reed, your theories have always been... imaginative. But Martians? Really?"

Elijah's hands trembled as he presented his findings. "I know what I saw. We must prepare!"

But his warnings fell on deaf ears. The world had moved on from Martian invaders to more terrestrial concerns. Once outside, Elijah's gaze fell upon the city. People went about their lives, oblivious to the danger from above.

As night descended, the meteors struck. This time, they were closer, their impacts shaking the very foundations of the city. From the fiery craters emerged not the advanced beings of yesteryear but grotesque, zombified creatures. Their limbs twisted in unnatural angles, their eyes glowing with a hunger for flesh. The city descended into pandemonium.

Elijah watched in horror as the creatures ravaged the streets. His mind raced - this was no mere invasion. It was an annihilation. He rushed to his car, the cacophony of sirens and screams filling the air. His only thought: to reach the military base on the outskirts of the city.

Arriving at the base, he was greeted by Captain Maria Alvarez, a woman whose reputation on the battlefield was both feared and respected. "Dr. Reed," she said, her voice steady amidst the chaos. "You were right. Now, what do we do?"

Elijah looked into her determined eyes. "We need a plan. But first, we need to understand what we're dealing with."

Together, they ventured into the heart of the base, where captured Martians were held. The creatures, once beings of intellect and technology, were now nothing more than mindless, undead husks. Elijah's mind raced with questions. What had turned them into these monstrosities? And more importantly, how could they be stopped?

As dawn broke, the base buzzed with activity. Plans were drawn, strategies formulated. But Elijah knew, deep down, that conventional methods would not suffice. This was a new kind of war, against an enemy humanity had never imagined.

Staring at the captive Martians, a thought struck him. These creatures, undead as they were, avoided certain substances present in the base's laboratory. "Bacteria," he muttered under his breath. "Could it be that simple?"

But before he could delve deeper, the base's alarms blared. The Martians were attacking, their numbers overwhelming. Elijah, Maria, and a handful of soldiers fought bravely, but they were forced to retreat, watching helplessly as the base succumbed to the undead horde.

As they fled into the unknown, Elijah's mind was ablaze with possibilities. The answer to humanity's survival lay not in the stars, but in the microscopic life teeming under their feet. The war of the worlds had begun, and Earth's smallest inhabitants might just hold the key to victory.

The world outside the military base was a grotesque tableau of destruction and despair. The streets, once teeming with life, were now overrun with the zombified Martian invaders, their grotesque forms a nightmare come to life. Elijah Reed and Captain Maria Alvarez, along with a band of survivors, navigated the chaos, their hearts heavy with the weight of a world falling apart.

As they huddled in an abandoned warehouse, Elijah's mind was a maelstrom of thoughts. "We need a new approach," he said, his voice barely above a whisper. "Traditional weapons are useless. We're fighting a war we don't understand."

Maria, her face smeared with soot and determination, nodded in agreement. "We've seen them adapt to every move we make. It's like fighting an enemy that evolves with each strike."

The group, a mix of soldiers and civilians, looked to Elijah with a mix of fear and hope. Among them was a young girl, no more than ten, clutching a tattered doll. Her eyes, wide with terror, met Elijah's. In them, he saw a reflection of his own fear, and a burning need to protect what little they had left.

"We use their strength against them," Elijah said, an idea forming. "Sun Tzu, in 'The Art of War', spoke of using the enemy's tactics to your advantage. We draw them in, make them think they've won, and then we strike."

Maria's eyes lit up. "A trap. But how do we lure them?"

Elijah's gaze fell on the young girl. "We use ourselves as bait."

The plan was risky, audacious. They would create a false refuge, a beacon of hope to draw in the Martian zombies. Once concentrated, they would unleash a barrage of explosives, hoping to decimate their ranks.

As night fell, they set their plan into motion. The warehouse was rigged with explosives, and lights were set ablaze, piercing the darkness like a beacon. The group hid in the shadows, their breaths shallow, hearts pounding.

The Martians came, their twisted forms silhouetted against the flickering lights. As they converged on the warehouse, Elijah's hand trembled over the detonator. Maria's hand found his, her grip firm. Together, they pressed the button.

The explosion was deafening, a blinding fury that tore through the night. As the smoke cleared, they emerged cautiously. Bodies of the undead Martians littered the ground, but their victory was short-lived.

From the shadows emerged more Martians, their numbers seemingly undiminished. And with them came a new horror - a leader, towering and grotesque, its eyes burning with malevolence.

The group retreated, their plan in ruins. The Martian leader seemed to mock them, its resilience a stark reminder of their underestimation.

Hiding in the ruins of a once-grand library, Elijah's mind raced. "We need something more," he muttered. "They adapt too quickly."

Maria, her face etched with fatigue, sighed. "What do we have that they haven't seen?"

Elijah's eyes widened. The bacteria. The Martian's aversion to bacteria-laden areas in the base. It was a clue, a piece of the puzzle they had overlooked.

"We need to turn their world against them," he said, his voice gaining strength. "Bacteria, the most basic form of life on Earth. It could be our weapon."

As they formulated a new plan, using bacterial agents to weaken the Martians, the Martian leader launched a relentless assault. The library became their fortress, a bastion of humanity's last stand.

But as they prepared to unleash their biological weapon, the Martian leader, in a display of terrifying intelligence, adapted once again. It led a concentrated attack, breaching their defenses, and cornering them.

In that moment, as they faced the monstrous visage of the Martian leader, Elijah's mind flashed back to the young girl's eyes, filled with fear and hope. He realized then that their fight was not just for survival, but for the future of a world teetering on the brink of oblivion.

The Martian leader loomed over them, its form a twisted mockery of life itself. Elijah and Maria stood side by side, their resolve unbroken despite the despair that gripped their hearts.

"This is it," Maria said, her voice steady. "We fight to the end."

Elijah nodded, his gaze meeting the leader's. "For Earth," he whispered.

And with that, they launched their final stand, a desperate battle against an enemy that threatened to extinguish the light of humanity forever.

The world outside seemed to hold its breath as Elijah Reed and Captain Maria Alvarez prepared for their last stand. The ruins of the library, their makeshift fortress, echoed with the distant roars of the Martian zombies. The Martian leader, a monstrous visage of death, stood at the forefront of the undead army, its eyes glowing with a hunger that seemed to consume the very air.

Inside, the air was thick with tension. Elijah clutched a vial containing a potent bacterial strain, his last hope. Maria checked her weapons, her face a mask of determination. The survivors huddled together, their eyes reflecting a mix of fear and resolve.

"This is it," Elijah said, his voice barely above a whisper. "We use the bacteria. It's our only chance."

Maria nodded, her eyes meeting his. "And if this doesn't work?"

Elijah's gaze was steady. "Then we fight until our last breath. For Earth. For humanity."

As the Martian zombies began their assault, Elijah and Maria sprang into action. They unleashed the bacteria, watching as it spread among the undead horde. For a moment, it seemed to work. The Martians faltered, their movements becoming erratic.

But the Martian leader, in a display of terrifying intelligence, resisted the bacterial attack. It advanced, unaffected, leading its army with renewed ferocity.

Elijah and Maria fought back-to-back, their weapons cutting through the swarm of undead. But for every Martian they felled, two more took its place. The survivors fought valiantly, but they were being overwhelmed.

In a desperate move, Elijah found himself face to face with the Martian leader. Its grotesque features were inches from his own. He could feel its fetid breath, a stench of death that seemed to suffocate the very air.

As the leader raised its clawed hand to strike, Elijah acted on instinct. He plunged the vial of bacteria into the creature's flesh. The leader howled in rage, its form writhing as the bacteria took effect.

But it was not enough. The leader adapted once again, its body overcoming the bacterial onslaught. Elijah was thrown back, his body crashing against the rubble.

As he lay there, dazed and injured, a realization dawned on him. His own blood. The unique strain of bacteria from his past research mishaps. It was a long shot, but it was all he had left.

With a strength born of desperation, Elijah rose to his feet. He faced the Martian leader, his eyes burning with a fierce determination.

"You want to know the strength of humanity?" Elijah shouted, his voice echoing through the ruins. "It's our ability to adapt, to overcome. You may take our world, but you will never extinguish our spirit!"

With that, he lunged at the leader, his own blood mingling with the creature's. The effect was immediate and devastating. The leader convulsed, its form disintegrating before their eyes.

The Martian zombies, now leaderless, faltered. The survivors rallied, pushing back with renewed vigor. The tide of the battle turned, the Martians retreating, their numbers dwindling.

As the last of the undead fell, a silence descended. The survivors emerged from their hiding places, their faces reflecting a mix of relief and disbelief.

Elijah collapsed, exhausted and wounded, but alive. Maria rushed to his side, her face etched with concern. "You did it, Elijah. You saved us all."

Elijah managed a weak smile. "No, Maria. We did it. Together."

As they looked out at the world they had saved, a new dawn broke over the horizon. The air was filled with the promise of a new beginning, a world reborn from the ashes of a war unlike any other.

Humanity had prevailed, not through might or technology, but through the unassuming power of the microscopic life teeming under their feet. In their darkest hour, it was the smallest among them that had led them to victory.

And in that moment, Elijah knew that the future was bright. A future where humanity would no longer take for granted the delicate balance of life on Earth. A future where they would stand united, ready to face whatever challenges lay ahead.

For in the war of the worlds, it was not the strong or the mighty that had triumphed, but the resilient spirit of humanity, undimmed and unbroken.

CHAPTER 15

THE 3 MUSKETEERS VS. ZOMBIES

"In the darkest corners of power, even the shadows fear to tread." -
Alexandre Dumas, reimagined.

The moon hung low over Paris, casting elongated shadows across the cobbled
streets that twisted like serpents through the heart of the city. D'Artagnan, his
cloak billowing behind him, moved with a purpose that belied his youth. The air
was crisp, filled with the promise of secrets yet to be unveiled. As he navigated
the labyrinthine alleys, a sense of unease crept over him, a prelude to the night's
ominous events.

His journey led him to the catacombs beneath Paris, a world away from the
glittering lights and gaiety above. Here, the air was musty, heavy with the weight
of history and death. D'Artagnan, ever the inquisitive soul, had heard whispers of
a gathering, a congregation of shadows that danced with the dead. His hand
rested on the hilt of his sword, a comforting presence against the unknown.

In the depths of the catacombs, he found them. Hooded figures stood in a
circle, their chants echoing off the ancient bones that lined the walls. At the
center, a man, his face obscured, led the ritual. With a flourish, he unveiled a
tattered tome, its pages yellowed with age and sin. D'Artagnan watched, hidden
in the shadows, as the man began to speak words that twisted in the air, words
that should never have been uttered.

The earth trembled, a silent scream from the depths. From the earthen floor,
hands, decrepit and clawing, emerged. Bodies, once resting in eternal slumber,
rose. Their eyes, empty of life yet burning with an unholy fire, scanned the
darkness. D'Artagnan's heart raced; he had stumbled upon a nightmare made
flesh.

He fled, the images of the undead etched into his mind. The streets of Paris,
once a comforting maze, now seemed to close in on him. He needed allies,
someone to share the burden of this unholy discovery.

The Three Musketeers, his friends, his brothers in arms, were his only hope.
Athos, the strategist; Porthos, the giant with a heart of gold; and Aramis, the

philosopher-warrior. They met at their usual haunt, a tavern where the wine flowed as freely as the tales of adventure.

"D'Artagnan, you look as though you've seen a ghost," jested Porthos, his booming laugh filling the room.

"Or perhaps something far worse," D'Artagnan replied, his voice a mere whisper. The laughter died as his friends saw the seriousness in his eyes.

He recounted the night's events, the hooded figures, the resurrection of the dead. Athos listened intently, his brow furrowed in thought, while Aramis, ever the skeptic, raised an eyebrow in disbelief.

"Raising the dead? That's the stuff of children's tales," Aramis scoffed, sipping his wine.

"But what if it's true?" Athos interjected. "We've seen enough in our adventures to know that the world holds more mysteries than we can fathom."

Porthos slammed his fist on the table, determination lighting his eyes. "Then we investigate. If there's a threat to Paris, to France, it's our duty to uncover it."

Their decision was made. The Musketeers would delve into the darkness, into a world where the dead walked and the shadows whispered. Little did they know, this adventure would test their bonds, their skills, and their very understanding of the world.

As they left the tavern, the moon still hung low, a silent witness to the beginning of a tale that would echo through the ages. The Three Musketeers, united in purpose, stepped into the night, towards a destiny that was as uncertain as it was dark.

The city of Paris, usually a vibrant tapestry of life and color, now seemed to D'Artagnan and his companions like a stage set for a tragedy. The news of the undead had not yet reached the ears of the common folk, but the air was thick with an unspoken dread. It was as if the city itself sensed the impending doom.

The Musketeers' first course of action was to gather intelligence. They split up, each delving into different corners of Paris, from the dimly lit taverns where secrets spilled as freely as wine, to the grandiose halls of power where whispers were as sharp as blades.

Athos, with his keen strategic mind, chose to visit his old contacts within the King's court. What he found was disconcerting. Courtiers spoke in hushed tones of strange occurrences, of shadows that moved of their own accord and figures seen roaming the palace halls at night.

Meanwhile, Porthos used his charm and connections in the lower parts of Paris. In a dingy tavern, he overheard a drunken soldier speak of a recent patrol where they had encountered what he described as "men who would not die." The soldier, pale and shaken, recounted how his blade had seemed to pass through them as if they were mist.

Aramis, ever the scholar, sought out ancient texts and forbidden lore. In a dusty library, he found a tome that spoke of rituals that could bind the dead to the will of the living. The book hinted at a power that could be wielded by those who dared to delve into the darkest corners of magic.

Their individual quests led them to one undeniable conclusion: the threat was real, and it was growing.

With the pieces of the puzzle coming together, the Musketeers regrouped. They shared their findings, each revelation more alarming than the last. It was clear that they were dealing with a force unlike any they had encountered before.

"We need to stop this at its source," Athos declared, his voice resolute. "These undead are but puppets. We must cut the strings."

"And for that, we need to find the puppeteer," added D'Artagnan.

Their plan was bold. They would infiltrate the catacombs, find the site of the ritual, and destroy it. To aid in their quest, they enlisted the help of an alchemist, known for his expertise in ancient and arcane substances. With his knowledge, they prepared alchemical bombs capable of destroying large swathes of the undead.

Under the cover of night, the Musketeers, along with the alchemist, descended into the catacombs. The air was thick with the stench of decay, and the silence was oppressive. They moved cautiously, guided by the flickering light of their torches.

As they neared the ritual site, the alchemist whispered, "Be on your guard. These catacombs have seen centuries of death. Who knows what horrors lurk in the shadows?"

Suddenly, they were ambushed. Undead soldiers, their eyes glowing with an unholy light, swarmed them. The Musketeers fought valiantly, their swords flashing in the dim light, while the alchemist hurled his concoctions, creating explosions of fire and light.

But it was a trap. More undead poured in, seemingly endless in number. In the chaos, the alchemist was struck down, his knowledge and expertise lost to them. The Musketeers were forced to retreat, narrowly escaping with their lives.

As they emerged from the catacombs, battered and disheartened, the gravity of their failure weighed heavily upon them. They had underestimated their enemy. This was no mere practitioner of dark arts; this was a force that threatened to engulf Paris itself.

They regrouped in their sanctuary, their spirits as bruised as their bodies. "We need a new plan," D'Artagnan said, his voice heavy with fatigue. "We can't face this enemy head-on. We need to be smarter, more cunning."

Athos nodded in agreement. "We have faced many adversaries, but this... this is something else. We must adapt, learn from our mistakes."

The night grew deeper, and the Musketeers sat in silence, each lost in their own thoughts. They were at their lowest point, outmatched and outmaneuvered. Yet, in the depths of despair, the seeds of hope were sown. For it is in the darkest of times that the true mettle of heroes is tested.

The dawn broke over Paris, a city now on the brink of an abyss. The streets, once bustling with life, lay silent, as if holding its breath against the coming storm. The Musketeers, weary yet resolute, gathered in their sanctuary, their minds set on a final, desperate plan.

Athos, his face etched with determination, spoke first. "We cannot face this enemy in a straight battle; we must strike at the heart, at Richelieu himself."

"But how?" questioned Aramis, his brow furrowed. "The Cardinal is well-guarded, and with the undead at his command, he seems untouchable."

D'Artagnan stepped forward, his eyes burning with a fierce resolve. "Then we must be as ghosts, unseen, unheard, until we strike." He laid out a map of the catacombs, tracing a path to where they believed Richelieu conducted his dark rituals. "We'll use the catacombs to our advantage, move beneath the city and take him by surprise."

Porthos, his usual jovial self buried beneath a grim seriousness, nodded. "Let's end this nightmare, for Paris, for the King, for France."

Their plan was a tapestry of daring and danger. They would split up, each taking a different route through the catacombs, converging at the ritual site. Time was of the essence; they had to reach Richelieu before he could unleash his full power.

As they delved once again into the catacombs' depths, the air grew colder, the darkness more oppressive. The stench of death was overwhelming, a stark reminder of the unnatural horror they faced.

D'Artagnan moved like a shadow, his every sense alert. The flickering torch in his hand cast eerie shadows on the walls, the ancient bones seeming to whisper secrets of the past. He could feel the weight of centuries around him, a tomb for forgotten souls.

Meanwhile, Athos, with his keen mind, navigated the labyrinthine tunnels, avoiding the undead that roamed like lost spirits. His sword was a silent promise of retribution, ready to defend the living against the corruption of death.

Porthos, relying on his brute strength, barreled through the catacombs, his heavy steps a stark contrast to the suffocating silence. His laughter, once a sign of his indomitable spirit, was now a battle cry against the darkness.

Aramis, ever the philosopher, pondered the nature of their enemy as he moved through the shadows. "What drives a man to such depths of evil?" he mused. His sword was not just a weapon but a tool to carve a path toward truth.

The Musketeers converged at the ritual site, a cavernous chamber where the air crackled with unholy energy. At its center stood Cardinal Richelieu, his hands raised high as he chanted in a language older than time.

The Musketeers charged, their battle cries echoing through the chamber. The clash of swords against the undead was a symphony of survival, each stroke a defiance of death.

Richelieu turned, his eyes alight with a mad fire. "You cannot stop what has been set in motion. The dead shall rule, and I shall be their king!"

The battle was fierce, the Musketeers fighting with every ounce of their skill and courage. They were a whirlwind of steel and determination, cutting down the undead that rose to defend their master.

Finally, D'Artagnan broke through, his sword aimed at Richelieu's heart. But as he struck, the Cardinal uttered a final, desperate incantation. A blinding light filled the chamber, and when it cleared, Richelieu lay dying, his plans undone.

The Musketeers stood victorious, but their celebration was short-lived. A chilling realization dawned upon them as they heard a groan from behind. Turning, they saw the King, his eyes empty, his skin pale. He had been bitten, turned into one of the undead.

Panic gripped their hearts. The King, the very symbol of France, now a creature of darkness. But D'Artagnan, ever the quick thinker, remembered the alchemist's antidote. With no time to lose, he rushed forward, administering the potion.

The King convulsed, then lay still. For a moment, all was silent. Then, slowly, life returned to his eyes. The antidote had worked; the King was saved.

The Musketeers emerged from the catacombs as dawn broke over Paris. They had faced the darkness and prevailed. But as they looked upon the city they loved, they knew that this was but one battle in a never-ending war against the shadows that sought to engulf the light.

Their victory was bittersweet, for in saving the King, they had uncovered a deeper, more sinister plot. Richelieu was but a pawn, manipulated by darker forces that lurked just beyond sight.

As they stood together, a new resolve took shape. The Musketeers would continue to defend France, not just from the enemies that marched in the daylight, but from those that whispered in the darkness.

For in a world where the dead could walk, the living must be ever vigilant, ever ready to stand against the night.

CHAPTER 16

THE TIME MACHINE VS. THE UNDEAD

"In the tangles of time, our greatest inventions are often our most tragic errors."

The late afternoon sun cast long shadows across the study of Dr. Edward Mallory, a room that bore the chaotic trademarks of a genius at work. Books, scattered papers, and intricate mechanical tools lay strewn across every surface, but the centerpiece was undoubtedly the machine. It stood there, a bizarre confluence of brass, glass, and whirring gears, pulsing with a light that seemed to beat like a mechanical heart.

Edward wiped the sweat from his brow and stepped back, admiring his creation. It was the culmination of years of toil and obsession, a physical manifestation of his belief that time was not a relentless march forward but a sea to be navigated. Tonight, he would unveil his masterpiece to the select few who had dared believe in his vision.

As the clock struck seven, his guests arrived, each as eclectic as the inventor himself. Among them was Professor Langdon, a skeptic, always quick with a dismissive quip, and Clara, Edward's confidante, whose sharp intellect was matched only by her beauty.

"Edward, I must admit, this is quite the spectacle," Langdon said, his voice echoing in the high-ceilinged room. "But I remain unconvinced. Time travel is a fantasy for novels and dreamers."

Clara, ever the mediator, smiled gently. "Perhaps, but if anyone can turn fantasy into reality, it's Edward."

Edward chuckled. "Thank you, Clara. Now, let me demonstrate the fruits of my labor."

With a flourish, he activated the machine. Gears turned, and lights flickered as a hum filled the air, growing steadily louder. The guests stepped back, their skepticism tinged with a hint of fear.

"This is madness, Edward," Langdon exclaimed. "You have no idea what might happen!"

Ignoring the protests, Edward set the controls. "I am off to witness the marvels of the future. If my calculations are correct, I shall return momentarily to your eyes, but for me, it will be much longer."

With those final words, he pulled a lever, and a blinding light engulfed the room. When their vision cleared, the guests gasped. The machine, along with Edward, had vanished.

In the year 2321, Edward Mallory reappeared, his machine materializing in a world unrecognizable. Buildings lay in ruin, overgrown with vegetation, the sky a murky shade of gray. He stumbled out, coughing, his mind racing to comprehend the scene before him.

As he ventured through the desolate streets, a chilling realization dawned on him. The people, if they could still be called that, were mere shells of their former selves. Their eyes were vacant, their movements erratic. They were undead, devoid of consciousness, yet eerily alive.

Edward's heart pounded in his chest as he retraced his steps, only to find his time machine damaged, its intricate components fried. Panic set in. He was trapped in this nightmarish future.

"Help!" he called out, his voice echoing through the empty streets. "Is anyone here? Anyone at all?"

From the shadows, a figure emerged, her movements swift and purposeful. She was different from the others, her eyes still held a spark of humanity.

"You shouldn't be here," she said, her voice a hushed whisper. "The undead, they're everywhere. You need to hide."

Edward, taken aback by her sudden appearance, nodded. "My name is Edward Mallory. I've come from the past, and I need to return. My machine is broken. Can you help me?"

The woman, sizing him up, finally extended a hand. "Ava. I can help you hide, but as for your machine..." She trailed off, her gaze falling on the broken contraption. "We have bigger problems than that."

Together, they retreated to a hidden shelter, an underground bunker that Ava and a small group of survivors called home. There, Edward learned the grim reality of this future - humanity had fallen, victim to a plague that turned them into the undead.

As the night wore on, Edward's mind raced. He had to repair his machine and return to his time, to prevent this future from ever happening. But first, he needed to survive. And survival in this forsaken future was a game played against the most relentless of opponents - time itself, and the undead it had spawned.

Edward's nights in the bunker were restless, his mind relentlessly replaying the desolation outside. Each morning, he would emerge with a new determination, sifting through the wreckage of his machine, scavenging for parts amidst the ruins.

Ava, who had become his unlikely ally in this dystopian nightmare, watched him with a mixture of curiosity and concern. "You really think you can fix it?" she asked one evening as they sat amidst the scattered remnants of technology.

"I have to," Edward replied, his hands ceaselessly working. "Not just to get back, but to stop this from happening. If I can return, I can change the course of history."

Ava shook her head, her expression grim. "I've seen what those things can do. You need more than just a working machine. You need a miracle."

It was during one of his forays into the desolate city that Edward realized brute force would not suffice. He narrowly escaped a horde, their movements eerily synchronized, as if controlled by a single, malevolent will. He returned to the bunker, shaken but enlightened.

"We need a plan," he declared to Ava and the other survivors. "These creatures, they're not just mindless zombies. There's something guiding them, something intelligent."

The survivors exchanged skeptical glances, but Ava's eyes held a spark of interest. "Go on," she urged.

Edward laid out his plan, inspired by the ancient stratagems of Sun Tzu. "We need to divide and conquer, use our environment to our advantage. Lure them into traps, strike where they're weakest."

Ava nodded slowly. "It's risky, but it's better than waiting to be picked off one by one."

Together, they embarked on a series of calculated strikes, each more daring than the last. They reclaimed small parts of the city, setting traps and ambushes, using the undead's predictability against them. For a time, it seemed they were turning the tide.

Flushed with their successes, Edward devised a grander scheme. "We can clear a path to my machine," he proposed. "Repair it and end this nightmare."

Ava, who had grown to respect Edward's ingenuity, agreed to the plan. They gathered their resources, rallying the survivors for one decisive push.

The day of the operation arrived with a heavy silence. The group, armed and resolute, moved through the city like shadows, avoiding the undead's roaming gaze. They reached the time machine, but as they began their work, the unthinkable happened.

The undead, in numbers greater than they had ever seen, descended upon them. Not randomly, but with purpose, as if drawn by an unseen force. The survivors fought valiantly, but they were outmatched, outmaneuvered.

In the chaos, Ava was captured. Edward, helpless, watched as she was dragged away by the creatures, her eyes meeting his in a silent plea.

The survivors retreated, defeated and demoralized. Edward, wracked with guilt, retreated to the bunker, his mind a whirlwind of despair and frustration.

It was then that he found it - a hidden room in the bunker, lined with ancient texts and forgotten lore. Among them was a tome describing a mystical 'Source,' a force that controlled the undead, bending them to its will.

"This is it," Edward whispered, a new resolve igniting within him. "This is how we turn the tide."

He shared his discovery with the remaining survivors, his eyes burning with a fervor they had not seen before. "We find this Source, we destroy it, and we free Ava. We free everyone."

The journey to the Source was fraught with danger. The undead, more numerous and aggressive than ever, seemed to sense their purpose.

As they neared their destination, the unthinkable happened. The undead, led by a mutated, intelligent creature - the Alpha - ambushed them. Edward was captured, brought before the very creature that controlled the fate of this future.

There, in the heart of darkness, he found Ava, her eyes vacant, her will subjugated by the Alpha. "Ava," Edward whispered, his heart breaking.

The Alpha, a grotesque parody of humanity, regarded him with cold intelligence. "You are the anomaly," it hissed. "Your presence disrupts the order we have created."

Edward, defiance flaring within him, met its gaze. "I will end this. I will free her, and all of you."

But as he spoke, he knew the odds were against him. Trapped in the lair of the enemy, surrounded by the very creatures he sought to destroy, Edward Mallory faced the darkest hour of his journey. The fate of the future, and of Ava, hung precariously in the balance.

In the oppressive gloom of the Alpha's lair, Edward's eyes never left Ava. Her once vibrant spirit seemed extinguished, her gaze hollow. Yet, he refused to lose hope. "Ava," he whispered, his voice a mixture of pain and determination. "I know you're still in there. I'll get us out of this."

The Alpha circled them, its grotesque form a nightmare come to life. "Futile," it hissed, its voice a chilling echo. "You cannot change what is destined."

Edward's mind raced, searching for a weakness, a chink in the creature's armor. He remembered the ancient texts, the lore of the Source. "You control them, don't you?" he challenged. "But you're also bound to them. Without them, you're nothing."

The Alpha paused, its eyes narrowing. Edward sensed he had struck a nerve.

Seizing the moment, Edward lunged towards a pile of debris, grabbing a sharp, metal rod. With a defiant cry, he charged at the Alpha. The creature, caught off guard, staggered back, its control over the undead faltering.

In that instant, Ava's eyes flickered with recognition. Fighting the Alpha's influence, she launched herself at the creature, giving Edward the opening he needed. He drove the rod into the Alpha, a howl of rage and pain echoing through the lair.

The undead, freed from the Alpha's grip, turned on it in a frenzied attack. Edward grabbed Ava's hand, pulling her away from the chaos. "We need to get to the machine," he shouted over the din.

They fought their way through the disoriented undead, reaching the time machine amidst the ruins. Edward frantically worked on the controls, his hands trembling. "I can fix this," he muttered. "I can still change everything."

Ava, her eyes clear for the first time since her capture, watched him. "Edward, what if this is our destiny? What if we can't change it?"

"We have to try," Edward insisted, his voice cracking with desperation.

As the machine whirred to life, a renewed roar from the Alpha signaled its approach. It was not yet defeated. Wounded and enraged, it charged at them, a terrifying specter of vengeance.

Edward pushed Ava behind him, facing the Alpha. His mind raced, calculating, strategizing. In a moment of clarity, he realized what he had to do.

With a swift movement, he redirected the energy of the machine, creating a vortex around the Alpha. The creature, caught in the pull of the time machine, howled as it was sucked into the temporal rift.

The machine, damaged and unstable, began to overload. Edward knew they had mere moments before it exploded.

"Ava, get out of here!" he yelled, pushing her towards the exit.

"No, I won't leave you!" she protested, tears streaming down her face.

Edward looked at her, his expression one of sorrow and love. "You have to. Tell them the truth. Prevent this from happening."

As Ava reluctantly fled, Edward turned back to the machine. His mind was clear, his purpose certain. He thought of his past, of the world he had left behind, of the future he had hoped to save.

In his final moments, as the machine reached its critical point, a horrific realization dawned on him. The virus, the source of this apocalypse, was within him, brought back from his first journey to the future. He was the paradox, the origin of the devastation.

With a bitter smile, Edward accepted his fate. He would end the cycle, even if it meant sacrificing himself. As the machine exploded, a blinding light enveloped him, and the world he knew was no more.

In an alternate 1895, a young Edward Mallory stood before a time machine, identical to the one lost in the explosion. Unaware of the alternate self who had just sacrificed everything, he prepared for his first journey, his eyes alight with excitement and curiosity.

The cycle was poised to begin anew, the threads of time weaving a complex tapestry of cause and effect. In the tangles of time, Edward Mallory's greatest invention was both a marvel and a tragic error, a paradox that would echo through the ages.

CHAPTER 17

UNDEAD MOBY-DICK

"In the heart of the sea, there lies a shadow, darker than the ocean's deepest trench, more ravenous than the fiercest storm." - Old Sailor's Proverb

The Pequod, a sturdy whaling vessel, cut through the murky waters like a knife through velvet darkness. Its weathered sails bore the scars of countless storms, and its crew, a motley assembly of hardened seafarers, went about their duties with the silent efficiency of men who had long ago made peace with the perils of the sea. At the helm stood Captain Ahab, a man whose very name whispered tales of obsession and dread across the ports of the world.

Ahab's gaze, piercing and relentless, was fixed upon the horizon, as if trying to unveil the mysteries of the deep. He was a tall, gaunt figure, his face etched with lines that spoke of storms weathered and battles fought, both against man and nature. His leg, lost to the very beast he now hunted, was replaced by a prosthetic made from the jawbone of a whale, a constant reminder of his vendetta against the leviathan of the deep - Moby Dick.

The crew, though seasoned, could not shake off an air of unease that clung to the ship like a shroud. They spoke in hushed tones about their captain's obsession, the unnatural pallor of his skin, and the haunted look in his eye.

One evening, as a crimson sunset bled into the sea, Ahab stood on deck, surrounded by his men. He raised his voice, a commanding tone that demanded attention.

"Men of the Pequod!" he began, his voice as deep and tumultuous as the sea itself. "You have been told we are here to hunt whales, the great behemoths of the deep. But our quest, our true quest, is far more dire. We hunt not just any whale, but a monster, a creature that transcends nature - Moby Dick."

The crew shifted uneasily, the name Moby Dick hanging in the air like a curse. Starbuck, the first mate, a man of reason and strength, stepped forward.

"Captain Ahab," he said, his voice steady but laced with concern, "we are whalers, not hunters of phantoms. This obsession of yours, it's leading us into uncharted waters, both in sea and in sanity."

Ahab's eyes flashed with a fierce light. "You think me mad, Starbuck? This whale, this demon of the sea, took my leg, left me less than whole. It is not just a whale; it's a manifestation of all that is evil in this world."

The crew listened, caught between loyalty and fear. Ahab's presence was magnetic, his madness tinged with a charisma that was hard to deny.

"Listen to me, all of you!" Ahab's voice rose like a tempest. "Moby Dick is no ordinary whale. It's a creature risen from the depths of hell itself. I have seen its eyes, red as the blood it spills, its skin, pale as the dead. We are not just hunting; we are battling a scourge that threatens the very essence of our world."

The men exchanged glances, their beliefs a whirlpool of doubt and fear. But in their hearts, the seed of Ahab's obsession began to take root.

As night fell, the Pequod sailed on, a lone sentinel in the vast, dark ocean. In his cabin, Ahab poured over ancient texts and charts, his mind a labyrinth of strategy and vengeance. The moon cast a ghostly glow on his face, accentuating his resolve, his unwavering determination to confront the horror that haunted his every waking moment.

The next morning dawned with a sense of foreboding. The sea was unusually calm, the air thick with the scent of an impending storm. Ahab stood on deck, scanning the horizon, his prosthetic leg tapping an impatient rhythm on the wooden planks.

Suddenly, a shout pierced the air. "There! On the horizon!"

All eyes turned to see a ghostly shape emerging from the mist. It was the zombified whale, Moby Dick, its massive form gliding through the water with a grace that belied its monstrous nature.

The crew, gripped by a mix of fear and fascination, watched as Ahab raised his harpoon, his eyes alight with a feverish glow.

"This is it, men! The battle we were born to fight!"

As Moby Dick drew closer, its undead nature became horrifyingly clear. Its skin was a ghastly pale, its eyes glowing with an unnatural light. It moved with an eerie intelligence, as if aware of the fate that awaited it.

Ahab hurled the harpoon with all his might, a primal scream tearing from his throat. The weapon struck true, embedding itself in the creature's flesh. But instead of a mortal wound, the harpoon seemed only to enrage the beast.

With a deafening roar, Moby Dick turned on the Pequod, its massive tail crashing down on the deck. The ship shuddered under the impact, men thrown like ragdolls in the chaos.

Ahab, undeterred, limped forward, his jaw set in a grim line. "This is just the beginning, men! The real battle lies ahead!"

As the sun set on the embattled Pequod, it was clear that this was no ordinary hunt. It was a war against a force beyond nature, a battle that would test the limits of man's courage and sanity. And at the heart of it all was Captain Ahab, a man consumed by a vengeance so fierce it bordered on madness.

The sea, once a place of wonder and mystery, had become a battleground, and the Pequod, a ship of ghosts, sailing into a nightmare from which there was no awakening.

The Pequod sailed on, a lone warrior against a sea turned hostile. Its sails, tattered and strained, bore witness to the struggle against Moby Dick, the leviathan of the undead. The crew, once men of the sea, were now soldiers in a battle they scarcely understood, led by a captain whose obsession was as deep as the ocean itself.

Captain Ahab, his face etched with the lines of sleepless nights, stood on the quarterdeck, his eyes never straying from the churning waters. The harpoon attack on Moby Dick had been but a prelude to the horror they now faced. The whale, bearing the scars of Ahab's wrath, had become an even more formidable adversary, its attacks more cunning, its movements unpredictable.

The first mate, Starbuck, approached Ahab with a caution born of witnessing the captain's growing fixation. "Captain, the men are weary, the ship is damaged. We must consider turning back," he implored, his voice barely above a whisper against the howling wind.

Ahab turned slowly, his gaze piercing Starbuck like a harpoon. "Turn back? Now, when we have the beast within our reach? No, Mr. Starbuck, we will not turn back. We will fight this demon until the very end."

Starbuck, troubled by the captain's fervor, nodded silently and retreated. He knew there was no swaying Ahab from his course, a course that seemed to lead them ever closer to the brink of doom.

In the days that followed, Ahab's strategy evolved. No longer content with mere harpoons, he delved into ancient lore, seeking weapons and tactics that bordered on the supernatural. He poured over the pages of obscure texts, muttering incantations and drawing symbols of power on the deck.

The crew watched with a mix of fear and awe as Ahab transformed the Pequod into a ship of war, unlike any that had sailed the seven seas. Chains inscribed with runes clanked against the hull, and the air was thick with the scent of strange herbs burned in rituals meant to protect and empower.

Then came the day of the second confrontation. Moby Dick, drawn by the ship's newfound aura, surfaced with a roar that shook the heavens. The sea boiled around its massive form, and the air itself seemed to shiver with malice.

Ahab, standing at the prow, his face a mask of determination, raised his arms and began to chant. The crew, each man armed with a weapon of dark design, joined their voices to his, creating a chorus that resonated across the waves.

The whale lunged, its jaws agape, revealing rows of serrated teeth that glinted like daggers in the sunlight. But this time, the Pequod was ready. From the ship's bow, a harpoon, glowing with an eldritch light, shot forth, striking Moby Dick in the eye.

The beast reeled, its cry of agony echoing across the sea. But instead of retreating, it attacked with renewed fury, its tail smashing into the ship, splintering wood and scattering men.

Ahab, undaunted, continued his incantations, his voice rising above the chaos. The crew, rallied by their captain's unyielding spirit, fought back with a ferocity that matched their foe.

But as the battle raged, it became clear that Moby Dick was no ordinary adversary. With each attack, it seemed to grow stronger, its undead nature allowing it to withstand injuries that would have felled any mortal creature.

The Pequod, battered and breached, groaned under the strain. Men fell, their cries lost in the roar of the sea. Starbuck, his face a mask of despair, fought alongside his crew, but his heart knew the truth - they were outmatched.

As the sun dipped below the horizon, casting a blood-red glow over the battlefield, Ahab, his body bruised and his spirit unbroken, faced Moby Dick once more. With a cry that was part rage, part plea, he hurled the last of his enchanted harpoons.

The weapon struck true, embedding itself deep in the whale's flesh. For a moment, the world seemed to hold its breath. Then, with a final, defiant bellow, Moby Dick dove beneath the waves, disappearing into the depths.

The crew, exhausted and battered, cheered, but their celebration was short-lived. As they looked to their captain, they saw not triumph in his eyes, but a dawning realization of the cost of their victory.

The Pequod, its hull breached, its sails torn, drifted aimlessly. The men, their faces gaunt, their eyes haunted, knew that their battle was far from over. They had wounded the beast, but at what cost?

Ahab, his leg aching from the strain of battle, limped to the helm. His gaze, once filled with the fire of vengeance, was now tempered with a somber understanding.

"We have fought well, my men," he said, his voice barely audible above the creaking of the ship. "But this is not the end. Moby Dick lives, and as long as it roams the seas, our fight is not over. We must regroup, repair, and ready ourselves for the final battle. For it is not just a whale we hunt, but a curse that threatens us all."

The men nodded, their resolve hardened by their captain's words. They set to work, patching the ship, tending to the wounded, each man driven by a newfound purpose.

As the Pequod sailed on, a silhouette against the setting sun, it was more than a ship. It was a beacon of hope in a sea of darkness, a testament to the indomitable spirit of man in the face of unimaginable horror.

And at its heart was Captain Ahab, a man who had looked into the abyss and found within himself the strength to fight back. The battle against Moby Dick was far from over, but as long as Ahab stood at the helm, the crew of the Pequod knew they would never face the darkness alone.

The Pequod, once a proud whaler now a ghostly vessel, carried its weary crew through the churning, ominous seas. Captain Ahab stood at the helm, his figure stoic against the relentless storm, his eyes fixed on the dark horizon. The ship, battered by their recent clash with Moby Dick, groaned beneath him, its timbers strained and weary.

Starbuck approached, his face etched with concern and exhaustion. "Captain," he began, his voice barely rising above the howling wind, "the men are spent, and the ship can barely hold herself together. We've done what no man has dared, but it's time we consider our own lives."

Ahab turned, his gaze piercing Starbuck like a shard of ice. "There is no turning back, Mr. Starbuck. We are bound to this quest, as surely as the stars are bound to the sky. Moby Dick is wounded, but so are we. The final battle awaits, and it is one we cannot flee."

As the Pequod sailed into the heart of the storm, the crew prepared for the inevitable confrontation. They knew their journey had transcended the hunt for a whale; they were now part of a saga that would be whispered in awe for generations.

The night fell like a curtain, and with it came a silence that was more foreboding than any storm. The sea became eerily calm, the air thick with anticipation. And then, with a sound that was a cross between a roar and a wail, Moby Dick emerged from the depths.

The whale, monstrous and spectral, bore the scars of their previous encounters. Its eyes, red and unyielding, fixed on the Pequod with a hatred that was almost palpable. Ahab, his face a mask of resolve, stepped forward, a harpoon clutched in his hand. "This is our destiny, men!" he shouted. "For good or ill, our fates are intertwined with this beast!"

The crew rallied, their fear transformed into a fierce determination. They took their positions, weapons at the ready, their eyes fixed on the leviathan that approached.

The battle that ensued was like none other. Moby Dick, empowered by its undead nature, struck with a ferocity that was terrifying. The Pequod, agile and defiant, danced around the whale's attacks, her crew responding with a barrage of harpoons and cannon fire. Ahab, at the forefront of the battle, fought with a ferocity that belied his age and his injuries. Each strike of his harpoon was guided by a lifetime of seafaring and a deep, unyielding hatred for the creature before him. As the battle raged, the Pequod took grievous hits. Men fell, their cries lost in the cacophony of the struggle. Starbuck, his face smeared with soot and blood, fought alongside his captain, his respect for Ahab mingling with a deep-seated fear for the man's sanity. And then, in a moment that seemed suspended in time,

142

Ahab's harpoon found its mark. The weapon, imbued with ancient energies, pierced Moby Dick's heart. The whale let out a sound that was half-scream, half-roar, a sound that echoed the pain of a creature that was more than just flesh and bone.

As Moby Dick thrashed in its death throes, the Pequod was caught in the backlash. The ship, already damaged, could not withstand the force of the whale's fury. Timbers snapped, the mast cracked, and the sea rushed in to claim its due.

Ahab, his face a portrait of triumph and tragedy, clung to the wheel. "We have won, Mr. Starbuck," he gasped, his voice barely audible over the din. "The beast is vanquished."

But as the crew celebrated their hard-fought victory, a chilling realization dawned. Moby Dick's body, now still, began to dissolve into a dark mist, seeping into the ocean, spreading like a plague. The men watched in horror as the water around them turned a sickly hue, the essence of the undead virus released into the sea. Their victory had come at a terrible price; they had unleashed a curse that would change the seas forever.

Starbuck, his face pale with the realization of what they had done, turned to Ahab. "Captain, what have we done? We sought to end a curse, but we have only begun another."

Ahab, his eyes reflecting the dark waters, looked out at the sea that had been his life. "We set out to conquer a monster, Mr. Starbuck, but in doing so, we have become the harbingers of a greater darkness."

The Pequod, her sails torn and her hull breached, drifted aimlessly. The crew, once hunters, now survivors of a battle that would haunt their dreams

, looked out at the sea with a new understanding. They had faced the abyss and had glimpsed the darkness that lay beyond.

As the first light of dawn touched the horizon, the Pequod sailed towards home, her journey at an end. But the sea, once a place of wonder and adventure, now held a new terror, a reminder of the price of obsession and the cost of battling the shadows of the deep.

And at the heart of it all was Captain Ahab, a man who had pursued his vengeance to the ends of the earth, only to find that some battles were never truly won, and some monsters never truly vanquished.

CHAPTER 18

TWIST VS. THE UNDEAD

"He Will Win Who Knows When to Fight and When Not to Fight:"

The London streets, once bustling with the clamor of daily life, now lay in a desolate silence, broken only by the occasional groan of the undead. Amidst this post-apocalyptic world walked a young orphan, Oliver Twist, his eyes holding a depth that belied his years. His thin frame, clad in tattered clothes, weaved through the maze of abandoned cars and crumbling buildings with a practiced ease.

Oliver's days at the orphanage were a monotonous blur of survival and solitude. But today was different. Today, he clutched a worn, leather-bound journal, its pages yellowed with age, a secret treasure he'd found hidden beneath a loose floorboard. The journal, filled with cryptic notes and faded photographs, hinted at a life Oliver had never known - a life before the outbreak.

As he wandered through the ghostly remnants of the city, he couldn't shake off the feeling of being watched. Turning a corner, he came face-to-face with a zombie, its pallid skin stretched over protruding bones. Oliver froze, but to his astonishment, the creature simply stared, a flicker of confusion in its lifeless eyes, before shuffling away.

"Oi, kid!" a gruff voice called out from behind a pile of rubble. Oliver spun around to see a scruffy man emerge, his eyes scanning the street warily. "You've got some nerve walking around here in broad daylight. Zombies or not, this place is crawling with scavengers."

Oliver's guard was up in an instant. "I can take care of myself," he replied defiantly.

The man chuckled. "I'm sure you can. But even a street rat needs allies in times like these. Name's Jack, by the way."

"Oliver," he replied cautiously, eyeing Jack.

Jack's gaze landed on the journal in Oliver's hand. "What's that you've got there? Looks ancient."

Oliver clutched the journal closer. "It's nothing. Just an old book."

Jack raised an eyebrow. "Doesn't look like 'nothing' to me. You know, in a world where the present is as grim as this, the past might hold some valuable secrets."

Oliver hesitated, then slowly opened the journal, revealing a photograph of a couple, smiling blissfully. "I think... they might be my parents."

Jack whistled softly. "Parents, eh? In this world, that's like finding a treasure trove. What are you planning to do about it?"

"I need to find out who they were... and why I was left behind," Oliver said, his voice barely above a whisper.

Jack nodded solemnly. "Well, kid, you're not the only one with unanswered questions. But be careful, curiosity in these parts can be as dangerous as those walking corpses."

As they spoke, a distant sound of shuffling feet and guttural moans grew closer. Oliver's instincts kicked in. "We need to move," he urged.

Together, they navigated through the labyrinth of the fallen city, dodging the undead with a stealth that came from years of survival. But as they moved, Oliver couldn't shake off the feeling that there was more to his past than just a couple of photographs and a mysterious journal. And deep down, he knew that the answers he sought might just change everything.

As they delved deeper into the heart of the desolate city, the skeletal buildings casting long, ominous shadows in the failing light, Oliver and Jack found themselves in a precarious world of survival and secrets. The city, once a vibrant tapestry of life and culture, now lay in ruins, its streets a labyrinth of danger and despair.

Oliver, with the journal clutched tightly under his arm, was driven by a need to unravel the mystery of his past. Jack, seasoned by the harsh realities of this new world, saw in Oliver not just a fellow survivor, but a glimmer of hope in the relentless darkness.

Their journey was fraught with peril. More than once, they narrowly escaped the clutches of the undead, their grotesque forms a constant reminder of the world's tragic fate. Each encounter left Oliver with more questions than answers. Why did the undead seem to disregard him? What secret did his past hold?

Determined to find answers, Oliver proposed a daring plan. "We need to get to the university," he declared one evening, as they huddled in the safety of an abandoned bookstore. "If there's any information about this outbreak, or about my parents, it's got to be there."

Jack looked skeptical. "The university? That's in the heart of the city. It's suicide."

"I know it's dangerous," Oliver replied, his eyes burning with determination. "But it's a risk I have to take. And I think... I think I can move among them without being noticed. I've seen it happen."

Jack considered Oliver for a long moment, then nodded slowly. "Alright, kid. But we're going to need help."

They spent the following days gathering a group of unlikely allies: a former military strategist, haunted by the loss of her family; a street-smart scavenger with a quick wit and quicker fingers; and a silent, enigmatic figure who seemed to understand the undead in ways no one else did.

Together, they devised a plan. Using Oliver's unique ability to blend with the undead, they would infiltrate the university, locate any information about the outbreak, and get out before they were overrun.

The plan was fraught with danger. As they made their way through the city, each member of the group faced their own demons. The strategist, Lieutenant Grace, grappled with the guilt of past decisions. The scavenger, Leo, fought the fear that had kept him alive but alone. And the enigmatic figure, known only as Shadow, moved with a purpose that none could fathom.

Their plan, however, began to unravel when they reached the university. The place was teeming with more undead than they had anticipated. In a catastrophic turn of events, their presence was detected, leading to a harrowing chase through the maze-like corridors of the university.

As they fought their way through, Oliver's heart sank. The information he sought seemed increasingly out of reach, the truth about his parents and his own existence buried under layers of chaos and danger.

Then, at the worst possible moment, their situation took a dire turn. The group was ambushed by a particularly intelligent and coordinated group of zombies. It was in this moment of desperation that the truth hit Oliver like a bolt of lightning.

They had underestimated their enemy. These weren't just mindless creatures; they were something more, something worse. The group was scattered, each member fighting for their life.

Oliver found himself cornered, his back against a wall, as the undead closed in. His heart pounded in his chest, his mind racing for a solution. But it was in this moment of sheer terror that Oliver's true nature revealed itself.

As the undead reached for him, they hesitated, their milky eyes filled with a confusion that mirrored his own. In that split second, Oliver realized that his unique ability was both a gift and a curse. It was his lineage, his connection to these creatures, that kept him safe. But it also meant that his very existence was tied to the outbreak.

In a desperate bid for survival, Oliver used his newfound understanding to navigate through the undead, leading them away from his friends and towards the heart of the university. There, in the depths of the abandoned research facility, he hoped to find the answers he so desperately sought.

But what he found instead was a revelation that would change everything. The university, once a bastion of knowledge and discovery, now held the darkest secrets of the outbreak. And at the center of it all was a truth that threatened to shatter Oliver's world forever.

As the undead swarmed around him, Oliver realized that the journey to uncover his past was far from over. It was only just beginning.

The air in the research facility was thick with the scent of decay and long-forgotten secrets. Oliver, his heart pounding in his chest, navigated the dimly lit corridors, the echoes of his footsteps a stark reminder of his solitude. The undead, their presence a constant threat, seemed to both follow and shun him, as if caught in a tumultuous dance of attraction and repulsion.

As he delved deeper, the whispers of the past grew louder, resonating through the hollow halls. He stumbled upon a laboratory, its walls lined with vials of strange liquids and papers strewn about in chaotic abandon. In the center, a large, dusty monitor flickered weakly to life as he approached.

The screen illuminated a series of video logs, each one a fragment of the story he was so desperate to understand. His heart skipped a beat as he recognized the faces in the videos - his parents, vibrant and alive, speaking passionately about their research.

"We've made a breakthrough," his father's voice echoed in the silent room. "A virus that could revolutionize medicine. But it's unstable. We need more time."

His mother appeared next, her eyes filled with a mix of fear and determination. "The virus has mutated. It's beyond our control now. We have to contain it, no matter the cost."

Oliver's hands trembled as he pieced together the tragic puzzle. His parents, brilliant scientists, had unwittingly unleashed the very plague that had brought the world to its knees. And in their final moments, they had made a desperate decision - to save their son.

A shuffling sound snapped Oliver out of his reverie. He turned to find himself face to face with the most fearsome of the undead - a sentient, almost human-like creature. Its eyes, a haunting mirror of his own, bore into him with a chilling recognition.

"You," it hissed, its voice a grotesque parody of human speech. "You are the key."

Oliver felt the weight of his lineage, a heavy burden he could no longer deny. His unique connection to the undead, his immunity, was no accident - it was a legacy, a final gift from his parents.

The creature advanced, and Oliver braced himself for the inevitable clash. But as they fought, a startling realization dawned on him. This creature, this abomination, was his mother - mutated, corrupted, but still bearing the faintest traces of the woman who had given him life.

The battle was fierce and heart-wrenching. Oliver, torn between horror and sorrow, fought with a desperate strength. But as he finally overcame the creature, delivering a merciful end to his mother's tortured existence, he felt a piece of his own humanity slip away.

The facility shook with the sounds of collapse, the virus containment systems failing under the strain of the battle. Oliver, his mission complete yet his heart shattered, knew he had little time. He gathered the research, the damning evidence of his parents' role in the apocalypse, and fled into the crumbling city.

The world outside had changed. The undead, sensing the loss of their queen, became disoriented, aimless. Oliver, emerging from the shadows of his past, saw a glimmer of hope amidst the chaos.

As he reunited with his companions, each bearing their own scars from the night's ordeal, Oliver knew that their fight was far from over. But now, armed with the truth and a resolve forged in the fires of loss and revelation, they faced the future with a new purpose.

Together, they would rebuild, not just survive. For in Oliver's hands lay not just the secrets of the past, but the keys to a new beginning. And as the sun rose over the battered skyline of London, Oliver Twist, orphan of the undead, stepped into the light, ready to face whatever challenges lay ahead.

CHAPTER 19

AROUND THE WORLD IN 80 ZOMBIES

"In times of chaos, the wise build bridges while the foolish build barriers," Phileas Fogg mused to himself, staring out of the rain-streaked window of his London townhouse. The night was dark, the kind of darkness that seemed to seep into the soul, filled with the distant groans and unrest of a city on the brink of collapse.

Phileas, a gentleman of considerable intellect and composure, found himself grappling with a reality far removed from his usual world of polite society and punctual trains. The streets of London, once bustling with carriages and the chatter of the gentry, were now desolate, save for the wandering hordes of the afflicted - the undead, as they had come to be known.

Inside the dimly lit drawing room, the ticking of the grandfather clock was a steady reminder of the passing time - time that was running out for Phileas' beloved fiancé, Aouda. She lay in the adjacent room, her breaths shallow and feverish, her once bright eyes now dull and distant. A local doctor, his face weary and lined with the toll of endless night shifts, had just left, shaking his head with a grim finality.

"There's nothing more we can do, Mr. Fogg," he had said. "This illness... it's like nothing we've ever seen. It's spreading fast, and once it takes hold, well... you've seen what happens."

Phileas hadn't needed to see the streets to know what happened. The transformation was gruesome, a fate he couldn't bear to imagine for Aouda. In his heart, a battle raged between despair and a desperate flicker of hope. It was this battle that kept him from succumbing to the paralysis of fear.

As he turned from the window, his eyes fell upon an old, leather-bound manuscript that lay on his mahogany desk. It was a relic he had acquired in his travels, filled with fragmented ancient texts and cryptic diagrams. Something about the manuscript had always intrigued him, but it was only now, in his hour of desperation, that a particular passage caught his eye.

"The cure lies in the journey, not the destination," it read, in barely legible script. A map sprawled across the next page, a map of the world with enigmatic symbols marking various locations.

A spark of resolve ignited within Phileas. He couldn't sit idly by, waiting for the end. If there was even the slightest chance that this manuscript held the key to a cure, he had to take it. He had to embark on this perilous quest, not just for Aouda but for humanity itself.

But doubt crept in, uninvited. The world outside was no longer one of order and predictability. It was a world overrun by chaos, where the dead preyed upon the living. Could he, a man of reason and science, navigate such a world? What did he know of fighting, of survival in the face of such horror?

These thoughts were interrupted by a sudden commotion outside the room. Phileas rushed to the door, opening it to find his butler, Passepartout, struggling to restrain a figure at the entrance - a figure whose ragged appearance and vacant, bloodshot eyes left no doubt of its affliction.

"Sir, I'm trying to hold him back, but I fear he's one of them!" Passepartout exclaimed, his usual composed demeanor replaced by a mix of fear and determination.

Phileas' heart raced as he realized the gravity of the situation. This was no longer a distant problem; the undead were at his very doorstep. With a deep breath, he stepped forward, grabbing a nearby fireplace poker. The creature lunged at him with a guttural growl, but Phileas, driven by a newfound resolve, managed to fend it off, pushing it back into the night from whence it came.

As he bolted the door, Phileas turned to Passepartout, his decision made. "Pack your bags, Passepartout. We're going on a journey, a journey around the world. There's a cure out there, and I intend to find it."

Passepartout, ever loyal, nodded, though his eyes betrayed his concern. "But, sir, the world is overrun with these... these monsters. How will we survive?"

"We'll survive by being smart, by being cunning," Phileas replied, his voice firm. "We will need to learn, adapt, and above all, we must never lose hope. For Aouda, for everyone, we must not fail."

As they prepared for their uncertain journey, the clock in the hall struck midnight, its chimes echoing through the house like a solemn reminder of the ticking clock of fate. And so, amidst a world plunged into darkness and despair,

Phileas Fogg set out on his race against time, a race to circumnavigate the globe and battle

the tides of undead, seeking a glimmer of hope in humanity's darkest hour.

The journey began under a cloak of darkness, as Phileas Fogg and Passepartout slipped out of London aboard a steam-powered dirigible, the city's sorrowful moans fading into the night. The world below was a patchwork of shadow and despair, a stark reminder of the mission's gravity.

Their first destination was Paris. The city of lights, now dimmed and desolate, greeted them with eerie silence. As they navigated the empty boulevards, Phileas's mind was awhirl with strategies and tactics, drawing inspiration from his extensive readings of 'The Art of War'. He knew brute force would not suffice; they needed cunning to survive.

In the heart of Paris, amidst the ruins of the Louvre, they encountered their first horde. The undead, with their soulless eyes and gnarled hands, were a grotesque mockery of humanity. Phileas, recalling a principle from Sun Tzu, used mirrors and light to create illusions, disorienting the zombies and allowing the duo to escape unscathed. Passepartout marveled at his master's ingenuity, though his heart raced with fear.

As they journeyed to Egypt, the riddles of the ancient manuscript loomed large in Phileas's thoughts. The Pyramids, standing tall against the sands of time, held their first real clue. Inside the labyrinthine corridors, they stumbled upon cryptic hieroglyphics, which Phileas painstakingly deciphered. But just as they neared a breakthrough, a sudden ambush by a swarm of zombies forced them to flee, the riddle unsolved and their spirits dampened.

Undeterred, Phileas charted a course to India, determined to not let their initial failures define their quest. In the bustling streets of Mumbai, they chanced upon a motley crew of survivors - a brilliant engineer named Aditi, who had turned her home into a fortress of ingenious traps, and a martial artist named Raj, whose dexterity with a sword was a dance of death for any undead that dared approach.

Together, they hatched a grand plan to retrieve an ancient artifact from a hidden temple in Rajasthan, believed to hold the key to the cure. The journey was fraught with peril, but under Phileas's leadership, they navigated through hordes of zombies using a blend of stealth, distraction, and sheer force.

Upon reaching the temple, they discovered the artifact - a mystic stone inscribed with forgotten languages. But their triumph was short-lived. As they made their way back, they were betrayed by one of Raj's acquaintances, who, unbeknownst to them, had been bitten during the journey. The artifact was a decoy, and the real one was in Japan. The betrayal hit them hard, not just in their failed mission, but in their trust in humanity.

The journey to Australia was a time for reflection and regrouping. Phileas realized that their approach needed to change. They could no longer rely on just strategy and brute force; they needed to be adaptable, to use the environment to their advantage. In the Outback, they honed their skills in guerrilla warfare, setting traps and using the terrain to evade and outsmart the undead.

Their newfound tactics were put to the test in Japan. The true artifact, a sacred scroll hidden within an ancient Shinto shrine, was within their grasp. But as they retrieved it, they were ambushed by a new type of zombie. These were not the mindless drones they had encountered before; these were faster, smarter, a horrifying evolution.

The team fought valiantly, but they were outnumbered and outmatched. Captured and brought before the leader of this new breed, they faced a creature that was the antithesis of everything Phileas had come to understand about the undead. It spoke, its voice a chilling echo of humanity lost.

"You cannot stop what has already begun," the creature hissed. "This world is ours now."

Bound and beaten, Phileas looked into the eyes of this evolved zombie, seeing in them a twisted reflection of his own fears. The artifact was taken from them, and as they were locked away in a decrepit cell, their mission seemed to reach its nadir.

But even in that darkest moment, Phileas Fogg's resolve did not waver. He knew that to save Aouda, to save humanity, he needed to fight, to outthink this new enemy. With his companions by his side, he began to plot their escape, their minds working together to overcome this unforeseen adversary.

As the night fell over their prison, a plan began to take shape, a plan born not just of strategy, but of hope, resilience, and an unyielding desire to reclaim the world from the clutches of darkness.

The moon hung low in the sky, casting a pale light over the decrepit cell where Phileas Fogg and his companions were held captive. Their situation was dire, but Phileas's eyes burned with an unwavering determination. He turned to his companions, speaking in hushed, urgent tones.

"We cannot let fear dictate our fate," he whispered. "We must use our wits and every skill we have acquired. Remember, in unity lies our strength."

Aditi nodded, her eyes reflecting the resolve that Phileas's words had ignited. "I can disable the locks. I've been observing the guards' patterns. There is a way," she said, her voice steady despite the danger that loomed.

Raj flexed his hands, the muscles in his arms tensing. "And once we're out, I'll take the lead. We'll need to be swift and silent," he added, his eyes scanning their surroundings, calculating their moves.

Their escape was a symphony of stealth and strategy. Aditi's deft fingers manipulated the lock, releasing them from their bonds. They moved like shadows, evading the undead guards with a blend of Raj's martial prowess and Phileas's tactical guidance. They navigated through the labyrinthine corridors of the fortress, each turn bringing them closer to the artifact and the creature that had orchestrated their capture. As they approached the heart of the stronghold, the air grew colder, the oppressive atmosphere thick with anticipation.

There, in a grand, dilapidated hall, stood the evolved zombie leader, the stolen artifact clutched in its grotesque hand. Its eyes, unnervingly human, fixed upon them with a malevolent intelligence.

"You are persistent, Mr. Fogg," it hissed, its voice a disturbing blend of human and monster. "But futile. Your world is gone. This is the age of the undead."

Phileas stepped forward, his gaze unwavering. "Our world is what we make of it. And I choose to fight for a world where humanity thrives, not one where it is consumed by darkness."

The creature laughed, a sound that sent shivers down their spines. "Then fight you shall," it sneered, signaling its minions to attack.

The battle that ensued was a maelstrom of chaos and fury. Raj's sword danced through the air, slicing through the undead with lethal precision. Aditi utilized her makeshift gadgets, creating explosions and distractions. And Phileas, with every move, demonstrated his mastery of strategy, outmaneuvering the horde at every turn.

But the true test came when the creature itself joined the fray. It moved with a terrifying agility, its strikes deadly and precise. Phileas found himself face to face with it, their duel a clash of intellect and brute force.

As they fought, a heart-stopping moment occurred. Aouda, her body partially turned, appeared amidst the chaos. Her eyes, once full of warmth and love, now glimmered with a haunting emptiness. She lunged at Phileas, but in her eyes, he saw a flicker of recognition, a battle within her between the woman she was and the monster she was becoming.

"Aouda!" Phileas cried out, dodging her attack. "I know you're still in there. Fight it!"

In that moment of distraction, the creature seized its opportunity, striking Phileas with a vicious blow. He stumbled, pain searing through his body. But as the creature moved in for the kill, Aouda, with a sudden burst of clarity, intervened, attacking the creature and giving Phileas the chance to recover.

The tide of the battle turned. With renewed vigor, Phileas fought alongside Aouda, their movements in perfect harmony. Together, they forced the creature back, Phileas delivering the final, decisive blow that sent it crashing to the ground, the artifact tumbling from its grasp. As the creature lay defeated, the artifact, a vial containing an ancient virus, began to emanate a soft, pulsating light. Phileas picked it up, his hands trembling. Without hesitation, he administered the contents to Aouda.

The effect was instantaneous. The virus in the vial, predating the undead plague, acted as a cure, reversing the transformation. Aouda's eyes cleared, the humanity within them returning as the monstrous features receded. Around them, the remaining undead began to collapse, the plague that had gripped them dissipating.

In the aftermath, as the first light of dawn broke over the horizon, Phileas, Aouda, Aditi, and Raj emerged from the fortress, weary but victorious. The world they stepped into was forever changed, the threat of the undead vanquished.

Phileas looked at Aouda, her hand in his, and knew that their journey had been more than a quest for survival. It was a testament to the resilience of the human spirit, a declaration that even in the darkest of times, hope could ignite a flame that burned brighter than any despair.

Together, they set forth to help rebuild society, Phileas penning a new 'Art of War' for a world reborn from the ashes of the undead plague, a world where humanity once again dared to dream of a future filled with light and life.

CHAPTER 20

DANTE'S UNDYING INFERNO

"In the darkest depths of despair, even the faintest whisper of hope can sound like a roar."

The night was unusually still in Florence as Dante, once a celebrated soldier, now a shadow of his former self, walked the cobbled streets. Haunted by memories of war and loss, he sought solace in the bottom of his wine cup, but found none. The moon hung low, casting an eerie glow on the ancient buildings, as if nature itself conspired to remind him of his solitude.

As he staggered through the narrow alleyways, a vision struck him. There, beneath the ghostly light, stood Beatrice, his long-deceased beloved. Her ethereal form shimmered, her voice a whisper that cut through the silence.

"Dante, you must journey to where few dare to tread," she spoke, her eyes pools of sorrow and hope.

Dante shook his head, trying to dispel the image. "Beatrice, you are but a dream, a cruel trick of my weary mind," he muttered, clenching his fists.

But the apparition persisted. "Your path lies beyond this world, Dante. In Hell itself, where tormented souls cry for redemption. There, you will find your own."

He wanted to laugh, to dismiss her words as the ramblings of a drunkard's guilt. But the intensity in her gaze, the unspoken pain, held him captive. With a heavy heart, he whispered, "Why me? I am no saint, no savior."

"You have seen the depths of human depravity, Dante. Your heart, though scarred, holds the key to understanding and empathy. You must free the souls trapped in eternal suffering, just as you seek to free yourself from your own demons."

Before he could protest, the ground beneath him trembled. Cracks appeared, opening like the jaws of some great beast. He stumbled, losing his balance, and fell into the gaping maw of the earth.

He plummeted into darkness, the wind howling in his ears, a symphony of terror and despair. When he landed, it was on cold, hard ground. Groaning, he stood, his eyes adjusting to the dim light. Before him stood the gates of Hell, towering and insurmountable, their inscription a chilling welcome: "Abandon all hope, ye who enter here."

Dante's heart pounded in his chest. "This cannot be," he breathed, his voice barely a whisper.

Yet, as he gazed into the abyss beyond the gates, he knew Beatrice's words were true. This was his path, a journey into the very heart of darkness.

With a deep breath, he pushed open the gates. The hinges groaned, echoing through the vast emptiness. Beyond lay a landscape of despair: barren, fiery plains, and the distant wails of the damned.

As he ventured deeper, he encountered the souls of the undead, their eyes hollow, their whispers like the rustling of dead leaves. "Why are you here, mortal?" hissed one, its form barely human.

Dante's hand went to the sword at his side, a reflex from his days on the battlefield. "I seek... redemption. For myself, and perhaps for you as well."

The creature laughed, a sound devoid of any mirth. "There is no redemption here, only eternal suffering."

Undeterred, Dante pressed on, determined to find a way to fulfill Beatrice's quest. But with every step, the horrors of Hell revealed themselves. Souls tormented by their own sins, their cries a constant reminder of the fate that awaited him if he failed.

In the distance, a river of fire flowed, its banks crowded with the damned. As Dante approached, a figure emerged from the flames. Charon, the ferryman of the underworld, his eyes like burning coals.

"Another soul for the crossing?" Charon rasped, his voice like the grinding of stone.

Dante met his gaze, his resolve unwavering. "I seek passage, but not as a soul to be damned. I have a mission, one that I cannot turn away from."

Charon regarded him for a moment, then nodded slowly. "Very well, mortal. But know this: the journey you embark upon is fraught with peril, and there is no guarantee of return."

Dante stepped onto the ferry, his heart heavy with the weight of his task. As the boat glided over the fiery river, he looked back at the fading gates of Hell, a final glimpse of the world he knew.

Ahead lay the unknown, a realm of darkness and despair. But within Dante burned a flicker of hope, a determination to face whatever horrors awaited him. For in the depths of Hell, he would not only confront the demons of the damned but his own as well.

The ferry slid silently through the fiery river, its passage undisturbed by the tormented souls that wailed along its banks. Dante, standing stern and resolute, watched as the infernal landscape unfolded before him. Charon's oar dipped rhythmically into the molten river, each stroke a reminder of the irreversible journey Dante had embarked upon.

As they reached the far shore, Dante stepped off the ferry onto the ashen ground. The air was thick with the stench of sulfur and despair. Before him lay the first circle of Hell, a desolate expanse that stretched into the horizon.

He ventured forward, his every step a descent deeper into the abyss. The souls he encountered were twisted shadows of their former selves, condemned to relive their earthly sins for eternity. Dante's heart ached at the sight, but he steeled himself. He must not falter; he must find a way to save them.

In his mind, Dante revisited the tactical knowledge he had acquired as a soldier. He began to formulate a plan, drawing on 'The Art of War' principles. If he could understand the patterns of this hellish realm, perhaps he could manipulate them to his advantage.

He scavenged for anything he could use as a weapon, fashioning a crude but effective arsenal. His first attempts to engage the undead were clumsy and fraught with danger. Each encounter left him more bruised and weary, but with each skirmish, he learned more about his foes.

Dante soon realized that brute force was futile. The undead were relentless, their numbers overwhelming. He needed a different approach, a strategy that could turn the tide in his favor.

With a newfound determination, Dante began to rally the repentant souls he encountered. They were meek, broken by their eternal torment, but in them, Dante saw a glimmer of hope. He spoke to them of redemption, of a chance to rise against their oppressors and seek a semblance of peace.

Together, they devised a grand plan. Dante would lead a revolt, a carefully orchestrated attack that would exploit the weaknesses he had observed in the undead ranks. The repentant souls, driven by the promise of redemption, lent their support, gathering resources and relaying information.

The day of the uprising dawned, a hellish sunrise that bathed the infernal landscape in a blood-red glow. Dante and his makeshift army launched their attack, striking at the heart of the undead horde. For a moment, it seemed they might prevail.

But Dante had underestimated his adversary. Lucifer, the ruler of this damned realm, had been watching, amused by Dante's audacity. With a wave of his hand, he unleashed his true might, turning the tide of battle in an instant.

Dante's forces were scattered, the repentant souls consumed by the renewed ferocity of the undead. He watched in horror as his plan crumbled, his hope turning to ash.

Defeated and alone, Dante fled, pursued by the relentless undead. He stumbled through the desolate circles of Hell, each more terrifying than the last. His thoughts were a whirlwind of despair and self-reproach. He had failed, and now he was nothing more than a hunted animal in this godforsaken realm.

As he reached the frozen wasteland of Cocytus, the final circle, a chilling realization dawned on him. He had been a fool to think he could outsmart the devil. And now, he was about to pay the price.

Lucifer appeared before him, a towering figure of darkness and malice. "You are a brave soul, Dante," he sneered, his voice echoing across the icy expanse. "But bravery alone cannot save you here."

Dante stood defiant, though his heart was filled with dread. "I will not bow to you, Lucifer. I will find a way to save these souls, even if it costs me my own."

Lucifer laughed, a sound that sent shivers down Dante's spine. "You are in no position to make demands. You are mine now, Dante. And I will enjoy breaking you."

With a flick of his wrist, Lucifer sent Dante hurtling towards the edge of Cocytus. Dante clawed desperately at the ice, but it was no use. He was slipping, falling into the abyss below.

In that moment, as he stared into the void, Dante felt a profound sense of despair. He had come to Hell seeking redemption, only to find himself facing eternal damnation. All hope was lost, and with it, the last of Dante's resolve.

As he dangled over the edge, his fingers numbing from the cold, Dante closed his eyes and waited for the end. But it was not to be. For in the depths of his despair, a spark of defiance ignited within him. He would not go quietly into the night; he would fight to the very end.

With a Herculean effort, Dante pulled himself back onto the ice. He faced Lucifer, his eyes burning with a fierce determination. "I may be damned, but I will not surrender. I will fight you, Lucifer, until my last breath."

Lucifer regarded him with a mixture of amusement and curiosity. "Very well, Dante. Let us see what you are truly made of."

And with that, the final battle began. Dante, armed with nothing but his will and a broken shard of ice, faced off against the ruler of Hell. It was a fight he could not hope to win, but he fought nonetheless, driven by a desire to redeem himself and the souls he had vowed to save.

The clash was epic, a dance of light and shadow on the frozen landscape of Cocytus. Dante's every strike was met with a counter from Lucifer, his every move anticipated and countered. But still, he fought on, refusing to yield.

As the battle raged, Dante realized the futility of his struggle. He was no match for Lucifer, and his efforts were but a mere annoyance to the devil. But even in the face of certain defeat, Dante found a sense of peace. He had faced his demons, both literal and figurative, and in doing so, he had found a measure of redemption.

With a final, desperate lunge, Dante struck at Lucifer, knowing it would be his last. Lucifer easily deflected the blow, sending Dante sprawling onto the ice.

As he lay there, broken and defeated, Dante looked up at the towering figure of Lucifer. "Do it," he whispered. "End this."

Lucifer loomed over him, a smile playing on his lips. "You are a fascinating creature, Dante. But your journey ends here."

And with that, Lucifer raised his hand, ready to deliver the final blow. But before he could strike, a blinding light filled the air, and a voice echoed through the frozen wastes.

"Enough, Lucifer. This soul is not yours to claim."

Dante shielded his eyes from the light, his heart racing. Who could challenge Lucifer in his own domain?

As the light faded, Dante saw her. Beatrice, radiant and ethereal, stood before him, her gaze fixed on Lucifer.

"Beatrice," Dante breathed, disbelief and hope mingling in his voice.

Beatrice turned to him, her eyes filled with sorrow and love. "Dante, you have fought bravely, but your journey is not yet over. There is still a chance for redemption, for you and for the souls of Hell."

Lucifer scowled, his form shifting and writhing in the light. "This is my realm, and this soul is mine. You have no power here, Beatrice."

But Beatrice stood resolute, her presence a beacon of hope in the desolate landscape. "I am here by divine decree, Lucifer. And I have come to offer Dante a choice."

Dante struggled to his feet, his eyes fixed on Beatrice. "What choice?" he asked, his voice hoarse.

Beatrice extended her hand to him, her touch warm and comforting. "You can choose to leave Hell, to return to the world of the living. Or you can choose to stay, to become a guardian of these lost souls, to guide them towards redemption."

Dante's heart ached at the thought of leaving Hell, of abandoning the souls he had come to save. But the prospect of returning to the living, of finding peace at last, was a temptation he could not ignore.

He looked at Beatrice, then at Lucifer, his mind racing. What should he do? What was the right choice?

In the end, Dante knew what he had to do. He turned to Beatrice, his decision clear in his eyes. "I will stay," he said, his voice steady. "I will be their guardian, their guide. I will help them find redemption, as I have found mine."

Beatrice smiled, a smile that warmed Dante's soul. "You have chosen wisely, Dante. And in doing so, you have fulfilled your destiny."

Lucifer howled in rage, his form dissolving into shadow. "You may have won this battle, Dante, but the war is far from over. I will be watching, waiting for you to falter."

But Dante was not afraid. He had faced his demons and emerged victorious. He was ready to embrace his new role, to guide the lost souls of Hell towards the light.

As Beatrice faded away, her final words a whisper on the wind, Dante stood tall, a beacon of hope in the darkness. The guardian of Hell, the guide of the damned.

In the frozen heart of Cocytus, Dante stood resolute, a newfound sense of purpose igniting within him. The landscape around him, once a symbol of despair, now served as a battleground for redemption. As Lucifer vanished into the shadows, the air around Dante seemed to thrum with a palpable tension, a silent acknowledgment of the monumental task he had accepted.

Dante's journey through Hell had transformed him. He was no longer a mere wanderer of the damned; he was their guardian, their hope. With each step, he felt the weight of his responsibility, the burden of countless souls seeking salvation.

The final battle was not just against the forces of Hell, but against the very essence of despair and hopelessness that pervaded this realm. Dante moved through the circles, his presence a beacon of light in the darkness, rallying the repentant souls to his cause.

As he journeyed, he encountered the most tormented of souls, those who had given in to despair. Dante spoke to them of forgiveness and redemption, his words a soothing balm to their tortured spirits. He did not fight them; he freed them, one by one, from the chains of their own making.

But as he approached the innermost circle, the air grew colder, the darkness deeper. Here, the souls were not just tormented; they were consumed by their sins, lost in an endless cycle of suffering.

Dante steeled himself, knowing that this would be his greatest challenge. He faced the souls, his heart heavy with empathy. "You are not forgotten," he proclaimed, his voice echoing through the icy chamber. "You are not beyond redemption. I stand with you, and together, we can find peace."

The souls hesitated, their forms flickering in the dim light. Then, one by one, they began to respond, their voices a chorus of pain and hope.

"We have waited so long," they whispered. "We had lost all hope."

Dante reached out to them, his touch a spark that ignited their spirits. The air around them shimmered with a newfound energy, a collective will to break free from their eternal prison.

But just as Dante began to lead them towards redemption, the ground trembled, and a deafening roar filled the chamber. Lucifer emerged from the shadows, his form more terrifying than ever.

"You dare defy me in my own realm?" he bellowed, his voice a tempest of fury. "These souls are mine, Dante. You cannot save them."

Dante stood his ground, his resolve unshaken. "I do not defy you, Lucifer. I defy the despair that you represent. These souls deserve a chance at redemption, and I will give it to them."

Lucifer laughed, a sound that chilled Dante to the bone. "You are a fool, Dante. But I admire your tenacity. Let us see how far it will take you."

With a wave of his hand, Lucifer unleashed his legions, a horde of tormented souls twisted by their own despair. They surged towards Dante, a tidal wave of darkness and malice.

Dante braced himself, his heart pounding in his chest. He knew he could not fight them all, but he would not back down. He would stand and fight, for as long as he could.

The battle raged, a maelstrom of light and shadow. Dante fought with every ounce of his strength, his every strike a testament to his unwavering spirit. The repentant souls rallied around him, their combined will a powerful force against the darkness.

But as the battle reached its climax, Dante realized that they could not win by force alone. He needed to reach the souls, to break the hold that despair had on them.

With a cry that echoed through the chamber, Dante raised his voice, not in anger, but in compassion. "You are not lost! You are not alone! I stand with you, and together, we can overcome this darkness!"

The words resonated with the souls, their forms flickering with uncertainty. Slowly, they began to withdraw, their aggression waning as Dante's words reached their hearts.

Lucifer watched in disbelief, his fury growing with each retreating soul. "No!" he roared. "You will not take them from me!"

Dante faced Lucifer, his eyes alight with a fierce determination. "I do not take them, Lucifer. I free them. And I offer you the same chance. Let go of your anger, your pride. Find peace in forgiveness."

Lucifer's form wavered, his resolve faltering for a moment. But then, with a snarl of defiance, he lunged at Dante, his form a whirlwind of darkness and rage.

Dante braced himself, ready to meet Lucifer's attack. But as their forms collided, a blinding light filled the chamber, and a voice rang out, clear and powerful.

"Enough, Lucifer. Your reign of despair ends now."

The light coalesced into

a figure, radiant and majestic. It was Beatrice, her presence a beacon of divine grace.

Lucifer recoiled, his form dissolving into shadow. "You cannot do this, Beatrice. This is my realm!"

Beatrice's gaze was unwavering, her voice a melody of hope and strength. "This realm belongs to no one, Lucifer. It is a place of passage, of transformation. And Dante has shown that even in the darkest depths, there is light."

The chamber was bathed in a soft glow, the souls around Dante lifting their voices in a chorus of gratitude and relief. Dante watched in awe as the darkness receded, the infernal landscape transforming before his eyes.

Lucifer, reduced to a mere shadow, vanished into the ether, his reign of despair finally at an end.

Dante turned to Beatrice, his heart full of wonder and gratitude. "Beatrice, I... I don't know what to say."

Beatrice smiled, her eyes shining with pride and love. "You have done what many believed impossible, Dante. You have brought light to the darkness, hope to the hopeless. You have fulfilled your destiny."

Dante looked around at the souls he had helped save, their forms glowing with a newfound peace. He knew his journey was not over; it had only just begun. But he was ready for whatever lay ahead, for he had found his purpose.

He was Dante, the guardian of Hell, the shepherd of lost souls. And he would lead them, one by one, towards redemption.

CHAPTER 21

MONGOLS VS. THE UNDEAD

"In the wake of conquest, shadows linger where light fears to tread." - An old Mongol adage.

The night air was crisp and jubilant, filled with the songs of victory as the Mongol horde celebrated yet another conquest under the indomitable Ghengis Khan. Laughter and the clinking of cups filled the camp, a stark contrast to the cold, unfeeling stars that twinkled overhead. Amongst these celestial bodies, a comet streaked across the sky, its fiery tail painting a blazing trail. The shamans, eyes wide with reverence, proclaimed it a sign of the Eternal Blue Sky's favor upon their Great Khan.

Ghengis Khan, seated upon his ornate throne, adorned in furs and intricate armor, watched his warriors revel. His face, a weathered map of battles won and lands conquered, remained impassive, but his eyes sparkled with a conqueror's pride. Beside him, his trusted general, Subotai, leaned in, "My Khan, the men believe this comet heralds an era of unparalleled conquest."

The Khan's response was a mere nod, his gaze still fixed on the heavens. It was then that a scout, breathless and wide-eyed, approached the throne. "My Lord Khan," he gasped, "a sickness... in the eastern camp. It's spreading fast."

Dismissing it as a mere ailment, Ghengis Khan ordered his healers to attend to it. But as night deepened, the festivity's warmth turned cold. The sickness was no ordinary plague. Those who fell ill rose again, their eyes void of life, their bodies moving with a hunger for flesh. The undead, as they came to be known, turned on their brethren in a mindless rage.

Panic ensued. The once-disciplined camp became a cacophony of screams and chaos. Ghengis Khan, atop his steed, surveyed the pandemonium, his mind racing. "Subotai, muster the warriors! This is no sickness; it's sorcery, a trickery of our enemies."

Subotai nodded, rushing to execute his Khan's command, but the tide of terror was relentless. By dawn, a significant part of the horde had turned. The living now stood outnumbered.

It was then that an old man, cloaked in a robe adorned with mystic symbols, made his way through the chaos to the Khan's tent. The guards, upon seeing him, hesitated, their superstitions battling their duty, allowing him passage.

Ghengis Khan, his face a mask of fury and confusion, confronted the stranger. "Who are you to enter my tent unbidden?"

The old man, unfazed, met the Khan's gaze. "I am known as the Eagle of the Steppes, a shaman of the old ways. What you face now, mighty Khan, is no enemy's trick, but a curse born from the heavens."

"A curse?" the Khan scoffed. "I am Ghengis Khan, ruler of all I survey. I fear no curse."

The shaman's eyes held a depth like the endless steppe. "This is a curse of your own making, Great Khan. Your conquests have angered the spirits. The comet was not a sign of favor, but a harbinger of retribution."

Ghengis Khan, though skeptical, felt a chill run down his spine. The reality of his undead warriors clawing at the fabric of his empire was undeniable.

"Speak, shaman. What must be done?" the Khan demanded, a hint of urgency in his voice.

The Eagle of the Steppes closed his eyes, whispering an ancient chant before speaking, "To break the curse, you must seek a balance between the conquest of the land and the conquest of the spirit. Only then will the horde rest."

The Khan stood, his hand on the hilt of his sword, a storm brewing in his eyes. "I have no time for riddles, old man. My empire is at stake!"

The shaman, unflinching, replied, "And it is your empire, your unquenchable thirst for it, that has brought this doom upon your people."

Ghengis Khan, his mind a whirlwind of thoughts, knew one thing for certain - he faced a threat unlike any before. A threat not from the outside, but rising from within the very heart of his mighty horde. As the sun rose, casting a pale light over the camp, the Great Khan knew that the battle he was about to fight would be against an enemy that was once his greatest strength - his own undead warriors.

The dawn broke over the Mongol camp, casting a sickly light on the faces of the undead, their grotesque forms a mockery of the mighty warriors they once were. Ghengis Khan, his heart heavy with a burden no ruler should bear, convened his remaining generals in his tent. The air was thick with desperation and the lingering scent of blood and fire.

"We must act," Ghengis Khan began, his voice a low growl. "These... creatures were once our brothers, our sons. Now, they threaten to unravel all we have built."

Subotai, ever the strategist, spoke up, "My Khan, our usual tactics of speed and ferocity will not avail us here. These undead feel no fear, no pain."

The generals murmured in agreement, a sense of hopelessness creeping into their hardened faces. It was then that Ghengis Khan, inspired by the tales of ancient wars and strategies, proposed a plan.

"We will use the land to our advantage. Lure them into the Valley of Shadows. There, we will trap them and use fire to cleanse this curse from our midst," he declared, his eyes alight with a fierce determination.

The plan was set into motion. The warriors, their spirits bolstered by their Khan's resolve, worked swiftly, setting up intricate traps and fire pits throughout the valley. As night fell, they baited the horde into the valley with a contingent of horsemen, their screams echoing as they sacrificed themselves to lead the undead into the trap.

The valley, once a place of serene beauty, transformed into a death trap. As the undead poured in, Ghengis Khan gave the signal. Fire roared to life, engulfing the valley in a hellish inferno. The night sky was illuminated by the flames, the screams of the undead piercing the air.

But the victory was short-lived. The undead, driven by a hunger that knew no bounds, continued their advance, unphased by the fire. The flames that were meant to be their end became a mere backdrop to their relentless onslaught.

"My Khan, the fire... it does not stop them!" Subotai yelled over the roar of the flames, his face a mask of horror.

Ghengis Khan watched in disbelief as the undead army, their bodies charred and ablaze, marched through the fire, setting their sights on the living.

Retreating to their camp, the Khan and his generals faced the grim reality. The fire, their last hope, had failed.

The Eagle of the Steppes, his presence almost forgotten, spoke, "Great Khan, you fight this battle with weapons of the world. This is a war of the spirit. Look within for your weapon."

Ghengis Khan, his mind a tempest of rage and desperation, realized the truth in the shaman's words. He had always conquered with might and strategy, but this enemy required a different approach.

Gathering his remaining forces, he addressed them, "Warriors of the Mongol horde, we face an enemy unlike any other. But we are Mongols, descendants of the Eternal Blue Sky. We will adapt, we will fight, and we will prevail!"

The warriors, their spirits reignited by their Khan's words, prepared for the battle ahead. Ghengis Khan, in a moment of introspection, understood that to defeat this curse, he would need to embrace change.

The undead horde advanced, their numbers seemingly endless. The Mongols met them with a new strategy, targeting the undead not with arrows and swords, but with tactics aimed at disorienting and dividing them. They used the terrain, leading smaller groups of undead into ambushes, exploiting their mindless nature.

But as the battle raged, a greater horror unfolded. The undead began to mutate, their bodies becoming grotesque parodies of warriors, stronger and more resilient. The Mongol warriors, though fierce and brave, fell one by one to the monstrous horde.

In the midst of this chaos, the Eagle of the Steppes was captured by the undead, his wisdom and guidance lost to the Mongols. Ghengis Khan, witnessing the capture, felt a deep sense of loss, not only for the shaman but for the hope he represented.

As the night drew to a close, the Mongol camp lay in ruins, the surviving warriors exhausted and demoralized. Ghengis Khan, sitting amidst the wreckage, realized that they had reached their lowest point. The undead horde, now more powerful than ever, loomed like a dark cloud over the remnants of his once-great empire.

The Great Khan, his eyes reflecting the flickering flames of the dying fires, knew that the dawn would bring the greatest battle of his life. A battle not just for his empire, but for the very soul of his people. The night was long, and in its dark embrace, Ghengis Khan prepared for the final stand.

As the first light of dawn crept over the horizon, painting the sky in hues of orange and red, Ghengis Khan stood amidst his weary warriors. His eyes, once full of the fire of conquest, now burned with a different flame - the flame of survival. He mounted his horse, his silhouette etched against the rising sun, and addressed his men.

"Today, we face not just an enemy, but our own past," he declared, his voice resonating with a somber intensity. "Our strength, our unity, will be our weapon. For our brothers, for our empire, we fight!"

The warriors, their spirits lifted by their Khan's words, let out a battle cry that echoed across the steppes. The undead horde, a grotesque mirror of the Khan's once mighty army, advanced with relentless hunger.

The battle that ensued was like none other. Ghengis Khan and his warriors fought not for glory or conquest, but for their very existence. The undead, unrelenting in their assault, swarmed the Mongol lines. But the Mongols, guided by their Khan's strategic genius, fought with a ferocity born of desperation.

In a pivotal moment, Ghengis Khan, realizing the connection between the undead and their past lives, made a bold decision. He rode to the forefront of the battle, tearing down his war banner, the symbol of his empire's might. As the banner fell, a wave of confusion rippled through the undead ranks. Many collapsed, their ties to their former lives severed.

The tide of battle seemed to turn. The Mongols, seizing the moment, redoubled their efforts, cutting down the disoriented undead. But just as victory seemed within grasp, a new horror emerged.

The Eagle of the Steppes, now one of the undead, led a renewed assault. His presence invigorated the undead horde, restoring their ferocity. The Mongols, caught off guard, faltered under this unexpected onslaught.

Ghengis Khan, facing the undead form of the shaman, felt a pang of sorrow. "Eagle of the Steppes," he called out, "I sought to conquer the world, but I did not seek this. Forgive me."

The undead shaman, his eyes void of the wisdom they once held, lunged at the Khan. The battle raged around them, a maelstrom of steel and fury.

It was then that the truth of the shaman's prophecy echoed in Ghengis Khan's mind. The curse would end only with a sacrifice - the sacrifice of his empire.

With a heavy heart, Ghengis Khan made his decision. In the midst of the battlefield, he renounced his title, his conquests, his dreams of empire. "I am no longer your Khan," he shouted to the heavens. "Take my empire, but spare my people!"

As his words rang out, a mystical storm brewed. Dark clouds gathered, and a fierce wind swept across the battlefield. The undead, as if struck by an invisible force, began to collapse, their bodies turning to dust.

The Eagle of the Steppes, his undead form writhing in the storm's fury, locked eyes with Ghengis Khan one last time. In that moment, a flicker of recognition seemed to pass through his undead gaze, a silent acknowledgment of the Khan's sacrifice.

The storm raged, and as quickly as it had begun, it ended. The undead were no more. The Mongol warriors, battered and bruised, looked around in disbelief. Their enemy, their cursed brethren, had vanished, leaving behind a land scarred by battle.

Ghengis Khan, now a man stripped of his empire but not his honor, dismounted his horse. He walked amongst his men, no longer their Khan, but a fellow warrior. The weight of his decision lay heavy on his shoulders, yet in his heart, he knew he had made the right choice.

The Mongol Empire, without its unifying force, gradually fragmented, its once mighty presence fading into the pages of history. But the legend of the day when Ghengis Khan saved his people from a fate worse than death lived on.

Ghengis Khan, the man who had once sought to conquer the world, now wandered the steppes, a nomad once more. His gaze, turned towards the horizon, was filled with a newfound peace. He had learned the true cost of ambition and power, and in his heart, he carried the hope for a future where conquest was no longer the path to greatness.

The sun set on the steppes, casting long shadows over a land forever changed. In the twilight, Ghengis Khan rode on, his story a testament to the enduring battle between the conquest of the land and the conquest of the spirit.

CHAPTER 22

CAESAR VS. ZOMBIES

"If You Know Neither the Enemy Nor Yourself, You Will Succumb."

The blood of conquest still fresh on his hands, Julius Caesar stood amidst the smoldering remains of Gaul. His eyes, as cold and calculating as ever, surveyed the remnants of what was once a fierce resistance. The Gallic leader, Vercingetorix, knelt defeated before him, chains clinking softly in the deathly silence of the aftermath.

"Great Caesar," Vercingetorix spoke, his voice a mix of defiance and resignation, "in your victory, you have sown the seeds of an empire's demise."

Caesar's laugh was sharp, echoing off the burned-out husks of nearby dwellings. "Empires are built on the bones of the fallen, Vercingetorix. Your people will be but a footnote in Rome's glorious history."

As he signaled for the execution, a comet streaked across the sky, its fiery tail burning bright against the twilight. The Romans cheered, taking it as a sign of divine approval, but the Gauls exchanged looks of deep foreboding.

That night, the Roman camp was a cacophony of celebration, filled with the clinking of cups and the roars of victorious soldiers. Caesar, however, remained in his tent, pondering his next move in the great chess game of power.

A bloodcurdling scream shattered the night's revelry. Caesar rushed out, cloak billowing behind him, to find a scene of horror unfolding. Dead soldiers, those he had watched fall in battle, were rising, their bodies grotesque and twisted, eyes hollow with an insatiable hunger.

"Necromancy!" shouted one of his centurions, drawing his sword in a futile gesture.

"Impossible," Caesar muttered, eyes narrowing as he watched the undead swarm over a group of his men.

The camp erupted into chaos. The undead, relentless and seemingly impervious to pain, tore through the ranks. Caesar, ever the strategist, quickly ordered a retreat, his mind racing to formulate a plan.

As dawn broke, the full extent of the disaster became clear. The undead had spread throughout the camp, leaving a trail of devastation in their wake. Caesar, standing amidst his remaining men, felt a chill run down his spine. This was no ordinary enemy; this was a threat that could unravel the very fabric of the Roman Empire.

"Legates," Caesar addressed his commanders, his voice steady despite the gnawing uncertainty, "send word to Rome. We face an enemy like no other, one that threatens not just Gaul, but the heart of our civilization."

"But, General," protested a young tribune, "our men are terrified. We know not how to fight these...monsters."

Caesar's gaze was steely. "Then we shall learn, or we shall perish. Rome did not rise to greatness by cowering in fear."

As the news of the undead plague reached Rome, the city was gripped by panic. The Senate demanded action, and the people looked to Caesar for salvation. Caesar knew he stood at a precipice - the greatest challenge of his storied career awaited him. In the balance hung not just his legacy, but the survival of Rome itself.

"This is no ordinary conquest," Caesar mused to himself, staring into the distance, where dark clouds gathered on the horizon. "This is a war for the soul of Rome."

And with that, Julius Caesar, the conqueror of Gaul, the shaper of empires, set his mind to confront a foe that defied reason, a foe that could herald the downfall of all he had built. In the eerie quiet that followed, a sense of foreboding settled over the camp, for they all knew that this was only the beginning of something far greater and more terrifying than any of them could have imagined.

The legions of Rome, once unchallenged masters of the battlefield, now faced an enemy that defied all logic and strategy. Caesar, with a mind as sharp as the blade of his gladius, set his legionnaires to work, fortifying the camp with all the ingenuity that Roman engineering could muster. Yet, in the shadows of the night, fear lurked among his men, a foe as potent as the undead themselves.

"General, our men are skilled in the art of war, but this..." Marcus, one of Caesar's most trusted centurions, hesitated, searching for words. "This is unlike anything we've ever faced."

Caesar, eyes fixed on the dark woods where the undead roamed, replied, "Then we shall adapt. We are Romans. We bend, but we do not break."

He first attempted traditional tactics, formations designed to repel living enemies. But the undead, driven by a hunger that knew no fatigue, tore through his lines with a ghastly fervor. The Roman shield wall, once impenetrable, crumbled under the onslaught.

In the aftermath of these initial encounters, the mood in the camp grew grim. Soldiers whispered of cursed lands and vengeful gods. Caesar, ever the stoic, concealed his own doubts, presenting a façade of unshakeable resolve.

"It's as if we're fighting the very shadows of Hades," muttered a young soldier, his face pale in the flickering torchlight.

Caesar's next plan was born from desperation and brilliance in equal measure. Inspired by the ancient texts of Sun Tzu, he devised a strategy of luring large groups of undead into elaborately constructed traps. The legionnaires, using themselves as bait, would draw the creatures into pits filled with spikes and flammable materials.

For a moment, it seemed as though Caesar had outwitted the undead. The traps claimed hundreds, their moans echoing through the night as they were consumed by fire and steel. But then, the unthinkable happened.

"They're learning," gasped a scout, rushing into Caesar's tent. "The creatures... they set an ambush. They flanked our bait parties."

Caesar's expression darkened. This was a development he hadn't anticipated. The undead, it seemed, were not mindless after all.

The Roman losses were catastrophic. Entire cohorts were lost, and the morale of his troops plummeted. As Caesar walked among the wounded, their groans and cries filled him with a sense of foreboding.

"We underestimated them," Caesar admitted to Marcus. "This enemy is unlike any other. We must change our approach."

It was then that Caesar decided to capture a few of the undead, seeking to understand their nature. Under the watchful eyes of his Praetorians, the grotesque figures were bound and studied.

"Their senses are heightened," observed a young medicus. "They're drawn to noise and the scent of blood."

Armed with this new knowledge, Caesar formulated a plan that required not just bravery, but cunning and stealth. He ordered the construction of a new type of defense, one that relied on silence and subterfuge rather than brute force.

As they prepared, word came of a massive horde of undead, larger than any before, marching towards the Roman camp. The air was thick with tension as the soldiers readied themselves for what many believed would be their final stand.

The night was moonless, the darkness a cloak under which the Roman soldiers moved with hushed urgency. Caesar's plan was in motion, a gamble upon which rested the fate of Rome itself.

As the undead approached, the Roman soldiers held their breath, waiting in silence. At Caesar's signal, they sprung their trap, collapsing the ground beneath the horde, sending thousands of undead tumbling into a vast network of trenches and pits.

For a moment, victory seemed within grasp. But then, with a chilling roar, the ground shook. From the midst of the undead emerged a towering figure, its form grotesque and terrifying. It was Vercingetorix, or what remained of him, now a monstrous avatar of death.

The undead, as if invigorated by the presence of their fallen leader, surged with renewed ferocity. The Roman lines buckled under the onslaught, and all seemed lost.

Caesar, his face a mask of resolve, drew his sword. "To me, Romans!" he bellowed, rallying his men. "We fight not just for Rome, but for the very soul of humanity!"

The clash that followed was brutal and merciless. Roman discipline pitted against the relentless tide of the undead. Caesar fought at the forefront, his blade singing a deadly song as it cleaved through rotting flesh.

But even as they fought, the realization dawned upon Caesar and his men - this was a battle unlike any other, a struggle against an enemy that defied death itself. And in the heart of that terrible night, as the clash of steel and the cries of the damned filled the air, Julius Caesar understood that the true test of his leadership had only just begun.

The dawn broke with a grim promise, painting the sky in hues of blood and fire. The Roman camp, now a fortress besieged by death itself, braced for the final onslaught. Caesar, his face etched with the toll of sleepless nights, surveyed the horizon where the undead horde, led by the monstrous Vercingetorix, advanced like a relentless tide.

"Today, we make our stand," Caesar addressed his weary but resolute men. "Not as conquerors, but as guardians of life itself."

The plan was audacious. Caesar had ordered the construction of a massive pit, hidden by a thin veneer of earth and foliage, encircling the camp. It was to be their final trap, filled with oil and dry tinder, ready to be ignited.

As the undead drew near, the air filled with the stench of decay and the guttural moans of the once-dead. Roman soldiers, their faces set in grim determination, waited for Caesar's command.

"Steady," Caesar's voice cut through the tense air. "Hold until my command."

The undead horde crashed against the Roman defenses like a wave breaking upon the shore. At the critical moment, Caesar gave the signal, and the ground beneath the undead collapsed, sending thousands into the fiery pit. Flames leapt into the sky, casting a hellish glow over the battlefield.

For a brief, triumphant moment, it seemed as though victory was within reach. But from the inferno emerged the figure of Vercingetorix, his form now a twisted abomination of flesh and fire. The undead, undeterred by the flames, began to circumvent the pit, pressing in with renewed fervor.

Caesar, amidst the chaos, faced the undead chieftain. Their eyes met, a moment of recognition passing between conqueror and conquered, now united in this dance of death.

With a roar that echoed the battles of old, Caesar charged, his legionnaires following suit. The clash was titanic, a maelstrom of steel and fury. Caesar fought with a desperation born of fear and duty, his blade a whirlwind of destruction.

Yet, as the battle raged, a chilling realization dawned upon Caesar. This was a fight they could not win by force alone. It was then, amidst the cacophony of battle, that Caesar's mind, ever the weapon sharper than any sword, seized upon a desperate ploy.

"Retreat!" he ordered, his voice cutting through the din. "Lure them to the river!"

His legionnaires, trusting in their leader's acumen, fell back, drawing the undead horde towards the Tiber. Vercingetorix, in his monstrous form, followed, driven by a hatred that transcended death.

At the riverbank, Caesar's final gambit came into play. He had ordered his engineers to construct hidden dams upstream, and now, as the undead massed at the water's edge, he gave the signal.

The dams burst, and a deluge of water crashed down, sweeping the undead into the raging torrent. Vercingetorix, caught in the maelstrom, locked eyes with Caesar one last time before being consumed by the river.

As the waters calmed, a hush fell over the battlefield. The threat was vanquished, but the cost was etched on the faces of the surviving Romans.

Caesar, standing by the river, felt the weight of his victory. It was a triumph, yes, but one shadowed by the knowledge of what they had faced, and what they had become in the process.

"General, you have saved Rome," Marcus approached, his voice a mix of awe and somberness.

Caesar looked towards the rising sun, its light a balm to the scars of the night. "No, Marcus," he replied, a hint of melancholy in his tone. "We have saved Rome, but in doing so, we have glimpsed our own fragility. Empires, like men, are mortal. We have fought death itself, only to be reminded of our own."

As they returned to the camp, a sense of solemnity accompanied the soldiers. They had faced the abyss and emerged victorious, but the victory brought with it a reflection on their own mortality.

Caesar, as he walked among his men, knew that the comet's warning had been fulfilled in a way he could never have imagined. He had defeated an undead army, but in the shadows of that triumph lurked the specter of his own destiny, a reminder that even the greatest of men are but players on the stage of history, their roles fleeting, their legacies etched in the sands of time.

CHAPTER 23

VIKINGS VS. THE UNDEAD

"In the heart of the brave, fear and courage dance a delicate waltz." Old Norse Proverb

The sea was a restless creature beneath the longship, whispering tales of distant lands and battles fought. Einar, standing tall at the prow, watched the coastline of his homeland emerge from the mist. His heart, which had been a tempest of anticipation, now throbbed with a triumphant rhythm. The voyage had been long, the battles fierce, but the spoils were rich and the glory undeniable.

As the ship sliced through the waters, his mind replayed the battles won, the foes vanquished. A tapestry of blood, sweat, and cheers of victory. He imagined the welcoming fires, the feasting tables laden with ale and meat, the warm embrace of his wife, and the wide-eyed awe of his children.

But as the ship drew closer, something felt amiss. The usual plumes of smoke from hearths and the bustling sounds of the village were conspicuously absent. Instead, a suffocating silence hung in the air, thick and ominous.

The longship touched the shore with a gentle scrape, a stark contrast to the turmoil brewing in Einar's heart. His seasoned warriors, men who had laughed in the face of death, now stepped onto their homeland with a hesitant tread, sensing the unease of their leader.

The village was not as they left it. Buildings that once stood proud were now but charred skeletons. The vibrant tapestry of village life was replaced with a chilling emptiness. Einar's homecoming was not met with songs and cheers but with a haunting silence that clawed at his soul.

"Thor's wrath... what happened here?" murmured Bjorn, Einar's oldest comrade, his voice barely a whisper against the cold wind.

Einar's eyes, steely as the sword he wielded, scanned the horizon. His warrior instincts, honed by years of battle, felt the wrongness in the air. It was then they saw them - figures, human in shape but grotesquely misshapen, shuffling aimlessly among the ruins.

The warriors gripped their weapons tighter, their knuckles whitening. Einar stepped forward, his presence commanding yet cautious. He approached one of the figures, a sense of dread coiling in his gut.

"Erik?" Einar called out, recognizing the tattered remnants of what once was a vibrant villager.

The figure turned, and Einar's heart plummeted into an abyss. The face that greeted him was a grotesque mask of decay, eyes hollow and void of life. A guttural growl emanated from its throat, and with a sudden burst of speed, it lunged at Einar.

The clash of steel rang out as Einar's blade met the creature in a dance of death. More figures emerged, their movements jerky and unnatural. The air filled with the sounds of battle, steel clashing against what once was flesh and bone.

"Einar, these are not men!" shouted Bjorn, his axe swinging in a wide arc, decapitating one of the creatures.

"Aye, they are monsters wearing men's skin," Einar replied, his voice laced with a rage born of betrayal.

The warriors fought back the tide of undead, each strike a prayer for their fallen kin. As the last of the creatures fell, the village lay in ruins, a tombstone to a once-thriving community.

Einar, his chest heaving with exertion, sheathed his sword. His mind raced with questions. Who had done this? Why? The air, now still, seemed to hold its breath, waiting for answers.

"It's sorcery, Einar," said Astrid, a shieldmaiden whose wisdom was as renowned as her skill in battle. "Dark magic has touched this land."

Einar looked at the faces of his warriors, seeing their fear mirrored in their eyes. They were warriors, not mages. This was a battle unlike any they had fought.

"We must seek answers," Einar declared, his voice cutting through the uncertainty. "We will find who is responsible for this curse and make them pay with their blood."

The warriors rallied to his call, their resolve hardened. They had faced death before, but this... this was a darkness that threatened to swallow them whole.

Einar led them away from the ruins, his mind a whirlwind of strategy and vengeance. Little did he know that his true enemy was not one he could simply cleave with his sword. In the shadows, magic stirred, and eyes watched, cold and calculating. The battle for Einar's homeland had just begun.

The twilight cast long shadows across the desolate landscape as Einar and his warriors trekked through their ravaged homeland. The air was thick with an eerie quiet, a stark contrast to the chaos of their earlier battle. Einar's mind was a tempest of thoughts, strategizing, planning, wondering. The undead they had encountered were unlike any foe he had faced before. Brute strength alone would not suffice; this he knew with a certainty that chilled his bones.

As night fell, they made camp in the ruins of what once was a thriving farm. The men were restless, the flickering firelight casting ghostly shadows that played upon their fears.

"We cannot fight what we do not understand," Einar muttered, staring into the flames. "These... creatures. They're not of this world."

Bjorn nodded, his brow furrowed in worry. "We need a new plan, Einar. Our swords alone won't save us."

Einar's gaze was distant, his mind racing. "We need to adapt, to think like the enemy. We need to be as cunning as the fox, as relentless as the winter storm."

In the following days, Einar led his men in small skirmishes against the undead, testing different strategies. They used fire, which seemed to repel the creatures. They led the undead into traps, using the terrain to their advantage. But each victory was minor, and the undead seemed endless.

"We're fighting shadows," Einar growled in frustration after a particularly harrowing encounter. "For every one we fell, ten more take its place."

It was Astrid who came to him with a plan, her eyes alight with a fierce determination. "We need to strike at the heart, Einar. Find the source of this curse."

"And how do you propose we do that?" Einar asked, skeptical yet intrigued.

"We seek the wisdom of the ancients," she replied. "There are old runes, tales of dark magic and those who wield it. We must learn from these."

Reluctantly, Einar agreed. They journeyed to the ruins of an ancient temple, long forgotten by time. There, amidst the crumbling stone and moss, they found carvings, cryptic and ominous. They spoke of dark magic, of a sorceress from a distant land who wielded the power over life and death.

"Morgana," Einar whispered, the name tasting like poison on his tongue.

They prepared for the inevitable confrontation. Einar devised a grand strategy, inspired by the ancient tactics of war. He trained his warriors in the art of guerrilla warfare, hit-and-run tactics, using the environment to their advantage. They were no longer just warriors; they were hunters in the night.

The night they chose for their attack was moonless, the darkness their ally. Einar led his warriors through the forest, silent as the grave. Their target was a decrepit castle, perched atop a hill, shrouded in mist and foreboding.

The battle was fierce. Fire arrows arced through the sky, casting an eerie glow on the undead horde. Einar's men struck from the shadows, their attacks precise and deadly. But as they breached the castle gates, a chilling laughter echoed through the night.

Morgana appeared, her presence radiating malevolence. She raised her hands, and the dead rose again, their wounds knitting, their eyes burning with unholy light.

"You cannot defeat me, Viking," she hissed. "Your efforts are futile."

Einar fought valiantly, cutting down the undead as he made his way towards Morgana. But she was powerful, her magic a force that pushed him back, inch by inch.

In a desperate move, Einar lunged at her, only to be struck down by an unseen force. He lay on the ground, his body wracked with pain, as Morgana approached.

"You are strong, Viking," she sneered. "But not strong enough."

She raised her hand to deliver the final blow, but it never came. A sudden burst of light filled the room, and a figure emerged from the shadows. It was Astrid, wielding an ancient artifact they had found in the temple ruins.

Morgana screamed as the light enveloped her, her body disintegrating into dust. The undead, bereft of their master, collapsed into lifeless husks.

Einar lay there, panting, his mind reeling. They had won, but at what cost? His warriors were decimated, his homeland still a shadow of its former self. And he knew, deep in his heart, that this was not the end. The darkness had been pushed back, but it would return, perhaps stronger than before.

As dawn broke, Einar stood among the ruins of the castle, his resolve hardened. He would rebuild, he would prepare. For the next time the darkness came, he would be ready. The battle for his homeland was far from over.

The dawn light spilled over the land, casting long shadows on the remnants of the battle. Einar stood amidst the ruins of the castle, his heart heavy but his resolve unshaken. The victory over Morgana was a triumph, but it was a fleeting one. The darkness she had unleashed upon the land still lingered, a malevolent whisper in the wind.

"We have won the battle, but not the war," Einar said to his remaining warriors, their faces marked by exhaustion and loss.

Bjorn nodded, his eyes reflecting the smoldering ruins. "We've bought some time, Einar. We must use it wisely."

Einar knew their next move was crucial. He spent days poring over ancient texts and consulting with Astrid, whose knowledge of the arcane had proved invaluable. They needed to understand their enemy better, to anticipate its moves.

As they delved deeper into their research, a grim picture began to emerge. Morgana had been but a pawn in a larger game, a disciple of a far more powerful force. A force that was now aware of Einar and his warriors.

"We must prepare for what's coming," Einar declared, his voice a steady drumbeat in the silent room. "We train, we fortify, we gather allies. We make our stand here."

The days turned into weeks, and the weeks into months. Einar's village became a fortress, its people warriors. Word of their struggle spread, attracting others to their cause: swordsmen seeking redemption, shieldmaidens with scores to settle, even sorcerers with knowledge of the dark arts.

Then, on a night when the stars seemed to fade in the sky, it came. A horde unlike any they had seen before, creatures of nightmare, led by a being shrouded in darkness. The air crackled with malevolent energy, and the ground trembled under the weight of the approaching doom.

Einar stood at the forefront, his warriors at his side. "This is where we make our stand," he bellowed, his voice cutting through the night. "For our homes, for our families, for our very souls!"

The battle was a maelstrom of steel and sorcery. Einar fought with the fury of the storm, his sword cutting swathes through the enemy. Beside him, his warriors matched his ferocity, their cries a defiant challenge to the encroaching darkness.

But the enemy was relentless, and for every creature they felled, two more took its place. Einar felt a sinking feeling in his gut, the realization that they could not win this fight.

It was then that nature itself seemed to answer their call. A pack of wolves, drawn by the chaos, joined the fray. Their feral savagery turned the tide, their natural enmity for the undead giving them an edge no human warrior could match.

Einar saw his opportunity and pushed forward, cutting a path to the heart of the enemy's ranks. There, he faced the dark being, a shadowy figure whose very presence chilled the soul.

"You cannot win, Viking," the being hissed, its voice a cold wind. "I am eternal."

Einar's response was a roar of defiance. He charged, his sword a beacon of light in the darkness. The two clashed, a symphony of violence that shook the very earth.

In the end, it was Einar's will that proved stronger. With a final, desperate effort, he drove his sword through the heart of darkness, shattering it into a thousand pieces.

The horde crumbled, the creatures dissolving into dust. The night was silent once more, the stars shining bright in the sky.

Einar collapsed, his strength spent. His warriors gathered around him, their faces etched with relief and exhaustion.

"We have won," he whispered, his voice barely audible.

But as they helped him to his feet, a chilling realization dawned upon them. The darkness was not defeated; it was merely pushed back, biding its time. They had won a battle, but the war was far from over.

Einar looked out over the land, his heart heavy but his spirit unbroken. They would keep fighting, keep standing against the darkness. For now, they had earned a respite, a moment of peace.

But the battle for their souls, for the very fate of their world, was just beginning.

CHAPTER 24

KING LEAR AND THE UNDEAD MADNESS

"In times of chaos, it is the dead who shall inherit the earth."

Under the shadow of a brooding sky, the ancient castle of King Lear stood as a bastion amidst a land teetering on the brink of chaos. Inside its stone walls, heavy with the weight of history, the air was thick with anticipation. King Lear, with a crown that seemed too heavy for his aging head, addressed his court with a voice that echoed through the grand hall.

"My beloved daughters," Lear began, his eyes, once sharp as an eagle's, now clouded with the haze of age, "the time has come for me to lay down the burdens of this crown. But a kingdom divided is a kingdom weakened. Thus, I shall divide this land among you three."

Goneril and Regan, the elder daughters, exchanged glances, their smiles as sharp as daggers hidden beneath silk. Cordelia, the youngest, stood apart, her expression troubled. The courtiers whispered among themselves, their words a serpentine hiss in the cavernous hall.

"But father," Cordelia's voice cut through the murmurs, clear and strong, "what of the growing threat beyond our walls? Travelers speak of a plague, one that raises the dead and sows terror in its wake."

King Lear's face hardened. "These are but tales, Cordelia, meant to frighten children. Our concern is with the living, not fanciful stories of the dead walking."

"Your Majesty," Goneril interjected smoothly, "our sister means well, but she is young. She knows not the intricacies of ruling a kingdom."

Regan nodded in agreement. "Indeed, father. We are ready to bear the weight of your crown and protect this kingdom from any real threat."

Lear, swayed by their words, nodded slowly. "Then it is decided. To Goneril and Regan, I bequeath the larger portions of our realm. But to Cordelia, who has yet to understand the nature of sovereignty, I can give no land."

The court gasped. Cordelia's eyes met her father's, a silent plea in their depths. "Father, is love alone not enough to merit your favor? Must I speak honeyed words to prove my loyalty?"

"Love speaks not with words alone, but with actions," Lear retorted, his voice rising. "You offer me neither, thus you shall receive nothing."

The rejection stung like a slap. Cordelia, her heart heavy, turned to leave, her footsteps echoing her departure. As she walked, the heavy doors of the castle closed behind her, sealing her fate.

Outside, the world was a different beast. The wind carried whispers of unrest, and the distant moans of the afflicted broke the night's silence. Cordelia wandered through the villages, her royal garb replaced by a cloak of anonymity. The stories she had dismissed as mere tales now unfolded before her eyes in horrifying reality. The undead, their eyes void of life, roamed the land, turning it into a graveyard of despair.

In a small, hidden hamlet, she encountered a group of survivors, their eyes wary. An old man, his back bent but his spirit unbroken, addressed her.

"Young miss, you don't belong here. The dead don't care for crowns or lineage. They hunger for the warmth of life."

Cordelia's voice was tinged with desperation. "I seek to understand this curse, to find a way to protect my people. Will you not help me?"

The old man studied her for a long moment. "Help? Perhaps. But know this - the dead are but one threat. The living can be far more dangerous."

His words echoed in her mind as Cordelia lay awake that night, under a canopy of stars. The call to adventure had been sounded, not by trumpets or heralds, but by the silent moan of the wind and the whispers of the dead. She knew then that the path ahead was fraught with peril and uncertainty. But it was a path she must walk, for the sake of a kingdom that no longer claimed her as its own.

The moon hung like a silver sickle over the blighted lands as Cordelia, cloaked in the shadows of twilight, watched the undead roam. Their ghastly forms, grotesque parodies of their former selves, moved with a chilling purpose. The plight of her kingdom, now teetering on the edge of an abyss, weighed heavily on her heart.

As dawn broke, painting the sky in hues of crimson and gold, Cordelia gathered a motley crew of survivors. Among them was Alaric, a former knight, his sword arm as steady as his haunted gaze, and Mira, a young woman whose knowledge of herbs and healing made her invaluable.

"Our first task," Cordelia declared, her voice firm despite the uncertainty that gnawed at her, "is to reclaim the villages closest to the castle. We must push back these... creatures, and fortify our defenses."

But the path was fraught with peril. Goneril and Regan, wielding the dark arts, had turned the undead into pawns, a grotesque army that marched at their command. Cordelia's initial attempts to fight back were met with brutal force. Villages were lost, and with each setback, the shadow of despair grew longer.

"We cannot win this way," Alaric said one night as they camped in the ruins of a once-thriving town. "These are not battles of sword and shield, but of shadows and deception."

Cordelia's eyes burned with a fierce determination. "Then we must adapt. We must think not as soldiers in a field, but as strategists in a game much darker than any of us have played before."

Inspired by the ancient text of "The Art of War," Cordelia devised a grand, audacious plan. They would not only fight the undead but also infiltrate the castle and confront her sisters. It was a gambit fraught with danger, but the only path that promised a glimmer of hope.

The group gathered resources, rallying those who still dared to resist. Among them were skilled archers, cunning scouts, and brave souls who had lost everything to the plague and sought vengeance.

But as they executed their plan, a grave miscalculation became apparent. The sisters' control over the undead was far more potent than Cordelia had anticipated. The creatures moved with unnatural coordination, thwarting their every move. The assault on the castle turned into a massacre, with many of Cordelia's followers falling under the relentless onslaught of the undead.

Retreating into the woods, the survivors were a broken shadow of their former selves. Cordelia, her spirit battered but unbroken, tried to rally them. "We underestimated our enemy," she admitted, her voice heavy with grief. "But we will not make the same mistake again."

It was during these darkest hours that they stumbled upon a hidden enclave, a sanctuary where a group of survivors lived, not just in fear, but in defiance of their grim reality. These survivors had adapted to their cursed world with remarkable ingenuity.

"There's more than one way to fight," the leader of the enclave, an elderly woman with eyes sharp as flint, told Cordelia. "We have learned to move unseen, to strike where they least expect it. The undead are many things, but they are not cunning."

Cordelia absorbed their lessons, blending her strategic acumen with the guerilla tactics of the enclave. She transformed, no longer just a deposed princess, but a leader forged in the crucible of dire necessity.

Yet, as they prepared to strike anew, news arrived that sent shivers down their spines. Goneril and Regan, emboldened by their recent victory, had unleashed the full might of the undead horde. The kingdom was in its death throes, its people fleeing or falling before the relentless tide.

Cordelia stood atop a hill, watching the horizon burn with fires of destruction. Her sisters' treachery had turned their land into a living nightmare. But as she turned to face her ragtag army, her resolve hardened.

"This is our darkest hour," she said, her voice carrying over the somber faces of her followers. "But it is always darkest before the dawn. We fight not for glory or for crown, but for the very soul of our land. Tonight, we take back our kingdom from the jaws of death itself."

Her words, infused with a fierce determination, ignited a spark of hope in their hearts. They were ready to follow her, to the very gates of hell if need be.

The stage was set for a final, desperate confrontation. The fate of the kingdom hung in the balance, teetering between the living and the dead, between madness and salvation.

The air was thick with the stench of decay as Cordelia and her band of survivors prepared for what could be their final stand. The undead horde, an unending sea of grotesque creatures, surged towards them, driven by the sinister will of Goneril and Regan. The sky, a tapestry of menacing clouds, seemed to mourn for the land it shadowed.

Cordelia, her armor dented and her face streaked with the grime of battle, raised her sword. "Today, we fight not just for our lives, but for the very soul of our kingdom," she declared, her voice resonating with a conviction that belied the fear in her heart.

The battle was a maelstrom of chaos and bloodshed. Cordelia and her followers fought with the ferocity of those with nothing left to lose. Alaric's sword danced a deadly ballet, cutting down one undead after another, while Mira's arrows found their marks with lethal precision.

But even as they fought bravely, the tide of the undead seemed endless. It was then, amidst the cacophony of battle, that a lone figure appeared on the battlefield. King Lear, his eyes wild with madness, wandered among the undead, a tragic specter of a once-great monarch.

"Father!" Cordelia cried out, her heart lurching at the sight of him. But her call was lost in the roar of battle.

As the conflict reached its fever pitch, a sudden twist of fate turned the tide. Lear, in a moment of lucid clarity, saw the monstrous forms of his elder daughters, commanding the undead with wicked glee. With a cry that was both a roar of anger and a wail of sorrow, he lunged at them, disrupting their concentration.

The control over the undead faltered. Cordelia seized the moment. Rallying her forces, they pushed forward, cutting a swathe through the disoriented horde. The battle raged around the sisters, the air filled with the clang of steel and the cries of the fallen.

In the midst of this pandemonium, Cordelia confronted Goneril and Regan. "This ends now!" she shouted, her sword clashing against theirs.

"You cannot win, little sister," Goneril hissed, her blade a viper striking with lethal intent.

But Cordelia was undeterred. "I do not stand alone," she retorted, parrying a blow from Regan. "This kingdom is not yours to destroy!"

As they fought, Lear, his mind torn between madness and clarity, staggered towards them. "My daughters," he murmured, his voice barely a whisper in the din of battle.

In a moment of tragic distraction, Lear stepped between Cordelia and her sisters. Goneril, her eyes alight with malice, did not hesitate. Her blade found its mark, plunging into Lear's chest.

"Father!" Cordelia's scream pierced the tumult. The king's eyes met hers, filled with a heartbreaking mix of regret and love, before he collapsed.

The shock of Lear's death broke the last vestige of the sisters' control over the undead. The creatures, now leaderless, began to turn on each other in a frenzy of mindless violence.

Cordelia, grief-stricken, faced her sisters. "You have destroyed everything," she said, her voice thick with sorrow and rage.

In the ensuing chaos, Goneril and Regan met their demise, consumed by the very creatures they had sought to control. The undead horde, without direction, eventually succumbed to the relentless assault of Cordelia's forces.

As the sun rose over the battlefield, casting its light on the carnage, Cordelia stood amidst the ruins of her once-great kingdom. The undead menace was vanquished, but at a terrible cost. She knelt beside her father's body, tears mingling with the blood-stained earth.

"We have won, father," she whispered. "But the victory is hollow."

In the days that followed, Cordelia worked tirelessly to rebuild her kingdom from the ashes of war. She was crowned queen, not in a grand ceremony, but in a solemn gathering, her crown a heavy burden on her brow.

Her reign was marked by wisdom and compassion, a beacon of hope in a land scarred by tragedy. The kingdom, forever changed, began to heal, its people united in their resolve to never forget the horrors they had endured.

The story of Cordelia, the queen who rose from the ashes of a kingdom ravaged by the undead, became a tale told for generations. A tale of courage, sacrifice, and the enduring power of hope in the darkest of times.

CHAPTER 25

DON QUIXOTE VS. ZOMBIES

"In dreams, we often find ourselves knights of our own fables, but for Don Quixote, his dream was a prophecy cloaked in nightmare."

The moon hung low over the village of La Mancha, casting eerie shadows across the cobbled streets. Don Quixote, the self-proclaimed knight of the woeful countenance, sat upright in his bed, sweat beading on his furrowed brow. His sleep had been disturbed by visions most foul - a horde of undead creatures ravaging the land, their moans as hollow as the void in their eyes.

As dawn broke, Quixote, with a resolve as firm as the steel of his imagined sword, descended the stairs of his modest abode. The clanking of his makeshift armor, fashioned from the relics of a bygone era, broke the morning's silence. He approached his loyal but bewildered housekeeper.

"Good woman," he began, his voice trembling with urgency, "I have been visited by a vision of impending doom. A plague of the undead threatens to engulf our land. We must act!"

The housekeeper, accustomed to her master's eccentricities, sighed deeply. "Señor Quixote, surely this is another of your fantasies. There are no such things as zombies."

But Quixote was undeterred. He made his way to the village square, where the townsfolk gathered for their daily routines. Standing atop a fountain, he addressed the crowd with the fervor of a man possessed.

"Good people of La Mancha! Lend me your ears! A great peril approaches, a tide of undead creatures that will spare no soul! We must fortify our village, arm ourselves for the battle ahead!"

The villagers exchanged skeptical glances. One burly man stepped forward, a smirk playing on his lips. "Don Quixote, have you tilted at too many windmills? There are no zombies here, only the figments of your overactive imagination."

A murmur of agreement rippled through the crowd. All but one dismissed Quixote's warning. Sancho, a young orphan who had always marveled at

205

Quixote's grand tales of chivalry and adventure, approached the disheartened knight.

"Sir," Sancho said, his eyes wide with a mix of fear and admiration. "I believe you. If there is a threat to our village, I will stand by you."

Quixote's eyes gleamed with a mix of surprise and gratitude. "Brave Sancho, your courage will be the beacon that guides us through these dark times. Together, we shall face this scourge and protect our beloved La Mancha."

With Sancho at his side, Quixote set about preparing for the impending doom. They gathered what they could - old farm tools which Sancho ingeniously modified into weapons, books of strategy and lore which Quixote pored over, seeking guidance from the ancient texts.

Days turned into weeks, and still, no zombies appeared. The villagers' mockery grew, but Quixote's determination never wavered. He trained Sancho in the art of combat, blending the elegance of knightly duels with the practicality of peasant brawls.

One evening, as they practiced in the moonlit square, Sancho asked, "Sir, are you certain of this vision? Could it have been just a dream?"

Quixote paused, his gaze drifting to the stars above. "Sancho, in our deepest dreams lie the truths we dare not face in daylight. This is no mere figment of my imagination. It is a call to arms, a plea for salvation. We must be ready, for when the darkness descends, it will be upon us to light the way."

In that moment, under the watchful eye of the moon, Don Quixote and Sancho stood not as a madman and an orphan, but as guardians of a village unaware of the shadow that loomed over it, waiting, just beyond the horizon, to engulf their world in terror.

The days in La Mancha rolled into weeks, and the weeks into months, yet the undead horde of Don Quixote's nightmares remained absent, a specter on the horizon that refused to materialize. The villagers' laughter grew louder, their jests sharper, yet Quixote's conviction remained unshaken, a steadfast rock against the relentless tide of their ridicule.

Sancho, his unwavering squire, stood beside him, a beacon of youthful optimism amid the sea of doubt. "Sir," he said one evening as they sat outside Quixote's house, their makeshift weapons lying beside them, "perhaps the danger has passed? Maybe your dream was just that–a dream?"

Quixote shook his head, his eyes fixed on the distant hills, silhouetted against the setting sun. "No, Sancho. I fear it is yet to come. We must continue our vigil, for when complacency takes root, disaster often follows."

Their determination, however, was soon to be tested. On a journey to gather more information, Quixote and Sancho stumbled upon an ancient, forgotten library, its dusty tomes filled with arcane knowledge and lost prophecies. Within its cobwebbed shelves, Quixote found a parchment that spoke of a dark curse that would awaken the dead and spread ruin across the land. The prophecy resonated with his dream, reigniting the embers of his resolve.

"This is it, Sancho!" Quixote exclaimed, his fingers trembling as he held the ancient script. "This prophecy speaks of our plight. We must prepare, for the threat is real and ever-nearing."

With newfound urgency, they returned to La Mancha, where Quixote, fueled by the prophecy, rallied a band of outcasts and misfits. They were an odd assortment–a blacksmith with a penchant for ale, a widow skilled in herbal lore, a pair of twin brothers who knew no fear, and others, each drawn to Quixote's cause by their own unseen threads of fate.

Under Quixote's guidance, they trained in combat and strategy, melding his knightly knowledge with Sancho's pragmatic ingenuity. They fortified the village, setting traps and preparing for an onslaught that only they believed was coming. But as time wore on without sign of the undead, doubts began to creep in, even among the faithful few. The villagers' taunts turned to outright hostility. "You're scaring our children with tales of ghosts and ghouls!" they accused. "Leave us be with your madness!"

Then, on a night when the stars seemed to dim, their fears were realized in the most unexpected way. They were not attacked by zombies, but by a band of marauders, drawn to the village by tales of a mad knight hoarding treasures for an imaginary war.

The village was ill-prepared for such an assault. Quixote and his band fought valiantly, but it was a losing battle. As the marauders set fire to the homes, Quixote's heart sank. "We prepared for the wrong enemy," he lamented amidst the chaos.

In the aftermath, as the village licked its wounds, Quixote's spirit was shattered. The prophecy, he thought, had led them astray. Sancho, however, refused to let his mentor succumb to despair.

"Sir," he implored, "this is but a setback. Our true foe still lurks. We must not falter now."

Quixote looked at Sancho, seeing in his young eyes a reflection of his own once unquenchable fire. He nodded slowly. "You are right, Sancho. We must rise from these ashes, stronger and more resolved."

In the weeks that followed, they rebuilt the village, their efforts now focused not just on the undead, but on any threat that might come their way. The villagers, chastened by the marauders' attack, began to view Quixote in a new light—not as a madman, but as a protector, albeit an unconventional one.

Then, on a night as silent as a whispered secret, the prophecy fulfilled itself. They awoke to a nightmare made flesh. The undead, in all their grotesque glory, descended upon La Mancha. The villagers, frozen in terror, watched as Quixote and his band sprang into action, their preparations now their only lifeline.

The battle was fierce and unforgiving. Quixote, at the forefront, fought with a ferocity that belied his age, his sword cutting through the rotting flesh of the zombies. Sancho, his fear conquered by loyalty, stood by his side, his improvised weapons reaping a grim toll.

But as the night waned, a chilling realization dawned upon them—the undead were not mindless creatures but were being controlled by a darker, more sinister force. From the shadows emerged a figure, cloaked in darkness, its eyes burning with malevolent glee.

The necromancer, the true architect of their doom, had come to claim La Mancha.

In a desperate fight, Sancho was captured, his cries echoing in Quixote's ears as he was dragged into the night. The villagers, now fighting alongside Quixote, found themselves outmatched and overwhelmed.

As the dawn approached, with the necromancer's laughter ringing in his ears, Quixote fell to his knees, his sword slipping from his grasp. Around him, the village lay in ruins, the undead closing in. It seemed, at that moment, that all was lost—that the prophecy was not a warning, but a prelude to their inevitable doom.

The first light of dawn cast a pale glow over the ravaged village of La Mancha, revealing the true extent of the nightmare that had unfolded. Don Quixote, his armor dented and his spirit waning, stood amidst the ruins, the sounds of the undead still echoing in the cold morning air. The necromancer, shrouded in dark robes, watched from a distance with a sinister smile, his eyes reflecting a malevolent triumph.

Sancho, bound and gagged, struggled against his captors, his eyes meeting Quixote's in a silent plea for help. Quixote's heart clenched at the sight of his faithful squire in peril, igniting a fire within him that he thought had been extinguished by despair.

Gathering his remaining strength, Quixote rose to his feet, his gaze fixed on the necromancer. "You may have brought despair upon us, but I will not let you claim victory. I stand for La Mancha, for the innocent, and for the memory of chivalry that still burns within me!"

The necromancer laughed, a sound as cold as the grave. "Foolish knight, you fight a battle you cannot win. Your chivalry is as dead as the creatures I command."

With a rallying cry, Quixote charged, his sword raised high. The undead, sensing their master's intent, moved to intercept him. The village, inspired by Quixote's bravery, rallied behind him, their farming tools turned into makeshift weapons once again.

The battle that ensued was fierce and brutal. Quixote carved a path through the undead, each stroke of his sword fueled by a blend of desperation and determination. Sancho, seizing an opportunity, wriggled free from his captors and rejoined the fray, fighting back-to-back with Quixote. As the sun climbed higher, the tide began to turn. The villagers, emboldened by Quixote's heroism, fought with a newfound ferocity, pushing the undead back with each passing moment.

Finally, Quixote reached the necromancer, their swords clashing in a dance of death. "Your reign of terror ends here," Quixote declared, his voice a thunderous vow.

The necromancer sneered, his skills in dark magic evident as he parried each of Quixote's blows. "You cannot defeat me, knight. I am beyond your mortal comprehension."

The battle raged on, the clash of steel echoing like a dirge for the fallen. Then, in a moment of unforeseen fortune, Quixote's sword found its mark, piercing the necromancer's defenses and wounding him grievously. As the necromancer fell, his control over the undead faltered. One by one, they collapsed, lifeless once more. The villagers cheered, their cries of victory mingling with sobs of relief.

Quixote, exhausted and wounded, stumbled towards Sancho, clasping his squire's shoulder in a gesture of gratitude. "We did it, Sancho. We saved La Mancha."

Sancho smiled, his eyes brimming with pride. "We did, sir. Together."

But their triumph was short-lived. As they turned to leave, the necromancer, with a final act of defiance, lunged at Quixote, a dagger in hand. Quixote reacted instinctively, his sword plunging into the necromancer's heart. As the necromancer lay dying, a startling revelation shook Quixote to his core. The necromancer's face morphed, revealing not a monster, but a mirror image of Quixote himself, aged and twisted by darkness.

Quixote staggered back, his sword clattering to the ground. "What sorcery is this?" he gasped, his voice barely a whisper.

The necromancer, with his last breath, spoke a truth that chilled Quixote's soul. "I am what you could have become, a knight consumed by his own madness and despair."

With those final words, the necromancer vanished, leaving Quixote grappling with the realization that the greatest enemy he had faced was the darkness within himself.

The villagers, now free from the nightmare, gathered around Quixote, their eyes filled with a new respect. They had witnessed not only the defeat of a tangible foe but the triumph of a man over his inner demons.

As the sun set on the village of La Mancha, a sense of peace descended. Quixote, his journey at an end, knew that while the battle against the undead was over, his fight against his own shadows would continue. But he was not alone. Sancho stood beside him, loyal as ever, ready to face whatever challenges lay ahead. Together, they would guard La Mancha, protectors not just of its people, but of the ideals that had guided them through their darkest hour.

And so, the legend of Don Quixote, the knight who conquered an army of the undead and his own inner turmoil, was woven into the tapestry of La Mancha's history, a tale of courage, redemption, and the enduring power of an unbreakable spirit.

CHAPTER 26

UNDEAD PINNOCHIO

"In every creation, there lies a secret that even the creator fears to know."

Under the golden hue of a setting sun, in a quaint village where time seemed to pause, Geppetto's workshop stood as a testament to a life dedicated to the art of craftsmanship. The walls, lined with shelves, bore witness to countless wooden figures, each carved with meticulous attention to detail, yet none as dear to the old craftsman as Pinocchio.

Geppetto, with his wrinkled hands and a heart heavy with years of solitude, often found himself speaking to Pinocchio as if he were a living boy. "Ah, Pinocchio, if only you could speak back," he sighed one evening, his eyes reflecting the flickering candlelight.

On this particular evening, as Geppetto organized his tools, his hand brushed against a peculiarly ancient scroll, hidden behind a pile of old wood carvings. Its leather was cracked, the script upon it indecipherable and eerily inviting. Curiosity, a trait that had never faded in Geppetto's aging heart, took hold.

"Perhaps this is just a relic of the past," he murmured, unrolling the scroll with a mixture of reverence and intrigue. The script, though foreign, seemed to dance before his eyes, compelling him to read aloud. The words felt powerful, resonating through the workshop's timeworn walls.

As he spoke the final syllable, a sudden gust of wind blew through the room, extinguishing the candles. The darkness was complete, oppressive, as if the very essence of night had descended upon them. Geppetto's heart raced, a sense of dread building within him.

"What have I done?" he whispered, fumbling for a match. The striking sound echoed, followed by the timid glow of a flame. It was then he noticed Pinocchio's eyes gleaming unusually in the dim light, as if they held a life of their own.

"Father?" a voice emerged, hesitant yet clear. It was Pinocchio, his wooden lips moving with an unnatural fluidity.

Geppetto stumbled back, disbelief etching his features. "This... this cannot be!"

"Father, why do you fear?" Pinocchio asked, a hint of sadness in his voice.

"It's not fear, my boy," Geppetto stammered, "It's wonder, utter wonder!" Emotions swirled within him - joy, fear, and a creeping sense of foreboding.

As they conversed, a distant, unsettling noise crept into their haven. It was a chorus of groans, low and guttural, growing louder with each passing moment. Geppetto peered out the window, his heart sinking at the sight before him.

Emerging from the shadows of the nearby crypt, figures stumbled forward. Their movements were jerky, unnatural, their eyes hollow and devoid of life. The undead, awakened by the very incantation Geppetto had read, were now descending upon their peaceful village.

"We must do something, Father!" Pinocchio urged, his wooden body clattering as he moved.

Geppetto, still grappling with the reality of his living puppet and the nightmare unfolding before them, felt a heavy weight of responsibility. "This is my doing, Pinocchio. I have unleashed this horror upon us."

"But we can face it together!" Pinocchio exclaimed, his voice laced with determination. "I may be wood, but I am not without courage."

Geppetto looked into the eyes of his creation, seeing not just wood and paint, but a spark of something truly alive, something brave. "Then we shall face it together," he resolved, a mix of fear and determination in his voice.

As the night grew darker, and the groans of the undead grew nearer, Geppetto and Pinocchio readied themselves. They were no warriors, just a craftsman and his wooden boy, standing against an ancient evil neither fully understood. Yet in their hearts burned a flicker of hope, a belief that even in the darkest of nights, courage and love could still prevail.

The village, once a haven of tranquility, had transformed into a tableau of horror. Shadows danced grotesquely as the moon cast its pale light over the undead. Geppetto and Pinocchio, standing at the threshold of the workshop, gazed upon the advancing horde with a mixture of terror and resolve.

"We must do something," Geppetto said, his voice barely above a whisper. "We cannot let these... creatures destroy our home."

Pinocchio nodded, his wooden face set in a determined expression. "I may have the body of a puppet, but I will fight like a warrior."

Their first attempt was simple yet cunning. Geppetto, utilizing his knowledge of carpentry, rigged a series of traps around the workshop. Pinocchio, agile and fearless, served as the bait. The traps, however, were only momentarily effective. The undead, driven by a relentless hunger, seemed to learn, adapting to each new obstacle with chilling efficiency.

"We need a better plan," Pinocchio said, frustration evident in his voice as they retreated back to the workshop.

Geppetto's mind raced, flipping through the pages of every book he had ever read. Inspiration struck from an unlikely source - "The Art of War." He concocted a grand strategy, leveraging the village's landscape and his own creations. "We'll use fire, decoys, and the river. We'll lead them into a trap they cannot escape."

The villagers, few but brave, rallied behind Geppetto and Pinocchio. Together, they worked, setting up barricades, digging trenches, and preparing their homespun arsenal. As night fell, they took their positions, hearts pounding with anticipation and fear.

The undead came like a tide, relentless and overwhelming. The initial phase of Geppetto's plan worked flawlessly, with the creatures falling into trenches and being swept away by the river. But as they pushed forward, the tide of battle turned. The lead zombie, grotesque in its decay, seemed to command the others, orchestrating a counterattack that turned Geppetto's traps against them.

Chaos ensued. Flames intended to ward off the undead instead spread to the village, creating a fiery hell-scape. The villagers, though valiant, were ill-equipped for such a battle. Amidst the screams and the clash, Pinocchio fought valiantly, using his wooden limbs to fend off the attackers.

"We underestimated them," Geppetto gasped, despair gripping his heart as he witnessed the destruction around them. "This is my fault."

"No, Father," Pinocchio said, his voice firm despite the chaos. "We fight together."

In the midst of battle, Pinocchio's keen eyes noticed something peculiar about the lead zombie. It seemed drawn to him, as if sensing something within the wooden boy.

"Father, the scroll," Pinocchio cried out over the din of battle. "It's linked to me. That's why they keep coming!"

The revelation hit Geppetto like a physical blow. His creation, his beloved Pinocchio, was the key to this nightmare. Before he could process this, a sudden, violent clash threw him to the ground, a searing pain coursing through his body.

"Father!" Pinocchio shouted, rushing to his side.

Geppetto's vision blurred, his breath coming in ragged gasps. "Pinocchio, you must go on. Stop them."

Pinocchio, tears of sap streaking his wooden cheeks, looked down at his creator, his father. "I cannot leave you."

"You must," Geppetto whispered, his voice fading. "You are the only one who can end this."

As Geppetto lay wounded, the world around Pinocchio seemed to slow. The groans of the undead, the crackling of the fire, the cries of the villagers - all faded into a distant echo. He stood alone, the weight of their only hope resting on his wooden shoulders.

With a newfound resolve, Pinocchio turned to face the horde. His wooden body, once a symbol of a puppet's limitations, became his greatest asset. He moved with surprising speed and agility, his limbs a blur as he struck at the undead.

The lead zombie, a monstrous figure of decay and malice, advanced towards Pinocchio. It was clear that the final battle would be between them. Pinocchio, fueled by love and desperation, prepared to face the creature that held the fate of the village in its rotting hands.

The village, once a sanctuary of life and laughter, was now a battlefield of shadows and flames. Amidst this chaos, Pinocchio, with the heart of a hero and the body of wood, faced the monstrous lead zombie. His creator, Geppetto, lay wounded, his life hanging by a thread.

"You cannot win, wooden boy," the lead zombie hissed, its voice a chilling echo of death. "You are nothing but a puppet."

Pinocchio's wooden eyes blazed with a fierce determination. "I may be a puppet, but I am my father's creation. And I will protect what he loves."

The battle between Pinocchio and the lead zombie was a clash of wills, a dance of death. Pinocchio, agile and fearless, used his extendable limbs to keep the creature at bay, while the zombie, with its unnatural strength, relentlessly pressed on.

As they fought, Pinocchio's mind raced. He remembered the scroll, the words that had brought him to life, and the revelation that his existence was tied to the undead. The realization was a heavy burden, yet it sparked an idea, a desperate plan.

"Father," Pinocchio called out, hoping Geppetto could hear him. "I know what I must do. I have to reverse the spell."

Geppetto, struggling to stay conscious, heard the resolve in Pinocchio's voice. "No, my son," he whispered, tears in his eyes. "There must be another way."

"There isn't," Pinocchio replied, his voice laced with sorrow. "This is the only way to save everyone."

With a heavy heart, Pinocchio engaged the lead zombie in a final, desperate confrontation. He baited the creature, leading it into the heart of the burning village square, where the remnants of the scroll lay beside Geppetto.

In a moment of eerie silence, amidst the flickering flames and the groans of the undead, Pinocchio grabbed the scroll. His wooden fingers trembled as he began to recite the reversal incantation, each word a goodbye to the life he had come to cherish.

The lead zombie lunged at Pinocchio, but it was too late. The words of the scroll took effect, a blinding light enveloping Pinocchio and the undead. The creatures, one by one, began to crumble into dust, their reign of terror ending as abruptly as it had begun.

As the light faded, a miraculous transformation occurred. Pinocchio's wooden body turned to flesh and blood. He had become a real boy, a final gift from the magic that had given him life.

Geppetto, witnessing this transformation, mustered his strength. "Pinocchio," he gasped, reaching out with a trembling hand.

Pinocchio, feeling the warmth of life in his veins, turned to his father with a smile. "Father, I..."

But the joy was short-lived. As the magic left him, so too did his life. Pinocchio collapsed beside Geppetto, his eyes closing slowly.

"No, my boy, stay with me," Geppetto cried, cradling Pinocchio in his arms. "You can't leave me now."

But it was too late. Pinocchio's sacrifice had saved the village, but it had cost him everything. In his final moments, he had experienced what it meant to be truly alive.

The dawn broke over the village, casting light over the devastation. The undead were gone, but so was the brave puppet who had become a hero.

Geppetto, surrounded by the villagers, mourned his son, his creation. In Pinocchio's sacrifice, he had found the courage and love he never knew he possessed. The village would rebuild, stories of Pinocchio's bravery passing down through generations. And in the heart of the old craftsman, the memory of a wooden boy who became real would live on forever.

The night embraced the city like a shroud, hiding the sins of the past and the horrors of the present. Within this abyss, Dracula and Van Helsing moved with purpose, their unlikely alliance a testament to the desperation of their cause.

In a derelict warehouse, Dracula had convened a gathering of the most unlikely allies. Among them were vampires of various lineages, their features ranging from the aristocratic to the savage, and a handful of human survivors, their eyes wide with a mix of fear and awe. At the center of this motley crew stood Dracula and Van Helsing, an image so surreal that it seemed ripped from the pages of folklore.

Dracula addressed the assembly, his voice a commanding echo in the vast emptiness. "We face an enemy unlike any other. These zombies, mindless as they may seem, are relentless. Our survival, both vampires and humans alike, depends on our ability to work together."

A murmur of dissent rippled through the crowd, the vampires visibly uncomfortable at the notion of aligning with humans. A burly vampire, with scars crisscrossing his face, stepped forward. "Why should we trust these mortals, Dracula? They are prey, nothing more."

Van Helsing, his eyes scanning the crowd, spoke up. "Because, without their help, you won't have a food source. The zombies are wiping out humanity, and with it, your chance at survival."

A tense silence fell upon the gathering. It was a truth they all knew, but none dared to voice.

It was the young vampire, the one Dracula had saved earlier, who broke the silence. "We need a plan, a strategy. We can't keep fighting these... things, in random skirmishes."

Dracula nodded, turning to Van Helsing. "The hunter is right. We need to be smart, strategic. We strike where they are weakest and protect what remains of the humans."

Van Helsing pulled out a map, spread it across an old table. "The zombies seem to be converging towards the city center. We believe there's something, or someone, controlling them."

A ripple of shock went through the crowd. The idea of a sentient force behind the zombie horde was a chilling prospect.

"We strike at dawn," Dracula declared. "We draw them out, thin their numbers, and then find and destroy this... puppet master."

The night passed in a flurry of activity. Weapons were distributed, plans were drawn, and alliances were forged in the fire of necessity.

As dawn broke, the streets echoed with the sounds of battle. Vampires and humans fought side by side, their combined forces pushing back the undead tide. The initial skirmishes were successful, the element of surprise working in their favor.

But as the sun climbed higher, the tide began to turn. The zombies, far more numerous than anticipated, began to swarm the fighters in overwhelming waves. The supposed weakness they had hoped to exploit was nowhere to be found.

In the thick of battle, Dracula fought with a ferocity born of centuries of warfare. Beside him, Van Helsing dispatched zombies with clinical precision. But it was becoming increasingly clear that they were losing ground.

A sudden explosion rocked the battlefield, sending a shockwave through the ranks of both the living and the undead. From the smoke emerged a new horror: zombies, not just mindless drones, but coordinated, almost intelligent.

Dracula's eyes widened in realization. "They've evolved," he hissed, dodging a lunging zombie. "This changes everything."

Van Helsing, his coat singed and his hat lost in the fray, looked around at the chaos. "We need to retreat, regroup. We underestimated them."

The retreat was chaotic, a desperate scramble for survival. They fell back to their stronghold, a fortified cathedral in the heart of the city. The heavy doors slammed shut, locking out the groaning horde outside.

Inside, the mood was somber. They had lost many, both vampires and humans. The young vampire, her clothes torn and bloodied, approached Dracula. "What now, my lord? We can't win this way."

Dracula looked at the faces around him, each one marked with fear and exhaustion. "We need a new plan, something drastic. And for that, we need more information."

Van Helsing stepped forward, his expression grave. "I may have a lead. Before the outbreak, there were rumors of a laboratory, one that was experimenting with... biological weapons."

A hush fell over the room. The implications were clear to all.

"We infiltrate this lab, find out what they were working on, and use it against the zombies," Van Helsing continued.

It was a dangerous plan, one that reeked of desperation. But it was all they had. The group set out under the cover of night, moving through the shadowy streets with a silent urgency. The laboratory was located on the outskirts of the city, a fortress of concrete and steel.

Infiltrating the lab was a task that required both the stealth of the vampires and the technological expertise of the humans. They worked in tandem, a dance of shadows and light, until they breached the inner sanctum.

What they found within the lab was beyond their wildest fears. Rows of vats containing grotesque experiments, documents detailing unholy fusions of science and necromancy, and at the center of it all, a figure suspended in a tank, its features an unsettling blend of human and zombie.

"This is it," Van Helsing whispered, his voice laced with horror. "The source of the outbreak."

They gathered evidence, took samples, anything that could help them turn the tide. But as they prepared to leave, an alarm blared, the sound echoing through the empty halls. They were not alone.

The ensuing escape was a nightmare of close calls and harrowing encounters. They fought their way out, each step a battle for survival.

As they emerged into the night, the laboratory a burning pyre behind them, they knew the hardest part was yet to come. The truth they had uncovered was a weapon in its own right, but how to wield it remained a question unanswered.

Back at the cathedral, the group pored over the documents, their faces lit by the flickering light of candles. The truth was there, hidden within the pages, a truth that could either save them or doom them all.

As dawn approached, Dracula stood at a window, watching the first light of day touch the broken city. His mind was a whirlwind of strategy and doubt, the weight of their survival resting on his ageless shoulders.

Van Helsing joined him, his expression grim. "We have a plan, Dracula. But it's going to require everything we have."

Dracula turned to face him, his eyes reflecting the dawning light. "Then we shall give it everything we have, hunter. For in this war, there is no other choice."

And with that, they turned to face the gathering allies, their resolve steeling them against the coming storm. The battle for survival was far from over, and the true enemy still lurked in the shadows, waiting for its moment to strike.

The cathedral's ancient walls, scarred by centuries and now witness to this strange new war, echoed with the hushed voices of those gathered within. Dracula and Van Helsing stood at the forefront, maps and scattered papers laid out before them like a battle-worn tapestry. The air was thick with anticipation, each heart - whether beating or still - weighed down by the gravity of what was to come.

"We strike at the heart," Dracula's voice cut through the silence, as commanding as the night itself. "The information we gathered from the laboratory points to one thing - there's a central consciousness controlling these creatures."

Van Helsing, his eyes scanning the room, added, "It's our best chance. We take down this... puppet master, and the horde will fall into disarray."

Murmurs of agreement rippled through the group, but it was the young vampire who voiced the unspoken fear. "And if we fail?"

Dracula's gaze met hers, unflinching. "Then we shall fall with honor, defending what remains of this world."

The plan was daring, a final gambit in a game where the stakes were nothing less than their very existence. They would split into two groups - one led by Dracula to assault the central hive, the heart of the zombie swarm, and the other led by Van Helsing to create a diversion, drawing as many of the undead away as possible.

As night fell, cloaking the city in its merciful shadow, the two groups set out. The city, once a vibrant testament to human achievement, now lay in ruins, its streets a labyrinth of death and decay.

Dracula's group moved with supernatural stealth, weaving through the city like ghosts. They reached the hive, a towering edifice of steel and glass, its windows dark and foreboding.

Inside, they were met with a sight that chilled even Dracula's ancient heart. Rows upon rows of zombies, standing motionless, their eyes empty yet somehow aware. And at the center, a figure suspended in a network of cables and machinery - the puppet master.

As Dracula and his team prepared to strike, the figure's eyes snapped open, a malevolent intelligence shining within. The zombies stirred, turning towards the intruders.

"Now!" Dracula bellowed, and the night erupted into chaos.

Meanwhile, Van Helsing's group enacted their part of the plan. Explosives, set at strategic points, roared to life, sending shockwaves through the zombie ranks. The diversion worked, drawing a large swath of the horde away from the hive.

Back in the hive, the battle raged. Dracula fought with a ferocity borne of millennia, his every strike lethal and precise. But the puppet master was not defenseless. It controlled the zombies with a mere thought, sending wave after wave against them.

In the midst of the fray, Dracula locked eyes with the puppet master, a silent challenge passing between them. With a final, powerful thrust, he broke through the undead ranks, reaching the figure entwined in machinery.

The puppet master, its form both grotesque and pitiable, sneered. "You cannot win, ancient one. I am evolution, the future."

Dracula, his face inches from the creature, replied, "You are an aberration, a perversion of nature. And I am its reaper."

With a swift motion, Dracula plunged his hand into the heart of the machine, tearing out the core of the puppet master. As it shrieked, a sound that was both digital and agonizingly human, the zombies faltered, their movements becoming erratic.

Outside, Van Helsing witnessed the horde's sudden disarray. Seizing the opportunity, he led his group in a final, desperate charge, cutting down the confused zombies.

As the puppet master's shrieks faded, its control over the undead broke. The zombies collapsed, one by one, like marionettes with their strings cut.

The battle was won, but the victory was bittersweet. The cost had been high, too high for some. The young vampire lay among the fallen, her eyes staring blankly at the night sky.

As the first light of dawn began to paint the sky with strokes of pink and orange, the air was thick with the aftermath of battle. The streets, once overrun with the undead, now lay silent, a grim reminder of the night's ferocity. Amidst the ruin, Dracula and Van Helsing stood, two warriors on the brink of a tenuous peace.

Dracula, his form weakened by the exertions of the night and the approaching dawn, turned to Van Helsing. "It's over, hunter. The world breathes again, though the cost has been dear."

Van Helsing, his eyes scanning the horizon, nodded slowly. "Yes, it is over. But for us, there can be no peace, Count Dracula. Not after centuries of bloodshed."

A flicker of understanding, and perhaps resignation, passed through Dracula's eyes. "Then do what you must," he said, his voice a low rasp.

Van Helsing reached into his coat, his hand wrapping around the handle of a weapon forged for one purpose - to end the immortal life of Dracula. "You know I must do this. It is my destiny, as it is yours to resist."

Dracula faced the hunter, his posture one of noble acceptance. "Then let it end, Van Helsing. Let it end where it began, in the light of a new day."

As Van Helsing stepped forward, weapon in hand, the first rays of the sun crested the horizon, casting long shadows across the battlefield. The light, lethal to a vampire of Dracula's stature, began to sear his flesh, the sizzling sound a grim accompaniment to the morning chorus.

Dracula, his face contorted in pain but his gaze unflinching, met Van Helsing's advance. "Do it now, hunter, while you have the chance," he urged, his voice a mix of pain and defiance.

Van Helsing, with a swift motion, plunged the weapon into Dracula's heart. The count's eyes widened, not in fear, but in a final, profound understanding. A mix of emotions played across his features - regret, relief, and perhaps the faintest glimmer of something akin to gratitude. As the weapon did its grim work, Dracula's form began to disintegrate, his centuries-long existence coming to an end under the light of the dawn. His last breath was a whisper lost in the wind, a final farewell to a world he had both terrorized and protected.

Van Helsing stood there, the weapon in his hand and the ashes of Count Dracula at his feet. He looked up at the rising sun, feeling the weight of his actions. He had fulfilled his destiny, but at what cost?

Around him, the city began to stir, the survivors emerging from their hiding places. A new day had dawned, a day of peace and rebuilding. But for Van Helsing, it was a day of reflection and mourning.

For in his victory, he had not only ended the reign of a monster but had extinguished the flame of a being as complex and tragic as the night itself. In that moment, Van Helsing realized the true burden of his legacy - a life spent in pursuit of shadows, only to find himself alone in the light.

And as the city awoke to a new beginning, Van Helsing walked away, his figure slowly disappearing into the dawn, a solitary hunter in a world no longer haunted by the specter of Count Dracula.

CHAPTER 27

THE DEATH OF THE MAYAN EMPIRE

"In the heart of shadows, even the bravest light must flicker." - Ancient Mayan Proverb

The sun, a fiery orb of life, hung low in the sky over the lush jungles of the Yucatan Peninsula, casting elongated shadows that danced upon the ancient stone structures of the Mayan Empire. It was a civilization in its zenith, a tapestry of art, science, and spirituality woven into the very fabric of the jungle. But on this day, as a rare solar eclipse approached, a sense of foreboding gripped the air, palpable as the humid breath of the forest.

In the heart of this empire stood Xbalanque, a warrior whose name was whispered with reverence and fear. His eyes, dark as the obsidian blade he wielded, scanned the horizon from atop a towering pyramid. Today, he was more than a warrior; he was the chosen guardian of a sacred ritual, one believed to ensure prosperity under the celestial omen of the eclipse.

"Xbalanque, the gods watch us," intoned Ahuil, the high priest, his voice echoing amidst the stone and foliage. "Your blade must guide our prayers to the heavens."

Xbalanque nodded, his gaze never leaving the darkening sky. The air vibrated with the chants of priests and the rhythmic beating of drums, a symphony that seemed to summon the very eclipse itself. As the sun began to vanish, swallowed by the moon's shadow, a hush fell over the gathered crowd.

Then, amidst the darkened silence, a scream pierced the air. It was guttural, filled with an anguish that clawed at the soul. Xbalanque spun, his warrior instincts honed to precision, and what he saw chilled his blood. From the edge of the jungle, figures emerged, their movements jerky and unnatural, their eyes void of life. The dead had risen.

Panic erupted as the undead horde descended upon the crowd. Xbalanque leaped from the pyramid, landing amidst the chaos. He swung his blade with lethal grace, each strike a dance of death. But for every undead creature that fell, another took its place.

"We must protect the city!" Xbalanque shouted to his fellow warriors, his voice cutting through the terror.

They rallied to him, forming a barricade with shields and spears. But doubt gnawed at Xbalanque's heart. These were no ordinary enemies; they were an abomination against the natural order.

As night fell, and the eclipse receded, leaving a sliver of moon to witness the horror, Xbalanque led a retreat to the heart of the city. The once-mighty empire stood besieged, not by rival kingdoms or European conquerors, but by a force as old and relentless as time itself.

In the council chamber, lit by flickering torches, Xbalanque met with the city's elders. Fear hung heavy in the air, a cloak that smothered hope.

"We cannot fight this enemy with traditional means," Xbalanque argued, his voice a low growl of frustration. "Our blades do not deter them. We need a new strategy."

"The gods are angry," the high priest Ahuil interjected, his eyes wild with fear. "We must appease them with sacrifices. More blood must be spilled."

Xbalanque slammed his fist against the stone table. "No! This is no wrath of the gods. This is something else, something... unnatural."

But his words fell on deaf ears. The elders, swayed by the high priest's fervor, decreed that more sacrifices would be made. Xbalanque stormed out of the chamber, his heart heavy with the knowledge that his people were blinded by superstition.

Outside, the city braced for another onslaught. Xbalanque stood alone, gazing at the stars that peeked through the jungle canopy. The night air was thick with the scent of impending doom. He knew he faced an enemy that defied understanding, an enemy that could spell the end of his glorious civilization.

And in that moment of solitude, Xbalanque made a vow. He would defend his people, not just with blade and bravery, but with cunning and strategy. He would find a way to turn the tide against this unholy menace. For in the heart of shadows, even the bravest light must flicker, but it need not be extinguished.

As the dawn broke with a hesitant light over the besieged city, Xbalanque stood on the ramparts, his eyes scanning the horizon where the jungle met the stone structures of his once unassailable empire. The night had been long, filled with the cries of the undead and the clash of desperate battle. Now, in the eerie calm of morning, Xbalanque knew that the respite was but fleeting.

He descended the steps of the pyramid, his mind churning with plans and strategies. The city's walls, built to withstand the assaults of mortal enemies, offered little reprieve against the relentless undead. Xbalanque gathered his most trusted warriors, men and women who had fought beside him through countless battles.

"We cannot hold them back with force alone," Xbalanque addressed his warriors. "We must be cunning, use our knowledge of the land to our advantage."

The warriors nodded, their faces etched with determination and fear. They dispersed, moving to enact Xbalanque's orders, fortifying weak points, and setting traps at strategic locations.

But as the sun climbed higher, casting its merciless gaze upon the city, the undead returned. They came in waves, a tide of death that seemed to know no exhaustion. Xbalanque fought at the forefront, his blade a whirlwind of destruction. Yet for every undead creature that fell, another seemed to take its place.

The day wore on, a relentless cycle of attack and reprieve. As night approached, Xbalanque watched with growing despair as his strategies crumbled under the undead's tireless onslaught. The city's defenses, once thought impenetrable, began to falter.

Then, amidst the chaos, a new figure emerged. Clad in armor unlike any Xbalanque had seen, with a sword that gleamed with the promise of European craftsmanship, stood a man who seemed as out of place as the undead themselves. He was Hernán, a Spanish conquistador, his face etched with lines of battle and eyes that spoke of a thousand horrors.

Xbalanque approached the stranger warily. "Who are you, and why do you fight with us?"

Hernán looked at the Mayan warrior, his gaze assessing. "I am Hernán, a soldier of Spain. I was separated from my expedition. I fight for survival, same as you."

Xbalanque studied the conquistador, sensing an opportunity. "Your tactics, your weapons, they are different from ours. Can they turn the tide in this battle?"

Hernán sheathed his sword. "Perhaps. In my land, we have fought many wars, seen many sieges. Fire is a powerful ally against any foe."

Inspired, Xbalanque quickly formulated a new plan, blending Hernán's knowledge of siege warfare with his own understanding of guerrilla tactics. They worked through the night, setting up barricades and preparing fire traps in the narrow streets leading to the city's heart.

As the undead swarmed the city the next day, Xbalanque and Hernán unleashed their plan. Flames roared to life, consuming rows of the undead in a fiery inferno. For a moment, it seemed as though they might hold the horde at bay.

But the undead, driven by some unfathomable will, adapted. They began to avoid the traps, moving with a terrifying cunning that seemed impossible for creatures devoid of life. The Mayans' initial triumph turned to horror as the undead penetrated deeper into the city, overwhelming the defenders.

In the council chamber, now transformed into a makeshift command center, Xbalanque faced the elders, his expression grim.

"We underestimated the enemy," he admitted. "They are not mindless creatures. They adapt, learn. We need a new plan, something more drastic."

The high priest, Ahuil, his face haunted with the weight of his failed prophecies, spoke up. "The gods have abandoned us. We are doomed."

Xbalanque slammed his hand on the table, frustration boiling over. "No, we are not abandoned. We are challenged. I will go to the source of this curse, the sacred temple where the eclipse ritual was held. There lies our salvation."

Hernán stepped forward. "I will join you. Together, we might stand a chance."

As they prepared to leave, Xbalanque turned to his warriors. "Defend the city. Protect our people. This is not the end."

The journey to the temple was a gauntlet of horror. The undead, sensing their intent, converged upon them in droves. Xbalanque and Hernán fought back-to-back, their blades singing a deadly duet. But as they neared the temple, a massive horde of undead emerged, cutting them off from retreat.

Surrounded and outnumbered, Xbalanque looked into Hernán's eyes, seeing his own determination reflected there. "This is it," he said. "For our people, for our civilizations."

Together, they charged into the horde, their battle cry echoing into the night, a defiant roar against the encroaching darkness. As they fought, Xbalanque felt something he had not felt since the eclipse - hope. But it was a fragile thing, easily snuffed out.

And as Hernán fell, struck down by the relentless undead, Xbalanque realized the true depth of their peril. Alone, he stood at the threshold of the temple, the heart of the darkness, facing an enemy that seemed as eternal as the stars above.

In that moment, at the lowest point of his struggle, Xbalanque understood the true nature of his battle. It was not just for survival, but for the soul of his people, for the legacy of a civilization that stood at the brink of oblivion. With a final, determined breath, he stepped into the temple, ready to face whatever horrors lay within.

The air inside the temple was thick with an ancient, suffocating darkness. Xbalanque's footsteps echoed through the hallowed halls, each step a defiant challenge to the oppressive silence. The walls, adorned with intricate carvings, seemed to watch him, their stone eyes witness to a millennia of secrets. The warrior's heart pounded in his chest, a frenzied drumbeat in the quietude of the temple.

As Xbalanque delved deeper, the shadows writhed around him, as if alive. He clutched his obsidian blade tightly, the only comfort in this realm of despair. The echoes of the undead outside faded, replaced by a more profound silence, the quiet before a storm.

He found himself in a vast chamber, its ceiling lost to darkness. In its center stood an altar, upon which lay an ancient relic, pulsating with a sinister light. It was the source of the curse, Xbalanque realized, the heart of the darkness that had befallen his people.

But he was not alone.

From the shadows emerged a creature, a monstrous being, part human, part nightmare. Its eyes burned with an unholy fire, and its form was adorned with the remnants of Mayan armor, a grotesque parody of Xbalanque's own garb.

"You dare to challenge the gods?" the creature's voice boomed, a sound that shook the very foundations of the temple.

Xbalanque steadied himself, his resolve unwavering. "I challenge the curse that you have brought upon my people. Today, it ends."

The creature laughed, a sound like the clashing of thunder. "Foolish mortal. You cannot comprehend the forces you meddle with."

With a roar, it lunged at Xbalanque, who met its charge with the skill and ferocity of a warrior honed by years of battle. The creature was strong, its blows sending shockwaves through the chamber. Xbalanque danced around its attacks, his blade striking with precision, but the creature seemed impervious to pain.

As they fought, Xbalanque realized that brute force would not win this battle. He needed to outsmart the creature, to use the temple itself as his weapon.

Luring the creature toward one of the chamber's massive stone pillars, Xbalanque feinted, dodging at the last moment as the creature's fist collided with the pillar, sending cracks running through the stone.

With a series of swift, agile movements, Xbalanque led the creature on a deadly dance, striking at its weaknesses, avoiding its crushing blows, all the while leading it towards the relic on the altar.

As the creature realized Xbalanque's intent, it let out a bellow of rage and charged with renewed fury. Xbalanque, his energy waning, made a final, desperate lunge towards the relic.

Their hands met on the ancient artifact, a clash of wills as much as flesh. The relic pulsed with a blinding light, and with a cry that melded triumph and despair, Xbalanque shattered it. The effect was immediate. The creature howled, its form writhing as the dark energy that had sustained it dissipated. Around them, the temple shook, as if in the throes of an earthquake.

Xbalanque staggered back, his breath ragged, watching as the creature crumbled before him, becoming nothing more than dust and shadow. But victory was short-lived.

With a final, spiteful act, the creature's remains exploded in a burst of dark energy, sending Xbalanque flying across the chamber. He hit the ground hard, pain lancing through his body.

Through blurred vision, he saw the undead, who had followed him into the temple, pause, their forms collapsing as the curse that bound them unraveled. But as he tried to rise, a shadow loomed over him. It was the creature, reborn in a final, ghastly form, its essence clinging to existence with malevolent tenacity.

Xbalanque, his body screaming in protest, forced himself to stand. He faced the creature, knowing this was the true final battle. There would be no holding back, no quarter given.

They clashed, a maelstrom of violence in the heart of the temple. Xbalanque, driven by a mix of fear, desperation, and unyielding determination, fought with a ferocity he had never known.

And then, with a move that was part instinct, part divine inspiration, he found his opening. With a swift, decisive strike, he plunged his blade into the heart of the creature's shadowy form. There was a moment of absolute stillness, as if the world itself held its breath.

Then, with a shuddering, final scream, the creature dissolved into nothingness, its existence extinguished forever. Xbalanque collapsed, his strength spent. Around him, the temple began to crumble, its ancient magic undone. He crawled towards the entrance, each movement an agony.

As he emerged into the night, the stars overhead seemed to shine brighter, the air fresher. The city lay in ruins, but it was silent, the horror of the undead vanquished.

Xbalanque looked upon the fallen empire, his heart heavy with the cost of their victory. Beside him, the ghost of Hernán seemed to stand, a silent sentinel in the aftermath of their shared battle.

The warrior knew that the world would never be the same. The Mayan civilization, his people, had faced the abyss and survived, but at a price. The dawn of a new era beckoned, one where the old ways would blend with the new, where the lessons of the past would shape the future. And as Xbalanque gazed upon the first light of dawn, he understood that his battle was over, but his journey was just beginning. For in the heart of darkness, he had found not just fear and despair, but hope, resilience, and the enduring strength of the human spirit.

CHAPTER 28

ASTRONAUTS VS. ZOMBIES

"In the vast emptiness of space, I was closer to humanity than ever before. It was only upon returning to Earth that I found true solitude." Jack Collins

Jack Collins gazed out of the International Space Station's viewport, his eyes tracing the curvature of the Earth. The planet, a swirling canvas of blues and greens, seemed so serene from his orbital vantage point. Little did he know that beneath that tranquil façade, chaos had begun to unravel the very fabric of civilization.

The day started like any other in orbit. Routine checks, experiments, a bit of banter with fellow astronauts, and the ever-present communication with NASA. But as Jack reached out to Mission Control during his scheduled check-in, an eerie silence greeted him. The static of the line was like a whispered warning, sending a shiver down his spine.

"Mission Control, this is ISS. Do you copy?" Jack's voice was calm, yet edged with concern.

Minutes stretched like hours. Jack tried repeatedly, each attempt amplifying the unsettling quiet. He exchanged worried glances with his colleagues, their expressions mirroring his own anxiety. The space station, once a hub of constant communication and activity, felt like a silent tomb floating in the abyss.

Jack's heart raced as he noticed something alarming from the viewport - vast swathes of the planet plunged into darkness, like someone had flicked off switches in major cities across the globe.

"Something's wrong," he muttered, more to himself than anyone else.

NASA's voice finally crackled through, strained and urgent. "ISS, initiate emergency return protocol Echo-1. Situation on ground... critical. Immediate evacuation required."

The message was a jolt. Jack and his team scrambled, their training kicking in. They prepared the Soyuz for an immediate return to Earth, the gravity of the situation weighing heavily on them. As the descent began, Jack's mind raced with possibilities. What cataclysm could warrant such an abrupt end to their mission?

The landing was rough, the Soyuz capsule jolting violently as it hit the ground. Jack's first steps back on Earth were shaky, not just from readjusting to gravity, but from apprehension. The silence was deafening. No welcoming committee, no sound of helicopters, just a haunting stillness.

"Hello?" Jack called out, his voice echoing in the emptiness.

He trekked through desolate landscapes, the absence of life chilling. Cars abandoned on streets, lights off in homes, cities that once teemed with life now ghostly.

His first encounter with them was in a small town. He heard the shuffling first, slow and irregular. Turning a corner, he faced the unimaginable - people, if they could still be called that, with hollow eyes, their skin pale and decayed, moving with a grotesque purpose.

Jack's astronaut training hadn't prepared him for this. His heart pounded as the creatures noticed him, their groans filling the air. He ran, his breath ragged, his mind reeling. Zombies. The stuff of horror movies and fiction, now a terrifying reality.

Holed up in an abandoned store for the night, Jack found a battery-powered radio. He tuned in to static at first, then a voice, a beacon in the darkness.

"To any survivors, this is a broadcast for safe zones. The nearest is..."

Jack clung to the radio, the voice his lifeline. He was not alone. There were others out there, fighting, surviving.

As dawn broke, Jack set out, determination steeling his resolve. The world he knew was gone, replaced by a nightmare. But within him burned a glimmer of hope, a drive to find others, to survive.

"I was trained to explore new frontiers," Jack whispered to himself as he navigated the treacherous, zombie-infested streets. "This... this is just a different kind of exploration. One I never expected."

The journey was perilous, but Jack Collins was not one to back down. An astronaut by training, a survivor by circumstance, he was locked into an adventure far beyond the realms of space, on a planet he once called home, now a stage for an apocalyptic struggle for survival.

Jack's journey through the desolate streets was a testament to human resilience. The once-familiar sights of his hometown were now distorted by the apocalypse, storefronts boarded up, cars abandoned mid-escape. The haunting echo of his footsteps on the pavement was a constant reminder of his solitude.

His first few encounters with the undead were clumsy, fraught with near misses. He quickly learned that stealth was his ally, quiet movements his best defense. But for all his astronaut training, nothing had prepared him for the horror of confronting those once-human creatures. Their grotesque forms, the vacant gaze in their eyes, the guttural sounds they made - it was the stuff of nightmares.

One evening, as Jack scavenged for supplies in a ransacked supermarket, he heard a noise - distinct, deliberate. Hiding behind a toppled shelf, he watched in silent anticipation. A figure emerged, armed and alert. A survivor.

The woman moved with a purposeful grace, her eyes scanning the shadows. Jack stepped out, hands raised in a gesture of peace.

"Don't shoot," he said, his voice barely above a whisper.

The woman, startled, pointed her gun at him. "Who are you?" she demanded, her voice tinged with suspicion.

"I'm Jack Collins, an astronaut. I just got back from the ISS to... this." His gesture encompassed the chaos around them.

The woman lowered her gun slightly, her expression softening. "Sarah Walker," she introduced herself. "You're a long way from home, astronaut."

Together, they shared stories of survival, the world they lost, and the one they now inhabited. Sarah was a former military officer, her skills honed in combat - skills that were invaluable in this new world.

Jack proposed a plan to reach a rumored military safe zone. Sarah was skeptical but agreed, intrigued by Jack's determination. They set out, armed with makeshift weapons, scavenged maps, and a sliver of hope.

Their journey was fraught with danger. They navigated through zombie-infested territories, relying on each other's strengths - Jack's strategic thinking and Sarah's combat skills. They encountered other survivors, some friendly, others hostile, but they remained focused on their goal.

As they neared the safe zone, their anticipation grew. But nothing could have prepared them for the sight that awaited them. The military encampment was overrun, a smoldering ruin of what once promised safety. In the midst of their shock, they were ambushed. A group of armed men, ruthless and desperate, captured Sarah. Jack managed to escape, but not without injury.

Alone and dejected, Jack nursed his wounds in an abandoned warehouse. The failure of his plan weighed heavily on him. He realized brute strength and straightforward tactics wouldn't be enough. He needed to think differently, to use the environment to his advantage.

Drawing inspiration from his knowledge of the Art of War, Jack started to plan his rescue mission. He began to set traps, use decoys, and move through the city like a shadow. His approach became more calculated, more strategic.

He tracked down the group that had taken Sarah. They were holed up in a facility that appeared to be conducting experiments on the zombies - and possibly on humans.

As Jack infiltrated the facility, he was overwhelmed by the horror of what he saw. Rows of cages, some holding zombies, others holding people in various stages of transformation.

He found Sarah in a cell, bruised but unbroken. Their reunion was brief as the sound of footsteps approached. They prepared to fight, but they were outnumbered and outgunned. Captured, they were brought before the leader of this macabre operation - Dr. Morgan.

Dr. Morgan was a man twisted by the new world order, his moral compass shattered by the chaos. He saw the outbreak as an opportunity to test the limits of human endurance and transformation.

"You are strong survivors," Dr. Morgan mused, observing Jack and Sarah. "Perfect subjects for my next phase of experiments."

Jack and Sarah were thrown into a cell together, their situation grim. This was the lowest point for Jack - captured, his plan in ruins, facing a madman who saw them as nothing more than test subjects.

But even in the darkest moments, the human spirit can find a light. Jack and Sarah's resolve hardened. They were not going to be pawns in Dr. Morgan's twisted game. They were fighters, survivors. And they were going to fight their way out, no matter the cost.

In the dim light of the cell, Jack and Sarah sat in silence, their minds racing with plans of escape. The cold, metallic walls of their prison seemed to mock their predicament, echoing back their quiet breaths in taunting whispers. But beneath that veneer of despair, a fire was kindling - a fierce determination to not just survive, but to overthrow the twisted reign of Dr. Morgan.

"We need to get out," Jack whispered, his eyes scanning the cell for any weakness. "But not just escape. We need to stop him. For good."

Sarah nodded, her bruised face set in a determined grimace. "I saw a lab through the corridor. If we can reach it, we might find something to use against him."

Their plan was audacious, almost reckless, but they had little to lose. As they plotted, the door to their cell creaked open. Two of Dr. Morgan's guards entered, their expressions indifferent to the plight of their captives.

It was now or never.

In a flurry of motion, Jack and Sarah sprang into action. Jack tackled one guard while Sarah, with swift precision, disarmed the other. They moved with a synergy born of desperation, their actions fueled by a singular desire for freedom.

With the guards incapacitated, they made their way through the dimly lit corridors of the facility, a labyrinthine structure that reeked of death and despair. They encountered more of Dr. Morgan's men, but each obstacle was overcome with a blend of Jack's cunning and Sarah's combat prowess.

They reached the lab, a sterile room filled with beakers, vials, and ominous-looking equipment. Amidst the scientific chaos, Jack's eyes landed on a series of syringes filled with a luminescent liquid.

"This could be it," Sarah said, examining the vials. "Some kind of toxin or serum. We could use this."

They pocketed the syringes and continued, navigating towards Dr. Morgan's main control room. The confrontation was inevitable. As they entered the room, they found Dr. Morgan waiting, his face a mask of demented calm.

"So, the rats have escaped the maze," he sneered, his eyes gleaming with madness. "But you are too late. My work is nearly complete."

"We're shutting you down, Morgan," Jack said, his voice steady despite the pounding of his heart.

A brutal fight ensued, the confined space of the control room amplifying the chaos. Jack and Sarah fought with everything they had, but Dr. Morgan was not alone. His guards swarmed the room, turning the skirmish into a battle for survival.

In the melee, Jack found himself face-to-face with Dr. Morgan. The scientist lunged, a syringe in hand, aiming for Jack's neck. In a split-second decision, Jack managed to redirect the attack, plunging the syringe into Dr. Morgan instead.

The effect was immediate and horrifying. Dr. Morgan's body contorted, his screams filling the room as the serum ravaged him. In a grotesque transformation, he became the very thing he sought to control - a monstrous, raging zombie.

With Dr. Morgan incapacitated, the tide of the battle turned. Jack and Sarah fought their way out of the control room, the facility descending into chaos as the infected Morgan attacked his own men.

They made their way outside, the fresh air a stark contrast to the stifling atmosphere of the facility. But their relief was short-lived. Jack felt a sharp pain in his arm - a bite. He had been bitten during the fight.

"This is it, then," Jack said quietly, looking at Sarah. "I'm infected."

Sarah's face was a mix of fear and resolve. "No. We'll find a way. We have to."

As they prepared for the worst, something unexpected happened - or rather, didn't happen. Jack showed no signs of turning. Minutes turned into hours, and he remained himself.

"Why... why am I not changing?" Jack wondered aloud, his voice a mixture of disbelief and hope.

"The space station," Sarah realized. "Your time in space... it must have changed you. Made you immune."

The revelation was staggering. Jack's blood held the key to not just their survival, but possibly the survival of what remained of humanity.

With renewed purpose, Jack and Sarah set out to find other survivors. They carried with them the hope of a cure, a chance to reclaim the world from the clutches of the undead.

As they disappeared into the horizon, the sun setting behind them, their silhouettes were those of warriors - not just survivors of a zombie apocalypse, but harbingers of a new dawn.

ABOUT THE AUTHOR

In the shadowy corners of his teenage bedroom, lit only by the flickering light of a television screen, the young author found his first love amidst the groans of the undead and the desperate struggles of humanity's last stand. Zombie films, with their relentless suspense and tales of survival, became his sanctuary, a world where he could explore the depths of fear and the resilience of the human spirit. This fascination wasn't just a phase; it was the beginning of a lifelong obsession.

Now, as an established writer, he breathes new life into this macabre fascination by reimagining the classical characters that have long haunted the corridors of literature and history. In his latest work, "The Art of War vs. Zombies," he pits these timeless icons against the relentless tide of the undead. Imagine Sun Tzu's strategic genius confronting not just the armies of men but legions of flesh-hungry zombies, or Joan of Arc rallying not just the French but all of humanity against the encroaching darkness.

This author's journey from a wide-eyed teenager absorbing zombie lore to a visionary writer merging the classical with the apocalyptic is a testament to the power of passion. His work is not merely a novel; it's a battleground where the undead meet the undying legends of the past, a unique tapestry weaving together his childhood dreams with his creative prowess.

Through "The Art of War vs. Zombies," he offers readers not just a story, but a window into a world where every strategy and sword strike decides the fate of both the living and the dead. This is where his love for zombies transforms into an epic saga, marking him as a master storyteller for the modern age, bridging the gap between the horrors of the undead and the heroics of history.

FOR INQUIRIES REGARDING LICENSING
AND ADAPTATION RIGHTS: IP@EXTRA-EXTRA.CA

ISBN: 978-1-7382357-8-0

www.ingramcontent.com/pod-product-compliance
Lightning Source LLC
Chambersburg PA
CBHW050511260626
47157CB00004B/1276